Praise for *Interregnum*

'Jim Ring has produced a most compelling thriller — full of unexpected twists and turns on almost every page — and set against the ghastly prospect of the Nazi Occupation of Britain. This is not for the faint-hearted.' General Richard Dannatt, Baron Dannatt.

'It's horribly credible, cleverly full of real people and fake ones deftly mixed, and absolutely essential reading now, when nothing is as it seems.' Peter York, author, broadcaster, commentator and journalist.

'A fine contribution to the literature of alternative history, and a truly exciting read.' Sam Llewellyn, author, columnist and maritime historian.

GU00497817

ALSO BY JIM RING

NON FICTION

A NOTE ON THE AUTHOR

Jim Ring first came to prominence as the author of *Erskine Childers* (John Murray 1996) which won the Marsh Prize for Biography. He is the author of five further books: *How the English Made the Alps*; (John Murray 2000), *We Come Unseen: the Untold Story of Britan's Cold War Submariners* (John Murray 2001) which won the Mountbatten Prize; *Riviera,*(John Murray 2004) *Storming the Eagle's Nest,*(Faber & Faber 2013) and *How the Navy Won the War* (Seaforth 2018) which was shortlisted for the Mountbatten Prize.

We Come Unseen was the subject of a TV documentary to which Jim acted as script consultant.
In 2005 he founded a film production company, specialising in documentaries. *Incomers* (ITV 2008) dramatises the challenges faced by immigrants in the UK. He has made a series of films about nuclear energy, including one about the 2011 Fukushima Daiichi disaster.

He lives in Norfolk with his family.

Interregnum is his first novel.

ISBN: Hardback: 978-1-9162610-5-1
ISBN: Paperback: 978-1-9162610-3-7
ISBN: eBook: 978-1-9162610-4-4

Compilation & Cover Design by S A Harrison

Published by WriteSideLeft UK
https://www.writesideleft.com

Interregnum

Being a Record of the February Rising,
by General Sir Max Quick
Chief of the Imperial General Staff,
KCB, CBE, DSO and Bar, MC

Jim Ring

'Ask any man what nationality he would prefer to be,
and ninety-nine out of a hundred will tell you that they
would prefer to be Englishmen.'

Cecil Rhodes

write/left

For Gail Pirkis,
without whose encouragement and enthusiasm this
would never have been written

CONTENTS

Foreword

A word about the origin and authorship of this book.

In 1999 I began researching an account of Cold War submariners that became *We Come Unseen* (John Murray, 2001). This was a collective biography of the generation of British submariners who entered the Royal Naval College at Dartmouth in 1963. In the course of this work I asked my six subjects to produce any records that they had of their own careers. Some of them found next to nothing, others a treasure-trove of personal memorabilia. One discovered something utterly unexpected. Among a cache of papers, long untouched, that he had believed pertained only to himself, he found a memoir. It took the form of a manuscript written in a beautiful italic hand on yellowing lined foolscap bound together by thin red cord.

I still remember the excitement with which N---- came to me in the summer of 2000 with his discovery. He would have been the first to admit that he had little taste for the written word. He had leafed through the pages in a desultory way, and then — against his better judgement — become utterly engrossed. For the memoir turned out to be that of his late great-uncle, General Max Quick,[i] Chief of the Imperial General Staff during the Occupation. It was a chronicle and record of Quick's intimate involvement in the events that led to the downfall of the Third Reich in the late winter of 1946. These were the events known to the world as the February Rising. Although apparently intended for publication, there was no evidence that the account had actually appeared. Various reasons suggest themselves, not least the implications for the reputations of Sir Winston Churchill and President Truman, for General Quick's contemporary and sometime friend,

i General Sir Maximilian Hargrave Quick, KCB, CBE, DSO and Bar, 1894-1984.

Admiral 'Kit' Conway,[i] and — arguably — for Quick himself. Perhaps after he had completed his memoir the Quick family had second thoughts — the General himself or his formidable wife Lady Nancy Quick.[ii]

I read the manuscript at a sitting, that very afternoon. No sooner had I done so than the magnitude of N-----'s chance discovery became apparent. Although the Occupation and the Rising have been partially and sporadically chronicled by biographers and professional historians, it is a period of our national history that many over the past sixty years have felt best forgotten. Much the same happened in France, the Low Countries, Denmark, Norway and Poland. Only since the turn of the century and the death of many of the participants have these nations — and our own — started to come to terms with betrayal, defeat and collaboration. The subject of course remains proscribed in schools throughout England and Continental Europe — much as that of the 1921 -2 Civil War is in Ireland. Here, for the very first time, was — to all appearances — an accurate and authoritative record by a figure quite central to the events of the Rising. The book would be a worldwide publishing sensation. It would be akin to the publication in 1983 of Adolf Hitler's dazzlingly prosaic diaries, the authenticity of which the foolish still doubt.

N---- proposed that I should edit the chronicle for immediate publication. I demurred. N-----insisted. The result, much delayed by litigation the nature of which can detain us only in the epilogue, is the memoir that follows.

As to the events recounted therein, another word is required. The General was writing in 1946 for an audience primed with an all too intimate appreciation of the critical events, personalities and circumstances of invasion, national defeat and Occupation. For most of those in their eighties and above, the Occupation is a horrifying memory. For anyone

i Admiral Sir Christopher Patrick Conway, VC, 1895-1953.

ii Lady Nancy Catherine Quick, GC, 1908-1997.

younger it is barely a memory at all, something scarcely taught and barely spoken of.

For the benefit of the present generation, suffice to say here that in September 1939 Great Britain found herself at war with Nazi Germany. The immediate *casus belli* was the invasion of Poland on 1 September by the Wehrmacht forces under von Brauchitsch.[iii] This was a country whose borders Britain, under Prime Minister Neville Chamberlain,[iv] had guaranteed. In the course of the following eight months, all of Western Europe fell to Hitler's forces. Towards the end of May 1940, a British Expeditionary Force fighting alongside the French found itself encircled at Dunkirk on the Channel coast of France. On 26 May Hitler's idiosyncratic order to halt the advance on the Dunkirk sands of General von Rundstedt's tanks was rescinded.[v] A third of a million English and French troops lost their lives or were captured. No more than a handful, some 23,000, was rescued by the Royal Navy.

Our forces had little opportunity to regroup. In an admirably planned and co-ordinated amphibious operation, on 14 July 1940 German forces fell simultaneously on England's southern and eastern seaboards. The two invasion fleets sustained substantial losses at the hands of the Royal Navy and the RAF. The *Blücher*, *Graf Spee* and the *Königsberg* were sunk and Admiral Doenitz drowned.[vi]Winston Churchill, who had replaced Chamberlain as PM on 9 May, proved an inspirational leader. Nevertheless, he could not make bricks without straw. He predicted that we should fight the enemy on the beaches. We did. Yet once the Wehrmacht had established its beachheads at Newhaven, Portsmouth,

iii General Walther von Brauchitsch. 1881-1948.

iv Conservative politician, 1869-1940.

v General Gerd von Rundstedt, 1875-1953.

vi Karl Doenitz, head of the German submarine flotilla.

Lowestoft and Boston, resistance was patchy in the extreme. In the east, von Rundstedt found the coast virtually undefended. Within days, his Panzers had reached the industrial heart of England: Birmingham, Sheffield and Manchester all fell with little fighting. In the south, Rommel[i] was held briefly by Gort's forces at the bottom of the North Downs along the line that runs from Guildford to Reigate. It was here that Gort was severely injured, subsequently dying of his wounds and thus precipitating Quick himself into the post of CIGS[ii] at the modest age of forty-six. There were some severe engagements in the London suburbs, but by the end of the month the fight had gone out of England. The capital surrendered on 29 July. Churchill, the Cabinet and the Royal Family fled to Canada with the remains of the Fleet. A disastrous mischance left the young princesses, Elizabeth and Margaret, in the hands of the Wehrmacht. They were victims of a turncoat at their parents' Norfolk estate of Sandringham.

On 1 August, a party comprising Hitler, Josef Goebbels, Rudolph Hess and Hermann Goering[iii] flew into Hendon in west London. Hitler formally accepted the surrender of Gort's forces in a ceremony at the airfield. Within the next few days, Great Britain was declared a province of the Reich. At its head as Reichskommisar was appointed an early Nazi party member named Reinhard Heydrich[iv], the fascist Oswald Mosley[v] his English deputy. In early September the Duke and Duchess of Windsor, styled King Edward VIII and

i Johannes Erwin Rommel, 1891–1946. The best of the Werhmacht generals.

ii Chief of the Imperial General Staff.

iii The Nazi leader accompanied by his chief propagandist, his second-in-command and the air minister.

iv Reinhard Tristan Eugen Heydrich 1904–46.

v Sir Oswald Ernald Mosley, 1896–1946.

4

Foreword

Queen Wallis, were induced to exchange their Riviera villa for Blenheim Palace in Oxfordshire, the ancestral home of the Marlborough family and birthplace of Winston Churchill. For Hitler in his Bavarian lair in Berchtesgaden[vi] this was a *fait accompli*, and he turned his mind to Operation Barbarossa and the conquest of the Soviet Union.

General Quick's memoir opens five and half years later in January 1946. In these bitter years there was little to distinguish the Reich's occupation of England from that of Continental Europe. People went about their daily lives and business increasingly persecuted by the familiar machinery of the Nazi police state, albeit adapted to local conditions. The Wehrmacht occupying forces barracked in every major town and city were buttressed by the SS, SA, Abwehr and Gestapo.[ii] Concentration camps were established for dissenters of every hue, notoriously in Wakefield, Solihull, Peterborough, Swindon, Croydon and Malvern. In practice, though — as in France — the Germans discovered that a relatively modest number of garrison troops was required to keep the population subdued. In the case of both countries fewer than 100,000 men oversaw populations in the order of 40 million. For a period of eighteen months between the end of 1940 and the late summer of 1942, a mood of laissez-faire established itself. Collaboration flourished and fraternisation became the order of the day. The Jewish community in north London and elsewhere was persecuted from 1942 onwards, and the Harwich internment camp for onward transit to the East became the counterpart of Drancy on the outskirts of Paris. This caused rumblings of discontent among the British intelligentsia, such as it was. Yet not until the following year was anything that could be dignified by the name of Resistance established. It grew in fits and starts. By 1944, the equivalent of the French *maquis* and the Italian partisans was to be found in the English capital, the

vi Hitler's home in southern Bavaria.

ii The four principal Nazi intelligence agencies.

western Highlands, north Wales, Cornwall and a handful of the industrial cities. From this time onwards, Britain began to establish itself as a troublesome province.

Attempts that year to assassinate Heydrich and Mosley met with failure — at hideous cost to the perpetrators and their families. At much the same time, as the Wehrmacht struggled towards Moscow, industrial workers were deported in significant numbers from the Midlands to the labour camps of Germany. In late 1945, when the high hopes that rested with the United States in its struggle against Japan were dashed by the sinking of the US armada in Tokyo Bay, spirits in Britain reached a nadir. The graphic images of the 45,000-ton battleships *Iowa* and *Missouri* and the aircraft-carrier *Hermes* capsized in the shadow of Cape Futtsu seemed a propaganda masterstroke. The same might be said of the highly publicised deployment of the V1 and V2 rockets that tipped the balance of the war in eastern Europe. The 'wonder weapons' as they were dubbed. In January 1946, with the defeat of Marshal Zhukov[i] in Moscow by Rommel's forces, many thought that the age of barbarism had returned. Yet, as General Quick's memoir so graphically demonstrates, the embers of Resistance throughout Europe were — quite miraculously — about to burst once more into flame. Hand in hand, the Old World and the New climbed out of the abyss.

My hand as editor lies lightly on the text. I have not attempted to modernise the General's sprightly but somewhat dated style nor to censor sentiments no longer fashionable. I have merely clarified expressions no longer in common use, changed certain names and illuminated facts about the Occupation that have been forgotten. The title and epigraph are the General's own.

Jim Ring, Burnham Overy Staithe, June 2020

---

i Georgy Konstantinovich Zhukov, 1896-1974.

Part One

Drawing the Lots

It was Thursday, 30 January 1946, at a little after 0800.

As I'd suspected, the Cabinet's old War Rooms[i] deep under Downing Street lay quite untouched, indeed precisely as we had left them more than five and a half years before. The new stewards of the corridors of power had not discovered their existence, and no one had sought to enlighten them. The basement of the War Office in Whitehall was a labyrinth in which one more steel door here or there was unlikely to catch the eye of a Pomeranian grenadier. A few moments earlier I had slipped through its portals into that eerie little passage quarried with such haste in 1938 in the aftermath of the Munich crisis.[ii] I flicked a torch on its clammy walls, padded silently under Whitehall with my footsteps just echoing on the concrete, and climbed up the spiral staircase into the lobby. When I'd last been there—I think 28 or 29 July 1940 — it had been a scene of frenetic activity, crowded with dispatch riders, aides-de-camp, and typists with pursed lips and fixed expressions, organised chaos presided over by Churchill. Now all lay silent as the grave. In the map room, where we three gathered, lay the Ordnance Survey map of the southern counties of our green and pleasant land. The last positions of Field Marshal Gort's[iii] and Model's[iv] forces were neatly

i Opened to the public in 1984 at the behest of the Prime Minister, the Right Honourable Margaret Thatcher.

ii The debate over the future Czechoslovakia that culminated in the agreement signed on 30 September 1938.

iii Field Marshal Sir John Standish Surtees Prendergast Vereker, 6th Viscount Gort, VC, GCB, MVO, CBE, DSO and two Bars ,MC, 1886-1940.

iv General Walther Model, 1891-1948.

marked, a chinagraph pencil hovering over Deptford. The chairs were pushed back, the ashtrays full, and the unshaded light threw the stained brown filing cabinets that lined the wall into sharp relief. On the sideboard stood a bottle of Haig, a soda-siphon, and a glass. Was it my imagination, or could I still detect the faint aroma of a cigar? It was as though we had stepped out for ten minutes' fresh air, only to return to shelter from Model's howitzers on Constitution Hill as they finally got the range of the Household Cavalry dug in at the end of Charles Street.

'I'll call the steward.' Kit's social graces had stood him in good stead since Dartmouth, and I would have been surprised had they failed him even now, the voice warm and confident, still hinting of his West Country home. Kit Conway. Admiral Sir Christopher Conway. Of the three[i] of us, all now just on the wrong side of fifty, the First Sea Lord had changed the least. The raven-black hair was streaked with grey, the forehead more heavily lined, the clothes unspeakably shabby, but those burning bright blue eyes set in a jockey's frame still had that quality that some men call king. Straight from Dartmouth he had joined Lieutenant-Commander Gordon Campbell's famous Q ships, merchantmen that disguised their armour until their assailants were too close to escape. Kit had been with Ironside[ii] in Archangel, commanded his own destroyer at twenty-seven, and come close to being cashiered in 1932 for too close an association with drink and women. Only his preternatural talent kept him in the wardroom. Come 1939 he was a full admiral. He had had *Royal Oak* blown from under him in Scapa Flow, had come within an ace of ramming *Graf Spee* in the Channel when *Exeter* was ablaze virtually from stem to stern. He had survived two nights in a rubber boat in the Western Approaches after the great guns of Cape Griz Nez had dropped the curtain on *Belfast's* brief and inglorious

i The heads of the three Armed Services.

ii Field Marshal William Edmund Ironside, 1880-1959.

career. After the Gestapo had finished with him at Portishead[iii] it was Admiral Raeder[iv] and the Kriegsmarine who had had him set free. The Abwehr kept tabs on him, but he was far too fly for them. He was supposedly under house arrest with his family in Fareham — that settlement close to the Solent much favoured by naval types.

Alec Howe, the third of our number,[v] allowed himself a thin smile. The obituaries characterised him as a misanthrope. It's true he was one of those people more at ease with machines than men, and Howe certainly emerged poorly from his scrap with Halifax[vi] in that feeble man's last days at the Foreign Office. Yet it seems to have been forgotten that but for Howe in 1940 we would have been fighting Messerschmitts and Focke -Wulfs with Gloster Gladiators and Boulton Pauls. In 1929 he had been the only possible successor to Hugh Trenchard[vii] as Chief of Air Staff and, irrespective of the RAF's ultimate failure to quell the Nazi armada in July 1940, we were lucky to have him. To be flown by him was to witness an absolute master of his art. Others seemed to haul their machines into the air by brute force, struggling with the controls as though restraining a runaway horse. He coaxed, and seemed to fly by mere force of will, a man entirely at one with his machine. It was this rather than Howe's more conventional qualities as a leader that gave him his extraordinary hold over his men. If his jacket hung thinly on his shoulders, and the pallor of the years of Occupation lay heavy on his parchment cheeks

iii A town on the Bristol channel, site of a notorious interrogation centre.

iv Grand Admiral Erich Johan Raeder, 1886-1960. Head of the Kriegsmarine.

v Air Marshal Sir Alexander Coram Howe, KCB, 1900-1946.

vi Edward Lindsay Wood, 1st Lord Halifax: Conservative politician; Foreign Secretary during the Munich Crisis.

vii Hugh Montague Trenchard, 1st Viscount Trenchard, 1873-1956

and wispy hair, there was still light in his grey eyes. Heydrich assumed he was broken. Kit and I thought otherwise. 'Cards?' he asked, in his thin, high pleasant voice, by way of a reply.

He was right. Time might have stood still 110 feet beneath Whitehall, but not elsewhere. Hitler was not supposed to be in the country. Nevertheless, we had reason to believe that he would address the multitude that evening in the course of the rally in the Mall to celebrate the victory of the Nazi forces in Europe. Indeed, we thought — as we spoke that morning — that a reception party led by Reichskommisar Heydrich was already on its way to the airfield at Hendon to meet the Führer. We had to decide who was to have the privilege of helping the Corporal over the Styx[i] and perhaps take a seat himself on the ferry. We three, as heads of the Services, had been working since the Armistice on 1 August 1940 towards such an end. Now — God willing — it was time to agree which of us was finally to make an end of Mr Hitler. It was down to the luck of the draw.

*

I pulled up a chair, rolled up the map of England, and delved into my jacket pocket for the pack. Still in their cellophane wrapper, black on red, the cards couldn't have looked less like a death warrant.

'Banco,' said Kit, who had seated himself opposite me in his usual chair. He looked himself. Stocky and cocky as someone once said, yet shabby as ever in an old Harris tweed jacket and grey flannels. Alec raised a sceptical eyebrow, in a way I had often seen him do of old when reproaching a wing-commander who had presumed too much upon his station. 'I think we'll cut for the deal, old man.'

I opened the packet with the stem of my pipe-scraper, shuffled the cards, shuffled them again, and pushed them over the table to Alec. I couldn't quite catch his eye. He shuffled

i In Greek mythology, the river forming the boundary between earth and the underworld.

them again, and passed them on to Kit. He pushed them back to me, stubbing out his cigarette in the overflowing ashtray. I took three cards straight off the top of the deck. The first I gave to Kit, the second to Alec — now sitting slouched in his chair on my right. The third I took myself, turning it face up as I did so. It was the nine of spades.

Kit nodded, and turned over a ten — again spades. Alec again raised an eyebrow. Then he put his thumb under the corner of the card to expose a seven of diamonds. He shrugged, turned to Kit and said 'Banco.'

Kit's face assumed the sphinx-like calm that had seen him triumph over so many lesser players in the wardrooms of the Fleet when time hung heavy on the China Station. In what seemed a single movement he swept the cards from the table, created a single pack, cut it into two, reassembled it into one, and then spread out the cards like a fan on the table.

'Alec.'

Alec's hand seemed to move out of his jacket sleeve like a tortoise's head out of its shell. It hovered briefly to the left of the deck, moved right, then returned to the left. He took a card.

'Following suit, Max?' asked Kit, indicating the fan of cards.

'As you please.' I took the nearest, and turned it up for us all to see.

The three of diamonds stared lifelessly up at me.

Alec breathed in sharply and put his own card next to mine. Three of spades. No better.

Kit drew the ten of diamonds. It was the long straw. He was off the hook.

It was Alec who said: 'And then there were two.'

Kit scooped up the cards, lit a cigarette and repeated his trick. There was no significance in precedence. I drew a card. I left it face down. Alec, more decisively this time, drew another. He, too, left it face down.

'I'll see you,' he said to me.

Kit bent across the table and flipped my card over with his dirty thumbnail.

It was the four of hearts.

I couldn't see Alec's face. Perhaps a minute passed. Kit shifted slightly in his chair, and Alec turned over his card.

It was a two, a blood red two of diamonds. Alec had drawn the short straw.

We were all on our feet. I swear there was relief in Alec's face. He shook hands with us both, turned on his heel, and left the room without a word.

I turned to Kit, standing there casually, almost insolently, with a smile playing lightly across his face. 'So be it,' I remarked, tritely enough, picking up the cards and putting them in my pocket.

'Yes,' he said, taking me by the arm and drawing us both back to our seats. 'And no.'[i]

*

It had gone 1030 before I was back in my fourth-floor rooms in the War Office. These were provided for me by the Wehrmacht as a courtesy to my former rank and my existing role. They were also a convenience for Hauptsturmführer Brunner, to whom I reported. His offices, formerly occupied by General Gort, were a couple of floors above. From the moment of Brunner's arrival from Berlin in the summer, I had found myself at his beck and call. Indeed, that very day, my ADC's first words to me were: 'He's after you, sir.'

The role in this record of my ADC, Sergeant Nancy Sturridge, will emerge in due course. Suffice to say here that she was the only daughter of Lord and Lady Bibury (Bibury was an insurance wallah ennobled by Lloyd George for public services somewhat vaguely specified).[ii] The Sturridge girl and

---

i The omission from the narrative of the subsequent discussion with the First Sea Lord first is the first indication that the General is being less than entirely frank with his reader.

ii It was Prime Minister Lloyd George's habit to enrich himself by selling peerages. The practice continues to this day.

her two younger brothers had been educated for a time at home. Then, after finishing her schooling at Wycombe Abbey, she'd spent a couple of years with her uncle in Florence, studying art and Mussolini's brand of fascism and fascists in equal measure. She'd then been formally recruited into the security services in 1938 by her godfather, Sir Hugh----. A blue-eyed English blonde too slight for gross Teutonic tastes, she was mildly freckled and wore her hair shorter than was the fashion. In their slightly old-fashioned way, the Jerries regarded her as above suspicion. They had accepted her as part of the fixtures and fittings of the War Office when they had commandeered the building on the day after the Armistice. This was an oversight. I said, 'Very good, Sergeant. Tell him I'm on my way. Papers?'

One of the various functions of Room 504 was to provide Brunner with a senior English perspective on Anglo-German relations. This was an office that had its counterpart in all the Occupied countries, although it took slightly different forms according to the terms of the Occupation and the national temperament. The French had a place in the Quai d'Orsay quite similar to our own, whereas the Dutch and the Swedes managed to keep the Boche more at arm's length.

Sturridge had already been through a full set of German and English-language papers, marking up items for Brunner's interest and, of course, our own. *Der Grosse Krieg, Volkstimme, Der Angriff, Volkszeitung,* the *Morning Chronicle* and *The Times* lay on the table. Goebbels' hand[iii] had lain heavy on all these publications since 1941, when the London branch of his Berlin propaganda office had found its feet. In any case the news left little room for editorial manoeuvre. All led on *Tag des Sieges in Europa,* glossed by those printed in English as 'Victory in Europe Day'. The broadsheets gave it 40-point headlines. There was extensive coverage of the victory parades to be held up and down the country, the spontaneous celebrations by a grateful population of the final victory in the east, and certain

iii Josef Goebbels, 1887-1946. German politician and Minister for Public Enlightenment and Propaganda.

relaxations of the curfew imposed since the 'troubles' had begun in earnest in 1944. The foreign pages gave a few sparse details of the armistice in Russia. I read the leaders with some care, as Brunner often did himself. They tried to outdo each other in praise for the Führer who had finally led Europe into the Promised Land after six years of bitter struggle. All described him as resting after his labours in the Berghof,[i] much lauded by the Bavarian peasantry. Berchtesgaden was *en fête*. I commented, 'Nothing there then, Sergeant.'

By way of reply, she handed me the foolscap *Britons Awake!*, scrappily produced, amateurish, yet a beacon of hope for the Resistance movement ever since it had surreptitiously first appeared in the Tottenham Court Road at the end of 1941. That day's issue attempted to put the best possible gloss on events. The whole of the front page was devoted to a leader that took as its theme the darkest hour. It was a wonderful piece, written, I believe, by John Buchan.[ii] The back carried a dozen news items, the usual stuff about resistance activity up and down the country. One item caught my eye, and was to have a particular bearing on later events. It concerned a raid carried out on what was described as a naval base in a curiously remote location at the head of some Scottish loch. Faslane. It was the first time I'd heard the name.

'Whistling in the dark, sir,' commented Sturridge, with a smile in her voice.

I glanced up from my desk with a nod. 'Just so.' Sturridge was party to our plot and was distantly related to Buchan. Perhaps she had suggested the piece.

Sturridge piled up the papers and handed them to me. 'With my compliments to the Hauptsturmführer.'

With a pile of papers under my arm I walked briskly up the flight of stairs to Brunner's office. The Hauptsturmführer

i Hitler's home in the Bavarian mountain resort of Berchtesgaden.

ii John Buchan (1875-1947). A man of many parts, not least a writer of thrillers. Best known for *The Thirty-Nine Steps* (1915).

was not in the mood that the day and its news might have been expected to dictate. He sat silently writing at his desk as I was ushered in by one of his guards. 'The papers, General,' he said, without looking up. The War Office is poorly heated at the best of times and, with coal in shorter supply than ever, Brunner was sporting his full winter uniform, coat and all, a vision of rather ill-fitting black. Even so he shivered, adding in a second a decade to his thirty-odd years. I laid the papers on his desk and he scrutinised them for some minutes. Some turn of phrase in the *Volkstimme* seemed to amuse him slightly, but when he turned to *Britons Awake!* he looked up, glowering. As ever, it seemed to me that his face was slightly too large for its features, the eyes too beady, the mouth too small, the open expanse of forehead too blank. His reputation rested on his six months in Nice on the Côte d'Azur, where he had cleared the city of virtually all its Jews, to be dispatched God knows where. He was said to view the efforts of his predecessor to make Finchley and St John's Wood *judenfrei*[iii] as woefully inadequate.

'This rag… ' he began, tetchily rubbing his hands on the blotter to remove the ink deposited by the paper on his hands.

'Herr Hauptsturmführer.'

'How does it come here? How *does* it come here? Today of all days?'

He had heard my explanation many times before and sat well back in his chair, his fingertips touching, as I rehearsed my reply. The papers were delivered by the retailer who in turn received them from the wholesaler, who in turn received them direct from the various presses in Fleet Street. Every day the pile appeared, and every day a copy of livid subversion was interpolated into the pristine leaves of Goebbels' press. The chain of suppliers had been checked again and again. No one could explain its presence. Once, when Sergeant Sturridge had tactfully removed the day's copy, Brunner had asked where it was. In his more benign moods he declared himself

---

iii Literally freeing an area of Jews.

pleased to be made aware of all strands of opinion.

When I had finished speaking, he took up a file from his desk. 'I have often felt your presence here in this office ...' he seemed to be struggling for the right word.

'*Merkwürdig?*' I suggested.

'Absolutely. Anomalous,' he agreed. Brunner was a good linguist and prided himself on articulating the word. He returned to the file, which was evidently my own. 'You were born in Vienna in 1894, your mother from England and your father from Prussia. Diplomats. You were educated in Vienna. Your father was posted to London in 1912. You completed your education at Winchester. Is that a place or one of your schools?'

'Both,' I said, beginning to wonder where the conversation was going.

'Before Sandhurst. You won the Sword of Honour. You fought and were wounded at the Somme and Vimy, and you ended the war a Major. Interesting, General,' he concluded. 'You could have fought on either side.'

I caught his eye and held it. 'I've always been very clear where my loyalties lie.'

'Yes,' remarked Brunner contemplatively, leafing through the remaining papers in the file. 'You led your unit with great distinction at Newhaven. Then in Guildford you prevented the lynching of a platoon of Westphalians who didn't know east from west. How very tactful. You were promoted Chief of Imperial General Staff on Gort's death, at 46 the youngest ever holder of the post. You lost your wife and children in one of the *Baedecker* raids and after — after the inevitable conclusion of matters — it was deemed appropriate by the powers-that-be that you be retained as the principal military point of liaison between the offices of the Reichskommisar of Britain and the, ah, fortunate people of this country. Well, *mein* General, it isn't in the book, is it?' Brunner nodded towards von Brauchitsch's *Orders concerning the Organisation and Function of Military Control in Britain*, a copy of which adorned every desk in the building. 'Personally, I'd have sent you straight to the Tower.'

Drawing the Lots

'I'm sure the Reichskommisar… ' I began, knowing the passions into which Brunner fell from time to time, often for no apparent reason.

'Oh, we know all about your connections with Reichskommisar Mosley,' said Brunner dismissively. 'He was your fag at Winchester, wasn't he?'

'If the Haupt… ' I began again.

But at this Brunner completely lost control of himself. 'Guard!' he shouted. 'Guard!'

A young *Schütze*[i] arrived in seconds, throwing the door open and seeming to expect to find me throttling his master.

Brunner, still seated, but deeply flushed with anger, almost shouted. 'Search this man! Search him at once!'

There was nothing for it. I turned out my pockets and laid the contents on Brunner's desk. There was little enough. The key to the rooms in Cambridge Square, my ration book and *Ausweis*,[ii] the pipe cleaner and a tin of tobacco, a dog-eared Kodak of Dorothy and the children, the torch I'd used in the Whitehall passage, and the pack of cards. Nothing he could possibly take exception to. Brunner's fury subsided as quickly as it had erupted. Perhaps he was mad, I thought, not for the first time. The three of us stood looking at these unassuming symbols of an identity in Occupied Britain in 1946. I'm not sure who was the most embarrassed.

'You're a card player?' asked Brunner in the tone of one negligibly interested in the reply.

'Patience,'I said, promptly enough. 'It's a… '

Opportunely enough, at this moment the telephone rang.

'Brunner' was barked by its owner as a guttural. As the Hauptsturmführer listened he took a couple of notes and then, holding the receiver between his shoulders and his ear, placed the notebook and my file in his briefcase, a heavy black

---

i The lowest of the enlisted ranks, the equivalent of a private.

ii Identity card.

affair with a combination lock that Lobb's[i] had crafted after a hint from Mosley's staff. After a glance at my belongings, he left them alone. With a final '*Jawohl*' he replaced the receiver, shut the briefcase, and turned to me. 'Herr General, we will resume this matter later. I know where to find you.'

I trotted back down the stairs with my heart in my boots, pondering the meaning of Brunner's explosion. Back in Room 504 I remarked to Sturridge, 'Brunner's on to something.'

She was looking glum, her shoulders drooping. 'Afraid so.'

'How do you mean?' I shot back.

Sturridge coloured suddenly and dropped her eyes. 'I'm sorry, sir. I thought you must have been told. They've arrested Sir Alec.'

*

I was due on parade at Horse Guards at 12.00 sharp. I'd make it only if I took it at the double. Brunner had some sort of scent and nobody knew what Alec might say or do in Vine Street. If I wanted to precipitate my own arrest, nothing would help it more than absenting myself from the first of the day's ceremonies. I dashed down the stairs into Whitehall. It had been closed to such traffic as was still on the streets for two days now, and the street seemed to have assumed the monumental qualities of Berlin's Wilhelmplatz. Glancing up towards Trafalgar Square I caught site of that ghastly statue of Hitler atop Nelson's Column, a perpetual affront to any Englishman. There were swastikas everywhere, perhaps a couple of dozen on each side of Whitehall, narrow strips of red and black billowing from the flagstaffs sprouting from the mansard roofs. The sky had the leaden dullness I associate indelibly with Berlin. What with the War Office standing in for Goering's *Reichsluftfahrtministerium*[ii] and the Treasury

i John Lobb the bespoke boot and shoe maker in St James's.

ii The German Air Ministry run by Reichsmarschall Herman Goering, 1893-1946.

for the Chancellery, it was all too easy to imagine oneself in the heart of the Third Reich. All that was missing was the Brandenburg Gate.

In Horse Guards, Organisation Todt[iii] had been busy. Tier upon tier of scaffolding had been set up on the parade ground in a semi-circle centred on a podium. Most of the seats were already filled, principally with representatives of the Kriegsmarine, Luftwaffe and Wehrmacht, a few civilians too. Half a dozen were clearly Gauleiters[iv]. I spotted Kingsmill and Williamson among them. Model was still standing, talking to Admiral Canaris.[v] I clearly remember Otto Skorzeny,[vi] a head taller than the tallest man, right behind them. His name will recur in this narrative. I also thought I spotted the architect-cum-armaments minister Albert Speer: tall, diffident, black hair thinning, his head slightly bowed in conversation with some apparatchik. Mosley and Heydrich were somewhere at the front, identifiable less for themselves than by the posse of surrounding bodyguards.

It was 11.58 as we took our seats. Two minutes later, punctual to the second, the open Mercedes was turning in to the parade ground, a vision of chrome and black, swastikas streaming from the front mudguards. In the back sat the hunched figure the world knows too well. Without bidding, we all rose as a single man to our feet. There was absolute silence as the motorcade led by the Mercedes and flanked by a pair of motorcycles drew slowly to a halt in front of the podium. The driver got out, opened the rear door, and

iii The Third Reich civil and military engineering group named after its founder Fritz Todt.

iv The party leaders of a regional branch of the Nazi party. Hugh Kingsmill and Henry Williamson were early members of the British Union of Fascists.

v General Walther Model, 1891-1946, the exponent of mechanised warfare; Admiral Wilhelm Canaris, 1887-1946, head of the military intelligence agency, the Abwehr.

vi See page 59 where Skorzeny is properly introduced.

Goebbels walked in his clumsy way up the half dozen steps to the platform.

Everyone knows the slight, feral figure of the master propagandist, but I have to say that his actual presence is magnetic. He told us, of course, little we didn't know and, as it so turns out, little that was quite true. Operation Barbarossa,[i] he said, had ended in the triumph long foretold by the Führer. Rommel had put Zhukov's army to the sword in Moscow, the Soviet capital was a funeral pyre, and Stalin had retreated beyond the Urals. There he was beyond the range of Rommel's 'wonder weapon,' the V2 rocket, the *Vergeltungswaffe 2*.[ii] From the Berghof, Hitler had personally pronounced that all major combat operations in Europe were over. Following the abandonment after Christmas by the United States of its struggle against Japan in the aftermath of the Tokyo Bay catastrophe, no major threats seemed to threaten the Axis Powers. The Big Three, Hitler, Mussolini and Hirohito, would soon be meeting in Potsdam to agree their respective spheres of influence. All that remained to usher in the millennium was for those present to complete the work of subduing this troublesome province. So summarised it sounds bald enough. Goebbels, though, like his master, had the gift of tongues and bent that audience to his will — an audience which, after all, had much to celebrate. When he ended by praising the Führer's enduring vision for the Reich and reminding us that it was thirteen years to the day since Hitler's appointment as Chancellor, the little man had us on our feet. He gave the final *Heil Hitler* with a great shout. The crowd roared back. It was the Jerries' day.

There was a certain amount of jostling as we got up from the stand. In fact, I half thought my pocket was being picked before dismissing the thought as unworthy in a distinguished

i The Nazi plan for the invasion of Soviet Russia.

ii Literally revenge weapon.

Drawing the Lots

— or at any rate high-ranking — group.[iii] In any case, such was the press of the crowd that I couldn't turn to see who might have done such a thing. At the bottom of the steps I checked the pocket. I never use it anyway because even something like a carefully folded handkerchief ruins the line of the coat. Self-respect matters, even in defeat. Here, though, someone had placed something. A *billet doux*, a card, or — perhaps — a playing card. With a sense of foreboding I drew it from my pocket.

It was the four of hearts, the very card I had myself drawn not four hours ago. How it had got there and who had placed it I couldn't imagine. Its meaning, though — even then — seemed quite clear. I had perhaps nine hours to do what Alec could no longer accomplish.

iii A painful example of the General's naivety.

Smoke

To do the Boche justice, they'd done a tremendous job on the Mall. I'd heard about Speer's 'Cathedral of Light' at the Nuremburg *Reichsparteitag der Arbeit*[i] in 1938, but my imagination did little justice to what he had created in the heart of St James's. He had got hold of two hundred or so anti-aircraft search-lights from store, and the Todt engineers had erected them at sixty-foot intervals along both sides of the Mall, from Admiralty Arch all the way up to Buckingham Palace. Once upon a time they had picked out Dorniers, Heinkels and Messcherschmitts as they pounded the Docks and the East End. Now they soared vertically upwards to the heavens, serving as the pillars of the soaring outer walls of an ethereal building that existed only to the imagination of the eye.

In front of the Palace and the Queen Victoria Memorial immediately to the east, a podium had been erected, an altar for the celebration of the Nazis' high mass. There was a light breeze flecked with snow, and a galaxy of swastikas flapped lazily in the wind, casting flickering shadows over the massed ranks below. Shoulder to shoulder stood the implacable forces of the New Germany: grim-faced, austere, a vision of field-grey, a mechanised and — it seemed — scarcely human army. The coal-scuttle helmets gave them the air of automata. There must have been nigh on a 100,000 there, almost a fifth of the whole British garrison, together with — I believe — substantial contingents from France and the Low Countries. As I watched from Admiralty Arch, the snow began to fall harder and to settle lightly on their greatcoats.

They had closed Whitehall entirely. I had to cut across Trafalgar Square to Northumberland Avenue, down Victoria

i Rally of labour.

Smoke

Street and through Parliament Square before turning west again to access Petty France. The snow, which had fallen in showers for most of the day, had largely discouraged such crowds as might have felt under an obligation to appear. The *Ordnungspolizei*[ii] was out in force, there was security of sorts at most of the major junctions, and one or two of the *Geheime Feldpolizei*[iii] patrols. A platoon guarded the Tothill Street entrance to St James's tube. I passed close enough to smell whisky on their breath. Then, by now making tracks in the snow, I turned north up Queen Street towards Birdcage Walk and into Queen Anne's Gate. It had taken me almost half an hour to walk round from the Arch, a distance as the crow flies of no more than 500 yards. Equally, though, I was now no further than that from the podium. I glanced at my watch under a street lamp. It was 1948. In theory, at least, time enough.

No. 22 had once been an elegant house in the style that had given the area its name. Four floors in Portland stone, handsomely proportioned with the high sash windows of the period. It had been hit during one of the air raids at Christmas in 1939 when everything seemed still in the balance. The damage was sufficiently severe to make it uninhabitable, and the house had been provided with a pair of the usual timber buttresses against collapse. It was repairable, but yet to be repaired. It was this that had first struck Sergeant Sturridge when — for our own purposes — we had asked her to vary her route into work.

I glanced left and right up the street. Straight in front lay Queen Anne's Gate. Silhouetted against Speer's great cathedral was the familiar coal-scuttle helmet of a sentry. Birdcage Walk, too, was closed. But the light across St James's Park drew the sentry's eye like a moth to the flame. The coast

---

ii The regular uniformed German police. They had all but replaced the 'bobby on the beat' in the capital and the industrial cities. In the country the 'peelers' largely survived.

iii The GFP or military police.

was clear. The front door of No. 22 was boarded up. I slipped down into the area, then turned back on myself. The steps were stuccoed brick. A shrapnel fragment or something of the sort had hit the top of the third step, stripped off the stucco and exposed a brick. This and the pointing were disfigured with years of London grime. I worked the brick free with some difficulty. Underneath lay a latch key, brass glinting dully in the light. I glanced up out of the area. It was still snowing, and the snow would mask the tread of any approaching patrol. I walked quickly across to the far side of the area, and fitted the key into the latch. It turned surprisingly easily. I pushed opened the door, and was inside. It was an empty house or, if Alec had talked, conceivably a trap. I had the same feeling in my stomach as I'd had on that last day at Newhaven.[i]

*

It was pitch dark. I dared not use a light lest it be seen by a passing patrol. Sturridge had sketched the plan of the house but I'd never been there myself. I'd memorised the plan. So I simply felt my way through the kitchen, my hand in front of my face, shuffling forward foot by foot. It seemed a barn of a place and twice I nearly tripped on some debris. The room smelled abysmally of damp and — even now, I thought — cordite. I came to a thin zinc grill screening a door. This must be the larder, one of those Victorian walk-in affairs the size of a wardrobe. I pulled the door open and fingered my way round to the back wall. There it was, sure enough, under my fingers. The cold steel of some sort of weapons' safe. My fingers slithered round the edge, feeling for the latch. I eased it open and felt inside. It was quite empty.

For a couple of seconds I cursed Sturridge under my breath. Then half a dozen other reasons for the rifles' disappearance crossed my mind. Whatever the explanation, it

i An episode alluded to by Brunner on p18 of this volume and elsewhere. I have been able to find no references to it in the Regimental History.

26

scarcely mattered. Without them, Hitler's day might yet end in dreamless sleep.

I turned, as much disappointed as relieved, and groped my way out of the larder into the kitchen again. It was there that I caught the faintest whiff of smoke. To my right was an area that seemed even darker than the kitchen. Recalling Sturridge's plan, I thought it was the stairs to the rest of the house. I paused. Sure enough, it was smoke. Tobacco smoke.

I groped for the banister, found it, and began to feel my way up into the main body of the house. Gingerly as I moved, it was impossible to be entirely soundless. Sturridge had said that only the attic would do. A couple of the treads creaked as I pawed my way right up inside the ruined house. On the third floor the stairwell became narrower and the staircase steeper. Again a faint smell of tobacco. I crept upwards like a thief in the night. My head rose level with the attic floor, and I stopped. It was entirely dark, for the blackout blinds were still in place — a vestige of the night air-raids of early 1940. It was quite silent, but in the far corner of the attic, maybe twenty-five feet away, I thought I could see the faint glow of a cigarette. I shifted slightly, and the tread creaked. For a moment there was silence. Then I heard a familiar voice, with its soft West Country drawl.

'Evenin' Max.'

There was a flash of a match being struck, and Kit was momentarily illuminated. His face was quite expressionless. Then, in the darkness, came the voice again.

'I've been looking at your file, old man,' he said, as he kindled a candle. 'Marksmanship was never your long suit,' he continued, with a glance at the rifles that I now saw on the floor. 'And you can always trust the Army to miss.'

This was no time for explanations, and Kit offered none. We were there for one purpose alone.

*

27

God knows how Sturridge had got the rifles. They were Karabiner 98Ks[i] of the sort only issued to the Wehrmacht's top marksmen. I'd have been surprised if there were more than a couple of dozen in the country, and all of them jealously guarded by their owners. They had a 1,000-yard range, and were quite accurate until there or thereabouts. We had less than half that across the park.

Once we'd loaded them and extinguished the candle, Kit carefully removed the two blackout blinds. We peered out towards the podium. At once we saw how clever Sturridge had been. The Abwehr had doubtless made a minute intelligence study of the immediate surroundings of the Mall in preparation for the celebrations. It had posted its own marksmen on St James's Palace, Marlborough House, Admiralty Arch, Buckingham Palace and the Wellington Barracks next door. As Kit pointed out, those sharpshooters straight across the park in St James's Palace were clearly visible. The buildings further east of the Barracks they'd neglected because the Queen Victoria memorial is entirely screened by trees. Or rather, it had been when they'd undertaken the survey in the early autumn, when Hitler's visit had first been rumoured. Now, in January, from the top of No. 22, the line of sight was almost entirely clear. The Abwehr, for all its thoroughness, occasionally lacked imagination. Through Kit's glasses I could make out the feathers of the eagle that formed the lectern crowning the podium. It was an easy enough shot. In the piping days of peace, I'd have taken a stag at that sort of distance with scarcely a thought.

The trouble lay in following the course of the parade and preparing ourselves for its culmination. From where we were, we could occasionally risk peering out across to the podium. We could also hear the speeches by way of the tannoy system that carried variations on the theme of victory right down to Trafalgar Square. We couldn't, though, identify the speaker

i The General has a tiresome interest in military hardware. These are sniper rifles developed by the infamous German arms manufacturer.

28

until he actually stepped up to the podium. There was then a period of grace of no more than thirty seconds or so in which to get in a shot. This was the brief period between the Wehrmacht cheering in recognition of the new speaker, and silence falling for his speech. To fire at any other time would be suicidal. The sound of the shots would be traced all too quickly to our lair.

The attic was entirely unheated. By half-past nine it was so cold we could scarcely bear to touch the steel of the rifles. We kept ourselves warm with occasional nips of Scotch. It was a little before ten when the troops at Admiralty Arch began to roar. It was a sound that was given shape and volume as it moved at a stately pace westwards down the Mall, until it gradually became a hundred thousand mouths or more yelling '*Sieg Heil! Sieg Heil! Sieg Heil!*'

Kit and I eased ourselves down behind the rifles, both aimed a foot or so above the pedestal. We could see nothing but a thousand arms raised to the man whose writ now ran from western Ireland to the Urals, whose creed of National Socialism had vanquished freedom, democracy and Christianity in the Old World, and now perhaps threatened to do the same in the New. I got him in my sights as he climbed the steps up to the podium and passed in front it. I could feel Kit shifting slightly beside me, adjusting his aim. This was it. We had waited for five years for this moment, and I could scarcely bring myself to squeeze the trigger. The chanting, tribal in its intensity, a great song, a hymn, a paean of praise to the Führer's power, began slowly to die.

It was time, for there was our target stock still. Hitler began raising his arm for silence.

At that second there was a thunderous sound from four floors below us, what sounded like the front door being burst open and, before either of us could fire, the whole stage on which Hitler stood erupted into a ball of flame.

The Two Princesses

I was awake, but why and where I couldn't tell. I was lying in what seemed to be a tiny bed. It was dark. The walls, in as far as I could see them, seemed very close. At first I thought it was a cell into which I had fallen or been consigned, some ghastly incarceration courtesy of the Gestapo, some living death. I thought for a moment of Alec.

Then I realised there was something strange about my prison. It was alive. Every few seconds it pitched and every few seconds it rolled. It was noisy, too. Noises that at first puzzled me, and that at last I identified. The squeaking and groaning was of blocks, the flap was of heavy canvas, and the clank was of steering gear. A ship.

How I came to be afloat I couldn't think. I had slept, or been put to sleep, fully clothed. I felt in my pockets. Matches. I fumbled with the box, managed to extract one while dropping a dozen on the floor, and struck a light. I was in a wooden sleeping cabin barely six feet long and tapering away to almost nothing. Beside a couple of ancient linocuts of Gravesend, a brass clock was fixed to the bulkhead. It was just after 9.30. Whether in the morning or the evening I had no idea. A sudden lurch of the vessel almost threw me out of the bunk. I swung my legs over its side and stood unsteadily, almost cracking my head on the low deck above. I noticed then that I had a large bruise on the back of my head, from God knows where. I tried the door, a low panelled effort with a neat recessed brass handle.

It opened onto a blaze of sunlight pouring down a steep wooden companionway. The space in which I stood seemed empty, stretching fifty feet or so into the darkness, and smelt pleasantly of pitch-pine and tobacco smoke. A hold, I thought; a cargo hold. I clambered up the steps onto the deck and found myself in the bows of the vessel. Aloft, I could see a

The Two Princesses

great spread of rust-red canvas silhouetted against a sky of startling wintry azure. On either side stretched the muddy brown of a great waterway, edging into mudflats, reeds and a littoral sparkling with a light dusting of snow. Not a house was in sight. Astern at the wheel of the craft — forty foot or so from where I was — stood a figure with a fresh, boyish face, not yet quite a man's. With his clear complexion and blond hair, he could have passed for a young Prince of Wales.[i] He wore dirty blue dungarees and had a pair of binoculars round his neck. I was aboard that most English of vessels, a Thames sailing barge, forging through the water on a bright winter day. Spotting me, the lad at the wheel saluted with a smartness that belied his clothing. As I stepped over the deck, he spoke in the clipped and reassuring tones of a young English naval officer: 'Mornin' sir.'

I was at least in safe hands, but there was only one thing really on my mind.

'Is he dead?' I asked.

A grin flashed across the boy's face. 'He's dead alright.' He sounded happy as Larry.

'Certain?' I flashed back, scarcely willing to believe the news.

'On the Home Service, sir. BBC never lies, does it? Blown up at Buckingham Palace. Whole of the Reich's in mourning, so they say. Admiral'll fill you in. He's havin' breakfast below.'

I noticed a smudge of smoke far astern. 'Tilbury?'

'Stanford, sir. We're heading back west. We'll be in the Pool[ii] by dusk.' His voice quickened slightly. '*Kriegsmarine* permittin'.' I followed his gaze. With the naked eye I could see what I took to be a patrol craft of some sort a few hundred yards away. 'One of the E-boats on the prowl I should think, sir. Better get below.'

---

i Name traditionally granted to the heir apparent. Prince Edward became King Edward V111 on the death of his father, King George V1, in 1935.

ii The Pool of London: the stretch of the river Thames between Tower Bridge and Rotherhithe.

I slipped down the rear companionway into the stern of the barge. A door was ajar into what I was later told was the stateroom, a grandiose term for something the size of a stable, fitted out with a couple of bunks, sundry lockers and a stove. Within the little cabin I found Kit had made himself characteristically comfortable. He had found himself an indescribably dingy outfit of a hue apparently designed to harmonise with paraffin stains and anchor mud, and was getting himself outside a large plate of eggs and bacon. A chipped mug stood on the table, a copy of yesterday's *Volkstimmes* in front of him. He rose to his feet in welcome, almost upsetting his mug. 'My dear fellow! I quite thought you'd overslept.'

It was not the moment for Kit's pleasantries. 'We've got visitors,' I said. 'Your friends the *Kriegsmarine*. Any drill?'

Kit was calm itself. 'Revolvers in those lockers,' he said, resuming his seat and wiping his black hair away from his face. On the opposite side of the cabin were three or four lockers nestling right under the deck. Opening them at random, I found a couple of service Colts. By now we could hear the low grumble of the E-boat's diesels. A couple of minutes later, judging by the wallowing of the barge, the two vessels were side by side. Kit and I took station at the bottom of the companion and awaited events. Kit had a revolver in one hand and his mug in the other. I could hear little other than the yapping of what I supposed was a dog. Some sort of interrogation was taking place to which I could only make out the replies.

'Barge *Cabby*…Rochester…Rochester…Medway… yesterday… in ballast…East India Docks…mixed cargo… Maldon…Captain Yates…Y-A-T-E-S…north-easterly.

There was a thump of someone landing heavily on the deck. Kit raised an eyebrow. 'Better leave this to me,' he said, adding. 'Make yourself scarce.' He handed me his Colt, kept his mug and went up on deck. I retreated to the stateroom. Looking round, I noticed a small door, no more than four feet high, leading aft. I swung it open, and was greeted by the rich smell of diesel. I heard steps on the companionway. I stooped, scrambled into the minute engine-room, and closed the door. The Lister almost filled the compartment, a monstrous piece of ironmongery the size of a horsebox. I'd no sooner squeezed myself behind it than I heard more steps on the companion. A moment later, the door opened again. The beam of a torch flashed round.

'Since when did barges engines have, Kapitän?' asked a voice whose tongue was scarcely English.

'Since the wind stopped blowing where they wanted to go.'

This was met with laughter, and the door closed. There were steps again on the companionway, then on the deck right above. For a few moments I awaited events. All seemed quiet. Perhaps the boarding party had gone. I crept out of my hiding place just in time to hear the E-boat's engines throttling up. Back on deck, I joined Kit. We were rewarded by the sight of the steel grey hull settling down on its haunches with a flashing, bubbling wake spurting from its stern. The rear quarters were all but taken up by a couple of torpedo tubes and an anti-aircraft cannon, on which sat a liver-coloured dachshund enjoying the breeze. Mascot, I thought. What did they call them? I'd read about this somewhere. The *Morning Chronicle* had done a feature on German gun dogs in the early days of the Occupation before the relationship with the Boche had entirely soured. Ah yes, with characteristic lack of imagination, *Der Bordhund*. Within a few moments dog and boat had receded into a speck. [i]

Kit and I wandered aft and joined the fair-haired lad at the wheel. He proved to be an Anglicised Scot from Peebles, who answered to the name of Crawford.

'What was that about?' I asked.

'Normal estuary patrol, sir', replied Crawford. 'But they rarely bother with barges. Too many of 'em. Something's up. He was *very* particular about our being inbound. I think he'd

---

i An episode the significance of which does not seem to have entirely registered with the General. See epilogue.

clocked that the London river's a two-way street.'

Kit looked speculatively in the direction the E-boat had taken, the wind catching the dark thatch of his hair. He seemed unmoved by the incident. 'Very well, Crawford. Alright on your own for a bit?'

'I'll wake Hawkins when we have to tack,' was the reply.

'Hawkins?' I asked of Kit.

'Second Lieutenant Hawkins, the *Cabby*'s mate,' said Kit. 'Like young Crawford here, a very rising member of the SBS.'[i]

Back in the stateroom I settled myself at the table while Kit set to work on the little coal stove. Soon I was tucking into bacon, mushrooms and eggs. They had been procured, Kit said, from a waterside farm at Coryton near the mouth of the Thames which — according to Kit - did a black-market trade with passing bargees.

'Like your new quarters?' asked Kit, as I pushed away an empty plate.

'I'd like to know how I got there,' I said. Another thought crossed my mind, too. A thought about a playing card. 'Not to mention a line on the pickpocket who tipped me the wink in Horse Guards.'

'Well, well,' began Kit, lighting a cigarette. 'One at a time. Getting away last night was a bit of a close-run thing'.

'I remember nothing between seeing the podium go up in flames and waking up in your fore-peak.'

'You've got our mutual friend Sergeant Sturridge to thank for that,' began Kit slowly, inhaling deeply on his cigarette. 'She set up that house to a T, including the escape route. I don't suppose you saw the hatch for the service lift in the kitchen? No? Well, of course the shaft went straight up from there to the dining-room on the third floor. She'd taken out the platform itself, the pulley system and all the cables. The idea was if we were caught short we just bundled ourselves into the shaft. It was, what? Eighteen inches square. Jump down it and you'd have ended up a pile of broken bones at

i Special Boat Section. An army commando unit tasked with amphibious operations established in 1940.

the bottom. Press your shoulders and thighs to the side and it was a tight enough fit to give you a controlled descent — with a bit of effort. The balloon went up, Jerry pouring in through the front door without so much as a by-your-leave from the butler, and you and I in *flagrante delicto* with the Karabiners in the servants' quarter.' Now Kit was getting into his stride. 'So the riot squad's piling up the stairs and we're creeping down to the dining-room. We slip into the shaft and Bob's your uncle. We're away. Back on the streets of course, merry hell. Thousands of Hitler's finest picking the remains of their fearless Führer off their greatcoats. No time for two respectably dressed, well-spoken, middle-aged gentlemen, on their way home. Or, as it so turned out, to Charing Cross pier. For dear old *Cabby*,' he continued, referring to the barge, 'that's a request stop only. Young Crawford picked up my signal. There was a bit of a to-do with the pier guards as she came alongside, which is where you got your bump on the head. Come back to you?'[ii]

'Not a thing,' I said, as indeed was the case. Neither then nor later did I regain memories of the aftermath of the assassination.

'No matter,' said Kit. Rather dismissively, I thought. It was all very well him sitting there nursing his breakfast and stubbing out his cigarette. I might have been badly hurt. Still, there were matters of greater moment, I supposed. I changed the subject. 'Who killed the Corporal?'

'Ah yes,' said Kit thoughtfully. 'Who indeed? Well, assassination isn't a very reliable method of getting rid of people and — as we know — co-ordination between the resistance groups isn't all it might be.'

'It was us, then?'

Kit considered this for a moment, looking across to the far side of the stateroom. 'Would you put it past Himmler or Heydrich?'

'No,' I said, after a moment's hesitation. Personally I

---

ii The General appears to take his account at face value.

have my reservations about democracies. Still, it's difficult to believe that our own political system could have produced quite such a cut-throat crew as had emerged in Germany since the Corporal came to power. Von Ribbentrop[i] the former champagne salesman as Ambassador to the Court of St James; Herman Goering the elephantine drug addict with a taste for other people's *objets d'art*; Joseph Goebbels the club-footed philanderer and demon of the casting couch; Himmler the pig farmer with a sideline in mass murder. I ask you. They made Horatio Bottomley[ii] look good, and I wouldn't have put knocking off the Corporal past any of them. I wondered if Kit had a line on this. 'Intelligence' his job was once, I think, however much of a misnomer that might seem. Himmler or Heydrich? It was a fair question. 'Do you know?' I asked point-blank.

Kit raised his rather shaggy eyebrows, like his hair black tinged with grey. 'No Max, I don't.' He said this with some emphasis and finality, and there was a moment's silence.

I then searched my pockets. Yes. It was still there. I fished out the card, the four of hearts, and laid it on the table. 'Who gave me this in Horse Guards?'

Kit smiled at this, brushing his hair back from his face. 'Is this an inquisition? How should I know?'

I had been pondering this for some time. 'Must have been one of our circle.'

Kit stood up and began to clear the table. 'Aren't there some things it's best not to know?' [iii]

It was a point that had been made often enough over the last five years and for the moment our conversation went no

---

i Joachim von Ribbentrop (1893-1946). Germany's Foreign Minister from 1936 onwards. Hitler posted him to Britain to forge an alliance with the words, 'Ribbentrop, you have the trumps in your hand, play them well.'

ii Horatio Bottomley (1860-1933). Politician and swindler.

iii An interesting question.

further. Kit finished clearing the table in silence and dumped the plates and mugs in the tiny sink. Then he felt underneath the table, and there was a scrape of a latch. He hinged the table upwards to reveal a little wooden cache. Within was a buff foolscap envelope. He pulled it out and laid it on the table. It had a typed label that read Operation Nonesuch. The back of the envelope bore a heavy red wax seal. 'All yours,' he said. Some of the tension had gone out of his voice, I thought.

I broke the seal, took out a couple of dozen sheets of closely typed foolscap and began to read. I have here neither the space nor the freedom from the strictures of the Official Secrets Act to disclose anything approaching the substance of Operation Nonesuch. Nevertheless, its drift will be apparent from my narrative, and much of the thinking was in any case common knowledge in our circle. It's enough to say here that the orders had been drafted to come into force in the eventuality of Hitler's assassination by the Special Operations Executive.[iv] They assumed — hoped perhaps — that this event could provide the trigger for some sort of national uprising. With the King and Queen in exile with the Cabinet in Ottawa, the princesses Elizabeth and Margaret were likely to be taken as the figureheads of the movement — or could be represented as such. Their custody was accordingly of the first importance. That Elizabeth was heir to the throne was hardly a secret. Although there had been plenty of rumours, the public had not actually been told that the King was dying. This was the first time I had seen this stated as fact in an official document. If the rising was to have any chance of success, Nonesuch argued, the princesses had to be freed. The signature that appeared on the bottom was that of the Prime Minister himself, and I thought I saw his hand in the grandiosity of the operation's thinking and its very name.

Winston might be Winston but he was very good at over-reaching himself. What was that mad plan he had at

---

iv Founded by Churchill in 1940 as a commando unit to 'set Europe ablaze.' This is the General's first mention of the organisation of which he was a leading member.

the beginning of the war for floating mines down the Rhine? The trouble was he'd been at everything from the Battle of Omdurman[i] to the trenches, and he thought he knew my job. Come to think of it, Kit's and Alec's too.

Still, I read through the orders themselves very carefully a couple of times and they seemed less hare-brained than some I'd seen over the years. 'This plan', I said cautiously, handing the papers over the table to Kit, 'might conceivably work.'

*

With a light south-easterly behind us and the tide just about slack, we moved slowly up the wide lower reaches of the Thames, past Gravesend and Tilbury, Grays Swanscombe and Greenhithe. The thick scudding cloud and snow of the previous day had been followed by one of those sunny winter days that only England can provide, when the bare stubble and naked trees speak only of the promise of spring. The low winter sun gave a wonderful incandescence to the Thames's sandy downstream waters and cast long shadows on the barge's black-caulked decks. Crawford steered with one hand lightly on the wheel of the great vessel as the *Cabby* retraced the passage she had taken the night before. For Kit and me, on the deck behind him, backs against the mizzen mast, keeping a weather eye out for the Kriegsmarine, wondering at the seagulls' swirling flight, it was difficult to believe that Hitler had gone. We talked of Dorothy and the children, of the hiding we intended to give Mosley, and of Alec and Hauptsturmführer Brunner. Kit told me an unsuitable story about one of his débutantes. As we drew further west, past Purfleet and the dreary flats of the Rainham marshes, the shadows lengthened, the young flood carried us upstream at a greater pace, and a chill began to steal over the barge. We clattered down the companionway. This woke Hawkins, who we found asleep on some sacks in a corner. He proved to be

i Fought on 2 September 1898.

38

a tough little Geordie, freckle-faced, tousle haired and not yet twenty. We briefed him, and left him on deck with Crawford.

Under the companionway was a neat example of maritime joinery. A chart table, above which had been framed a matrix of three dozen pigeon holes. In each of these was a neatly rolled signalling flag. Kit thrust his hand into one of the holes and fiddled for a second. Then he hinged the whole matrix aside over the chart table. The entire space behind was filled with a steel-grey Pye wireless telegraphy set. I examined this with some interest as I'm a bit of w/t expert. 'Where's the aerial?' I asked.

'Runs right up the mast and the sprit. We're hooked up to a relay, and on a good day Crawford's picked up Ottawa.[ii] We'll try later.'

'Must be three and half thousand miles,' I said admiringly.

'Progress,' responded Kit, drily.

For the present, we tuned in to the BBC. Under Goebbels's personal direction, its preparation for the coverage of *Tag des Sieges* had been extensive; the coverage — if partial — will be remembered by those who heard it. The Corporation had apparently done nothing to plan for coverage of the Führer's death. You'd think it might have had contingency plans for such an eventuality, but that's Reith[iii] for you. All sound and fury signifying nothing. According to Kit it had been playing solemn music since dawn, interrupted with sparse news bulletins. Goebbels had evidently taken the view that, with thousands of witnesses, the Führer's death was a little difficult to conceal; for similar reasons that its circumstances were impossible to deny. The great man had been assassinated. To no group, faction or individual did he allow responsibility to be attributed; there was talk merely of the extermination (*'die Vernichtung'*) of the suspects. There had been other assassination attempts before, all with the

---

ii Capital of Canada and seat of Churchill's exiled government.

iii John Charles Reith, 1st Lord Reith, 1889-1971. Father of the BBC.

grisliest of consequences for their perpetrators. Kit flicked the switch that transported the announcer to oblivion. 'Time to try the oracle,' he said. For a few moments he busied himself at the console, getting everything ready to ensure that our time on air was kept to a bare minimum. The *Cabby*'s R/T had no encoder, and we strongly suspected that the Boche had detectors at Tilbury as well as Greenwich. Leaning forward, Kit spoke with unaccustomed urgency into the microphone.

'Watson to Moriarty. Watson to Moriarty. Over.' He flicked the switch from transmit to receive. He was met by a barrage of static. He tried again. 'Watson to Moriarty. Watson to Moriarty. Over.' Again he shifted to receive. There was nothing. Again and again he tried. Then, just as he flicked over the transmit once more, Ottawa responded. 'Moriarty to Watson. Moriarty to Watson. Over.'

Ottawa was audible, though heavily garbled.

'Watson to Moriarty. Hearing you Strength One, Interference Five. Over.'

'Moriarty to Watson. Confirm Nonesuch. Confirm Scylla. Over.'

'Nonesuch confirmed. Confirmed. Over.'

'Have you your or... '

'Repeat, please, repeat. Over.'

'Are you hearing me? Over.'

'Have you your orders? Over.'

'Affirmative, Moriarty. Have we permission to execute? Over.'

'Watson repeat. Over.'

'Have we permission to execute? Over.'

'Permission granted. Repeat. Permission granted. Over.'

'We receive your permission. Will you stand by? Over and out.'

Kit flicked off all the switches as quickly as he could. We'd been on air for perhaps ninety seconds. Probably not enough for the Boche to get a fix, but enough to arouse a few suspicions if anyone was on the case in Greenwich. Any half-way competent W/T officer would equate a signal of our strength with something the size of the battleship *Potemkin*,[i] check it against his shipping schedule and raise the alarm. It was a risk we had to run. 'Well, old boy,' said Kit rubbing his hands together with his usual enthusiasm for the fray. 'Looks like we're on.'

*

It seems scarcely worth rehearsing what a gruesome reputation the Tower had acquired by the beginning of 1946. When the SS took over the castle in 1940, they acquired a purpose-built prison in the centre of London that might have been designed for their needs. With its curtain walls and old moat, it was virtually impregnable either from within or without; it could accommodate almost a thousand prisoners enjoying considerable degrees of discomfort; and it was amply provided with *oubliettes*, torture chambers and dungeons dedicated to the purposes of execution.

The SS moved in, replaced the existing staff virtually to a man, and at a stroke they turned the clock back five hundred years. They found uses for the medieval thumbscrew, the rack and the iron maiden, and practised the casual dismemberment of eye, ear and nose so favoured by our Plantagenet predecessors. They refined the best methods of the Tudors and Stuarts with hose pipes, hooding, mind-altering drugs, sleep deprivation and water torture. It was there that Ironside, Gamelin, Dill, Cunningham and Montgomery[ii]1 all succumbed, and where Heydrich concluded that Alec was sufficiently broken to merit release. It was the chamber of horrors of the regime, the reputation of which was rivalled only when those strange rumours from Poland began to circulate

i The 12,500 ton battleship of Russia's Black Sea Fleet. Scene of the mutiny of 1905 that ushered in the Revolution of 1917.

ii Senior allied staff. Field Marshal William Ironside 1880-1942; General Maurice Gamelin, 1872-1943; Field Marshal Sir John Dill, 1881-1941; Major-General Bernard Montgomery 1883-1942.

last year about a place called Sobibor.[i] It was believed that the princesses had been held in the Tower since their capture at Sandringham; from here we were ordered to prise them.

*

As the early winter's dusk fell, we studied the plans of the Tower. MI5 had been unable to procure a ground-plan dated later than 1935, and we were obliged to assume that nothing much had been changed. The critical issues were the precise location and disposition of the SS forces within the walls and of course more particularly where the princesses were being held. With a prison population nigh on four figures and a garrison, we believed, of five hundred or so, few secrets could be kept absolute. The intelligence was that the Tower was garrisoned by the 109th SS-Totenkopf regiment under the command of Standartenführer Ludwig Goring. They were barracked principally in the Waterloo Block, with the White Tower used as an annex. The bulk of the prisoners were kept in the New Armouries; those deemed worthy of special treatment of one nature or another were in the Byward Tower or the Queen's House. The princesses themselves were said to be held in the latter.

The prospects of an open assault on the Tower succeeding were negligible in the absence of my battalion, decimated at Newhaven and then disbanded. The Tower had always been well guarded, and the SS would now be in a state of high alert. It could only be breached by means of a Fifth Column[ii] or subterfuge of one nature or another. If we had an advantage, it lay in our relatively detailed knowledge of the Tower and its workings that the Boche had had only a limited opportunity to acquire. The planners of Nonesuch also believed that whatever the strengths of the SS in guarding a *Schloss*, they

---

i The Nazi extermination camp in the Lublin district of Poland.

ii A group of people who clandestinely undermine the nation.

might be less imaginative in considering the possibilities of a river. Jerries don't really understand water. On three sides the Tower was guarded by walls that rose 30 feet from the empty moat. They were floodlit, and overlooked by sentries supposedly stationed in each of the corner towers: Bell, Devereaux, Martin and Salt, together with the turrets of the White Tower itself. On the fourth side streamed the river, a sleepless muddy sentinel deemed by those who had conceived the castle on the site of the Romans' Londinium Augusta as protection in itself. In the days of Edward I, a lower wall had been built along the Thames, and in this was set the water-gate. This was used when transport by river was infinitely easier than by road. It became the custom to land the Crown's enemies there. By the early seventeenth century it was known as Traitors' Gate.

In the nineteenth century it had gradually fallen into disuse and, since the Great War, it had been utterly neglected. There, though, it still stood. To the casual eye it looked unusable and impassable, like a bricked-up door. The plan hinged on Standartenführer Goring taking precisely that view.

On deck again the easterly had strengthened slightly, and with it the flood. We were carried west with the night towards our destiny. As the sun set in our eyes, dusk fell on the narrowing stream, and lights began to appear on the shore. We passed Woolwich town and Wren's great hospital at Greenwich. As we approached the Docks, the lights of ships in the fairway began to thicken, flares gliding in the water; green, red and white, pursuing, overtaking, joining and crossing one another. Most were steamers, but here and there we saw the great wing of a fellow barge, the rich tan of the sail shading into the starry night sky. Sometimes we heard the beat of a patrolling E-boat. We forged up the Blackwall and Limehouse Reaches and swept past Bermondsey and Wapping into London Pool. Here our way was barred by Tower Bridge, the carriage-way of which was too low for the *Cabby*'s great mast.

With Crawford at the wheel, Kit and I lowered the *Cabby*'s starboard lee-board,[i] and Hawkins on the foredeck prepared the capstan. Just in front of Butler's Wharf on the south bank, Crawford put the wheel right over. The barge described a tight semi-circle around the lee-board that brought her back into the wind and against the tide. Within seconds she'd lost all way and, with a splash, Hawkins at the capstan dropped anchor. In a trice, Hawkins and Crawford were together on the main halyard as they pulled the great flapping sail up to the sprit. In a few minutes the mainsail was brailed up, the topsail run down and clewed in, the foresails stowed and the riding light lit. The great barge was at rest.

As the *Cabby* settled gently to her anchor, I borrowed Kit's glasses and looked back over her stern. Under the bridge's carriage-way we could see the Tower in all its glory, the floodlit swastikas streaming from the four turrets of the White Tower in the wind. In a moment I spotted the water-gate, not much more than a semi-circular shadow in the north embankment. Behind it stood St Thomas's Tower.

It wasn't only Traitors' Gate that caught my eye. Just upstream was moored an E-boat. According to Crawford, there were at least a dozen in the Estuary squadron, and a number of others making passage through the Thames to the Channel or the German Sea. It could have been any of them. As it so turned out, though, it wasn't. On its stern, master of all it surveyed, was a small, liver-coloured dachshund. It was *Der Bordhund*.

---

i The lifting boards used to prevent the barge skidding sideways under pressure from the wind.

Traitors' Gate

Back in the stateroom, the four of us took stock. The E-boats used to patrol the estuary were based at the Royal Victoria Docks in the Plaistow marshes. There was no obvious reason why she should have been here, and it was curious that this particular one was. Her proximity to Traitors' Gate was a nuisance, but didn't make the plan of gaining entry to the Tower through the gate unworkable. According to Crawford and Hawkins, by German standards the Kriegsmarine E-boat crews were cowboys. They were more likely to be in the brothels in Shad Thames just across the river from the Tower in Southwark than doing sentry duty. Looking again at the plans of the Tower, it also occurred to me that the line of sight of the SS sentry in the Byward Tower down to the river and the gate would be blocked by the grey bulk of the *Schnellboot*. Either way, as Hawkins pointed out, short of casting her adrift, there was nothing we could do. Only to myself did I add the curiosity of the *Schnellboot* to the oddities surrounding the Führer's assassination, and the planting of the four of hearts.

It was time to make ready. Earlier in the day we had agreed our *noms de guerre*: Sturmbannführer Herman Koidl and Sturmbannführer[ii] Stephan Merkel. Given our ages and the need strut about the Tower late at night, we felt the rank seemed about right. Crawford fished out the uniforms, and I have to say that Gieves[iii] had done a wonderful job. They had Kit's and my measurements on file, so all they had to do was to turn out a couple of standard Sturmbannführer uniforms. They'd had plenty of practice over the last five years, I suppose. With a couple of fittings they'd have been

ii Storm unit leader, the equivalent of a Major.

iii Gieves & Hawkes, the Savile Row tailors.

perfect. Lobb had done a similarly good job on the boots. We packed everything into a couple of waterproof cases that Crawford had had run up in the SBS workshops in Chatham, a complex the Boche never quite fathomed. Provided they did not leak and we could actually get them into the Tower's precincts, we would be fine. The frogmen's suits were less satisfactory. Crawford's relationship with the quartermaster at the *Kleinkampfmittelverband*[i] didn't have quite the strength of that with the good tailors of Gieves. He had managed to procure a couple of von Wurzian's[ii] old diving outfits that had been downgraded from operational to training purposes. Both had slight cracks on the seams. They'd do. With a bit of luck we'd be out of them in ten minutes. Finally, we agreed the short strokes of the plan with Crawford and Hawkins. The heavy barge dinghy had been prepared, and was swinging on the davits ready to be lowered. They were to row Kit and me across to the north bank and get us as close to the water-gate as they could. Neither of us were strong swimmers and we couldn't possibly swim the cases very far. If we could effect an entry, the youngsters were to follow us and try to find an escape route from the Tower that could be used as easily by a couple of teenage princesses as by a pair of middle-aged military gentlemen slightly below their normal very high standard of fitness. If we couldn't use the water-gate entrance, they would be there to take us off immediately.

It had just gone 2130 as we climbed the companion steps up on to the barge's deck. It was a bright clear night with a thin crescent moon, but after the warmth of the stateroom with its gurgling stove, bitterly cold. Crawford, looking about twelve in the moonlight, had already lowered the dinghy and she stood bobbing by the side of the barge's black pitch hull, the river meandering silently past her. It was now just after high water, so we'd have the stream against us up to the gate. High

i German frogman units.

ii They were led by Alfred von Wurzian.

above the *Cabby*'s riding light, clearly silhouetted against the stars, soared the two towers of the bridge.

Kit stepped down the accommodation ladder on the side of the barge into the dinghy with the ease of a professional sailor. I handed down the two cases and followed more gingerly. The steps were slippery. Crawford was at the bow oars. Hawkins — a stocky little figure like a Dickensian street urchin - followed me down, loosed the painter and took the stern oars. From the river rose that wonderfully evocative smell of water vapour and Thames mud. At that moment, I thought I'd rather be there, doing what I was doing, than anywhere else in the world.

Crawford and Hawkins pulled strongly away from the barge, pointing upstream as the current swept us down, crossing towards the northern embankment of the great river. In a few minutes we were under the shelter of the northern carriage-way of the bridge. There we paused for a few moments, Hawkins taking a couple of strokes every now and then to prevent us being carried back downstream. We looked west, upstream. Ahead of us lay the embanked wall of Water Lane. It curved away slightly to the north, but we could just see the corner of the E-boat's stern. Water Lane itself was very well illuminated by the floodlights on the Byward, Waterfield and Develin Towers. As the Nonesuch planners had surmised, these lights spilled over only marginally to the river. Indeed, at this state of tide the Water Lane embankment threw a shadow of perhaps nine feet. Beyond this was a strip of light that shaded quickly into muddy brown and then black. Our course was too obvious to merit discussion.

Hawkins and Crawford set to their oars once again, and we crept silently upstream in the friendly shadow of Water Lane. With every stroke, slightly more of the transom stern of the E-boat was revealed: half in, half out of shadow. Closer and closer we crept until we could see the whole of the stern, her white riding-light and, a darker shadow within the shadows, the entrance to Traitors' Gate. If anyone in the *Schnellboot*'s crew had thought to take a turn on the bridge and glance aft, he would have been rewarded by the sight of the four of us skulking towards the water-gate right under the ship's stern. As it was, no one did, and history took a different course. A couple of seconds later Crawford pulled heavily on his starboard oar and nosed us right out of the waterway and away from prying eyes of the Kriegsmarine. We were in the ante-chamber of the water-gate, a tunnel rather longer than I'd expected, thirty feet or so running under Water Lane. Here the water lapped gently on steps that had been trodden by the sad feet of Cranmer.[i] Only the wooden lattice-work of the gate itself lay between us and the princesses.

At this point the judgement of the Nonesuch planners became paramount. The water-gate was designed to control the entrance and exit of water-craft. When the gate was withdrawn upwards into St Thomas's Tower, the waterway was clear to permit boats to dock at the tiny quay and steps that led up towards Wakefield Tower. When it was closed the passage was barred to vessels in both directions. For the gate to be effective it had to drop down to the surface of the water, no further. Obviously the height of the water surface above the floor of the chamber varied with the height of the tide. It was necessary that the bottom of the gate should be below the water even at the lowest of low tides. What wasn't necessarily needed was for the gate to touch the river bed. In their scrutiny of the Tower, the planners in Ottawa had been led to believe that at all states of tide there might be sufficient room between the river bed and the bottom of the gate to permit the passage of a man. If they were wrong, it was conceivable that it might be possible to raise the gate into the superstructure of the tower above. Whether the mechanism was still operable, nobody knew.

I glanced at my watch. It was now 2148. There was no time to lose if we were to find the princesses before they turned in. I was marginally a better swimmer than Kit. I was to go first. There was enough light from the Wakefield floodlight both on

i The martyr Thomas Cranmer, 1489-1556.

48

the river outside the embankment and the area immediately below the Tower within to see what we were doing. I lowered myself gingerly over the side of the dinghy and hung on with both hands. Even through the frogman's suit I could feel the bitter winter Thames gnawing at my vitals. Kit, without a word, handed me the waterproof case with my mask. Using the case as a float, I kicked the ten feet or so to the gate itself. With one hand I grabbed the lattice-work just above the water; with the other I held the case. I now reached down with my foot to try to find the bottom of the gate. I could feel the lattice-work extending towards the chamber base, but neither the bottom of the gate nor the river bed.

Well, it was high tide. There was nothing for it. I took a deep breath and pulled the mask over my nose and mouth. With the case in one hand I dived down towards the bottom, kicking as hard as I could.

I didn't make it.

The more I pulled down with my one free arm, the more that cursed case pulled up, buoyed with the air inside. Within seconds I was back on the surface again, spluttering like a hippopotamus. I might make it by myself, but not with the case.

I took another breath, shoved on the mask, and submerged. This time I used the lattice as a ladder, dragging the case after me. In no time at all the lattice-work suddenly came to an end. Fighting the desire to draw breath, I pushed myself down with my free hand. Through the suit under my feet I could feel the slush and silt of the river bed. Then I could hold my breath no more. I surfaced and splashed back to the boat. Kit leaned over the side and grabbed my hand. 'What's the form?'

'Just possible,' I gasped. 'Gap at the bottom of a foot or so. The problem's the cases.'

'Just the job for Crawford,' he said with his slightly lop-sided grin.

I have to say Crawford was very game. Of course we both gave him thirty years, and swimming was part of his job. The water, though, really can't have been much above freezing, and he had no diving suit. In a couple of moments he had stripped himself and swum the cases over one by one to the gate. Then he took each one, climbed down the lattice, and slipped the case under the bottom of the gate. In a moment the cases sat bobbing on the surface on the far side of the gate, awaiting our attention. Crawford sat in the dinghy trying to dry himself with his own clothes, his lank fair hair dripping over his eyes.

Now that we were unencumbered by the cases, getting ourselves under the gate was a piece of cake. Just as the clocks were striking ten, Kit and I were scrambling into our uniforms on the inside of the gate. A few minutes later we inspected each other. We looked like two perfectly presentable Sturmbannführers, albeit smelling moderately of Thames mud.

It was only after we had disappeared from his sight that Crawford noticed a new wiring loom running up the wall close to the steps. It looked as if the SS had taken the trouble to alarm the gate after all.

*

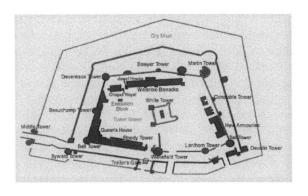

The next stage of the plan called for an effrontery that comes naturally to senior members of His Majesty's armed services. Having satisfied ourselves as to our appearance, we formed up and walked brazenly through the gateway in the Wakefield Tower that opened in front of us and gave into

50

the main courtyard of the Tower. Ahead, so heavily floodlit
that it actually took the hue that provided its name, stood
the White Tower. Its swastikas were now hanging limp in
the night calm, flickering just occasionally like the tail of a
cat. We swung left, our new boots scrunching on the gravel
beneath our feet. We strode in front of the Bloody Tower and
headed straight for what we thought was the main doorway
into the Queen's House. Glancing right, I saw the mass of the
Waterloo Barracks, with lights at just a couple of the windows.
All seemed quiet, and not a sentry was in sight. I assumed,
though, that we were being observed by the guards in the Bell
and Wakefield Towers. We both knew better than to look up.
The door, a very heavy affair of oak bound with iron, was
just ajar. I pushed it open with some effort, and we stepped
together into the Queen's House. Immediately on our right
was a tiny concierge's office. Within, busy over a kettle, was
a *Schütze*. He had one of those rough-hewn peasant faces, all
angles and flat planes, that one sees so much in Thuringia.
'*Guten Abend*,' said Kit and I as one.

The *Schütze* continued his efforts with the kettle, merely
giving us a grunt. He seemed utterly unsurprised at our
appearance in the Queen's House at this time of night. Wishing
to do nothing to raise his suspicions, we walked on into the
main body of the house, as though we knew exactly where we
were going. Ahead lay a wide stone-flagged corridor, its walls
panelled in oak. A picture of Himmler glared down at us from
one of the panels. The photographer had tactfully omitted
his pigs. We marched along with all the confidence we could
muster. In a couple of moments we found ourselves at the
bottom of a flight of broad stone stairs. These we stepped up
briskly. At the top of the flight, out of sight of the concierge,
we took stock.

According to our intelligence, there were only a couple
of suites of rooms in the complex that were suitable for
holding the princesses. Both were on the first floor. One lay
in the part of the building that dated back to Henry IV. The
other, a newer set, supposedly overlooked the river. We had

a hurried, whispered discussion. I suspected we were still in the older part of the house, but where I was not sure. As Kit helpfully pointed out, we couldn't go round knocking on the doors of all the bedrooms to find out. The only course seemed to be to explore this floor. We followed the upper corridor for fifty feet or so, past four closed doors. At its end it gave onto another corridor, curiously angled at about fifty degrees to the first. Just as we turned the corner we heard the click of a closing door. Ahead of us appeared an orderly, carrying a chamber pot. Kit rose to the occasion and for once was quite quick-witted. 'A present for Standartenführer Goring?'

He was a weedy-looking *Schütze* with steel-rimmed glasses, clearly rather more surprised by our appearance than the chap downstairs. I saw his eyes registering our ranks, and thanked God for Gieves and Hawkes. He managed a smile. 'Too good for him, sir. This is blue-blooded,' he said, glancing at his pot.

'Well,' I remarked pleasantly, 'they're only human.'

The *Schutze* permitted himself a smile, and made to move off.

'Goodnight, private,' said Kit dismissively. The man took the hint.

We walked on, relishing our stroke of luck. Two minutes later we knocked on what we assumed was the princesses' door, and thrust it open.

The room was carpeted and pleasantly furnished with a couple of Louis Quinze chairs and an escritoire. A small fire burned in the grate, and in front stood an *Unterscharführer*.[i] This chap looked alert. Kit and I both saluted. 'Evening, Sergeant. All quiet?'

He saluted, but looked at the pair of us with some surprise. It had gone ten, it was the night after his beloved Führer's assassination, and the Tower was on high alert, doubtless awash with rumour and gossip. The Tower might have been thought impervious to intruders, but here was he, the last line of defence in protecting an asset on which his masters clearly

i Junior squad leader: the first non-commissioned rank in the SS.

put a high price. It was a tricky moment.

Then I noticed a couple of things — his wound stripe and the regimental badge.

He was attached to von Mackensen's *Kavallerie*,[ii] whom I'd done my best to turn back into the sea at Hastings. 'I say, did you pick that up at Newhaven? We were on your right flank.'

'Lewes, sir,' he said, promptly enough. 'Just on the corner of the high street.'

'Where the HLI[iii] put up that stand?'

'Just there, sir,' he agreed.

'What's your name?'

'Zimmermann, sir.'

'Well, Zimmermann, we're sorry to drag you out tonight. We've just been having dinner with Standartenführer Goring. He wants a chat with the princesses.'

This he took entirely in his stride. 'I'll get them ready, sir.'

What happened next exceeded our expectations. Zimmermann knocked somewhat tentatively at what I presumed was the door into the main apartments. There was no response. He knocked again, somewhat more firmly. The inner door opened just a crack. I couldn't see inside. Zimmermann was forced to explain himself through the slit. The response was a tirade that began with an exclamation, continued in utterly vile language, and ended with the door being firmly shut.

'Who on earth's that?' I asked.

Zimmermann looked at me and, presuming rather on his rank I thought, rolled his eyes upwards. 'Lady Julia Manning.'

'Lady-in-waiting?' I asked.

'That's what they call her,' agreed Zimmermann. Assured of my credentials, he was forthcoming. 'Watchdog, more like. Bit my hand off more than once, I can tell you.

ii Field Marshal Anton Ludwig August von Mackensen, 1849-1945.

iii Highland Light Infantry. There is some evidence in the Regimental History to support this statement.

Doesn't approve of the girls going out at night, least of all to see the Kommandant, certainly not at this time.'

I glanced at Kit and chanced my arm. 'The Sturmbannführer speaks English of a sort. He may be more persuasive.'

The sergeant shrugged.

Kit knocked at the door. 'Lady Julia, may we have a word?' There was no response. 'Lady Julia, this is Sturmbannführer Koidl. We need to speak to you. Now.'

After a moment, the door opened and a woman, more girl than woman, slipped into the room. Other images have overlain my first impressions of Julia. I should say here that she was small, verging on stocky, very fresh-faced given that she presumably spent her time cooped up inside the Tower, and had short brown hair. A slightly square jaw gave an air of determination. She wore a green-flecked tweed suit, slightly threadbare. She might have been thirty, maybe a shade younger.

'What's the meaning of this?' she demanded in the commanding tones of her class. 'How dare you come barging in at half past ten at night asking us to tramp across to see old Ludwig. What on earth does he want now that won't wait till morning?'

'Now Lady Julia,' said Kit, 'as you very well know, that's not an attitude you can afford to adopt.'

This wasn't well received. She turned sharply to Kit. 'I'll adopt any attitude I think fit for the girls. And don't you dare patronise me.'

'If you have the princesses' best interests at heart...' Kit continued calmly in his best First Sea Lord manner.

Then this strange girl sat down cross-legged on the floor, and just stared at us. 'Who are you anyway? Who are these people, Zimmermann?'

This was not an avenue we wished to pursue. 'This is Sturmbannführer Herman Koidl of the Reiter-SS,' I said quickly, 'and I am Sturmbannführer Stephan Merkel of the same.'

She looked at us again appraisingly and in a manner I would not describe as flattering.

'Cavalry, eh? You smell like a couple of draymen.'

'Oh, come on,' said Kit coaxingly. 'Standartenführer Goring wants to see them for ten minutes — to satisfy himself over a little sporting matter we raised with him. We're not taking them to… ' — here he paused for a moment — 'Badminton.'

It was an expression that even then struck me as decidedly strange. The girl seemed to think the same. She looked more closely at Kit, then back at me, then back at Kit again. Then she shrugged her shoulders and got to her feet. 'Five minutes?'

'Five minutes,' confirmed Kit confidently. 'It's cold outside and they'll need their coats.'

A good twenty minutes later we were ready to go. The princesses I need hardly describe. I'd last seen them at a point-to-point at Holkham[i] in north Norfolk a year before the war. Then they were children, Elizabeth eleven or twelve and Margaret — I think — eight. Princess Elizabeth was now a young woman with all the freshness of morning upon her, not quite a beauty but with her clear complexion and well-cut features something very close. Her sister, smaller, more vivacious, had a hint of mischief in her eye. They had had a strange life, for of course no one had dreamed until 1935 that they might come close to the throne. Only the abdication of their uncle[ii] the following year in favour of their father had thrust them into the limelight of succession. It was a fairy-tale story that the public — then decidedly in need of a dose of innocent romance —adored. That night they were shy and sleepy.

We escorted them down the corridor back towards the concierge. Here, Zimmermann was our passport to freedom because the concierge could hardly let the girls past unquestioned without his presence. On the other hand,

---

i Seat of the Earls of Leicester, and only fifteen miles from Sandringham, where the pair had been captured in 1940.

ii King Edward V111. See page 151.

the veteran of Lewes might think it odd if we made for the water-gate rather than Standartenführer Goring's suite in the Waterloo Barracks. He would certainly think it strange when we all ended up in the *Cabby*. Zimmermann led the party down the stairs, with Kit and me forming the rearguard. I attracted Kit's attention and glanced at Zimmermann. Kit nodded.

At the door Zimmermann nodded to the concierge who, judging by the aroma, had concocted some sort of *Glühwein*. I could have done with one myself. No sooner were we all on the path outside than Kit fell in next to Zimmermann and engaged him in conversation. Moving at a stroll, I led the party off towards the Waterloo Barracks. These, I noticed, were now ablaze with light. A few moments later, Kit rejoined us, alone. I wondered if Zimmermann was still in the land of the living. Kit and I then drew Julia aside from the princesses. 'I'm sorry, Julia,' said Kit, sounding not in the least apologetic. 'I thought you'd remember Badminton.'

'Naturally,' she said, colouring slightly in the floodlight. 'Your friend?'

'General Sir Max Quick,' said Kit.

She took it calmly. 'Where are we going?'

'A place of safety,'

'Shall I tell the girls?' We glanced at the princesses, still standing hand in hand in the dark.

'You'll have to,' I said, thinking of the sentries in the towers surrounding us. 'We need to get out of this place.' I felt then how extraordinarily lucky we'd been. If it was to last we couldn't hang around within full sight of the sentries, looking like lost sheep. 'Let's get a move on,' I said.

*

We retraced our steps to the Queen's House, past the door and along the front of the building, towards the water-gate. Behind us the girls were whispering. Again our boots scrunched as we walked towards the Wakefield Tower. A couple of moments later we were in the sanctuary of the gate itself. Everything then began to happen very quickly.

At once I saw that Crawford and Hawkins had succeeded. The gate itself had been raised well above the water, and the way was clear for us to make our escape from the Tower. There were the pair themselves in the dinghy by the steps, Crawford beckoning furiously. Lady Julia apparently had no qualms about small boats and stepped briskly down the steps to the dinghy. The princesses hesitated momentarily at the top of the flight. Suddenly, the reason for speed became apparent. I heard the deep hum of a big electric motor starting up, the crunch of gears engaging, and the latticed gate began to drop slowly towards the water. At the same time, a klaxon, from somewhere very close, began to wail.

In a flash, the squat Hawkins was out of the dinghy and up the steps. With an utter lack of ceremony, he seized the two girls bodily and thrust them down the stairs into the dinghy. Kit and I were at his heels. With Crawford at the bow oars, Hawkins seized the boat's transom and pushed the dinghy firmly away from the steps at the same time as scrambling aboard. The lowering gate was now six or seven feet in front of us and fast nearing the water. 'Duck!' shouted Crawford above the scream of klaxon, abandoning his oars in the rowlocks and throwing himself beneath the dinghy's gunwale. Kit grabbed all three girls and forced them down. Behind us I could hear the sound of running feet. The bows of the dinghy just cleared the descending gate, but the gate skimmed the gunwale as we glided on, caught the rounded transom and began to force the stern of the boat down towards the water. Quick as thought, Kit pitched his weight into the stern, the transom cleared, and we were free. Crawford seized his oars and with a couple of strokes nosed the dinghy out of the mouth of the tunnel and into the shadow of the E-boat.

An hour earlier there had been no sign of life aboard the *Schnellboot*. Now, on her stern, smoking a cigar, stood an exceptionally tall man wearing an Oberführer's[i] uniform. It

i Senior leader, the equivalent of a brigadier.

was as though he had been waiting for us. At his feet sat a liver-coloured dachshund. I recognised Colonel Skorzeny at once. A couple of ratings, armed with submachine guns, stood just behind him. Their weapons were trained on our dinghy.

'Gentlemen, I congratulate you,' said the Colonel in a rather pleasant tone. 'You have saved me an infinite amount of trouble.'

Storm

Otto Skorzeny might have been taken as something from Hollywood if he had not been all too real. Born in Vienna in 1908, to the public the Colonel was known as the Waffen SS Commando who snatched General Chuikov[i] from his HQ in Stalingrad in January 1943, so ending Russian resistance in the city. Operation Rosselsprung they called it. Goebbels recognised this as a wonderful propaganda opportunity and played it to the hilt. The papers splashed the presentation of the Knight's Cross to him by Hitler at the Berghof, the rally at the Sportpalast in Berlin, and the tour of the munitions factories in Warsaw, Strasbourg, Lyons, Antwerp, Sheffield and Birmingham. There can't be many citizens of the greater Reich who wouldn't recognise a frame of which Frankenstein might be been envious, topped by the massive head with the iconic scar slashed indelibly across the left cheek. He looked like a human Panzer.

The reality was more complex. Although Hitler made much of their common Austrian parentage in the speech at the Berghof, Skorzeny's a Polish name and the Colonel was of Polish extraction. Far from being an automaton, he was highly intelligent, had been trained as an engineer and spoke German, Polish, French and — of course — English fluently. His famous scar wasn't the result of some squalid street brawl, but the badge of honour of an expert fencer who fought fifteen duels in Vienna during the '20s. Strange though it may seem, Herman Goering personally turned down Skorzeny for the Luftwaffe in 1939 because he was over the age limit of 30. This precipitated him into the Waffen SS. Joining one of its most famous units, the *Leibstandarte SS Adolf Hitler*, he was sent to the Eastern Front when Operation Barbarossa opened in 1941.

i Vasily Ivanovitch Chiukov,1900-1982, commander of the Soviet 62nd Army at Stalingrad.

He was wounded in a skirmish outside Kharov in May 1942, an episode that saw him decorated with the Knight's Cross for bravery under fire. It was while convalescing from his wounds in Berlin that he caught the eye of both Himmler and Hitler. Invitations to the Chancellery and the Berghof followed. It was the time at which the fall of Stalingrad seemed less than the inevitability it became. Hitler took heart from Skorzeny's confidence in the ultimate outcome and used this as a stick to beat General Paulus,[i] hunkered down with the Sixth Army on the outskirts of Stalingrad. Operation Rosselsprung seems to have been dreamt up by Hitler and Skorzeny at one of those meetings. The capture by Skorzeny's paratroops of Chuikov then proved the beginning of the end for his 62nd Army in the city. Skorzeny's preferment by way of promotion to Colonel naturally followed.

I believe it was Himmler who thought that Skorzeny might be useful in England. Despite the strictures of censorship, it is well known that by the spring of 1944 the Resistance in Glasgow was getting the upper hand. What is less well known is Skorzeny's kidnapping of Wingate and half a dozen of his circle, and their incarceration in Wakefield Concentration Camp. This was the reason for the collapse of resistance in Glasgow until very late last year.

Yet Otto Skorzeny, superficially the good and faithful servant of Hitler and Himmler, was actually something rather more. He was too educated and intelligent a man to be entirely taken in by the patent absurdities of National Socialism. He was also too personally ambitious to kowtow forever to Himmler and Hitler. Our own intelligence had suggested as much for months. When I saw his unmistakable figure on the stern of the E-boat that night, I knew that we faced a quite an opponent — in the struggle for both the princesses and the future of England. I was uncertain, though, what particular role he would play, where his allegiances lay.

i Friedrich Wilhelm Paulus, 1890-1957.

60

Storm

'Gentlemen, I congratulate you. You have saved me an infinite amount of trouble,' said Skorzeny. His English was clear and strong, but heavily accented, the voice richly confident. 'Just bring her alongside. If you would be so kind.'

I glanced at Kit, who shrugged his shoulders. The eyes of the girls, Hawkins and Crawford were on me. So were those of Skorzeny's ratings. The machine-guns brooked no argument. I looked up at Skorzeny. 'Very well.'

'By the bridge,' directed Skorzeny.

Crawford and Hawkins took a couple of strokes that brought the dinghy up to the E-boat's bridge. Here a temporary accommodation ladder had been placed. Skorzeny and the ratings followed us along the side-deck until they stood right above us. One of the ratings took the dinghy's painter from Crawford and secured it to a cleat on the deck. 'Now gentlemen,' said Skorzeny, 'If I might just relieve you of your precious charges.'

Lady Julia and the two princesses had remained admirably calm during the crisis. It was Lady Julia who got to her feet, wrapped her tweed coat more closely around herself and, steadying herself on Kit's shoulder, exclaimed, 'You must be joking.'

This evidently pleased Skorzeny, whose huge face broke into a grin. 'Really, Lady Julia, there is no other way.'

'How do you know my name, you shit?'

Skorzeny's eyes hardened slightly. 'There is little I don't know about the future Queen of England, her little sister and her entourage.'

'From that blabber Ludwig Goring, I expect,' she sneered.

'From the many of your fellow countrymen who see which side their bread is buttered,' retorted the Colonel calmly.

I interrupted. 'What guarantees do you give us of their safety?'

Skorzeny looked at me keenly. His giant figure was silhouetted against the Tower. 'General Quick?'

'The same,' I said.

'Your disguise is imperfect, General. And, if I may say so to a fellow officer, you're hardly in a position to be demanding guarantees.'

This was too much for Kit.

'Nevertheless, Colonel, we are.'

'Admiral Conway, too?' mocked Skorzeny, turning towards Kit. 'I'm surprised your dinghy hasn't capsized with such a weighty superstructure of top brass.'

'Your assurances, Colonel,' responded Kit bluntly, disengaging himself from Lady Julia, rising to his feet, discarding his cap and looking about as formidable as his bandy legs allowed.

At this, the Colonel stood up again, and nodded at the two ratings. Both slid back the safety-catches on their guns. I could almost hear my heartbeat rising. Skorzeny cast his eye over the dinghy. 'The princesses and Lady Julia are now in my custody. I take full responsibility for their safety. You have my assurance, Admiral — you, too General — that they will be appropriately treated.'

'Where are you taking them?' I demanded.

'Ruritania,'[i] quipped the Colonel.

Kit now turned to Elizabeth. She was still seated on the thwart next to her sister, still holding hands. 'Ma'am?'

There was a pause of some moments. She looked unblinkingly at Kit, then at me, as though seeking inspiration or guidance. Then, turning away, she said, 'I think we know the Colonel as a man of his word.' With this she stood up, grasped the accommodation ladder and clambered up onto the E-boat. It was an act of great courage. Her sister and Lady Julia were left with no option but to follow. They were helped up by the Colonel and the ratings. The three of them looked down at us from the deck.

'Thank you, ma'am,' I heard Skorzeny say.

No sooner had he done so than another couple of ratings

i The fictional European country in Anthony Hope's 1984 bestseller, *The Prisoner of Zenda*.

appeared on the bridge. As they led the three girls through the door at its side, Lady Julia turned and shouted, 'See you soon, Kit.'

The proximity or otherwise of the Admiral was a matter that must also have occurred to Skorzeny, now on the bridge. Within a few seconds we heard the diesels of the E-boat grumbling. The two ratings with the submachine guns ran fore and aft to cast her off, leaving us momentarily unguarded. To Crawford, still sitting in the bows at his oars, Kit hissed, 'The painter!' Crawford took in his meaning at a glance. We were still tethered to the E-boat.

Before Crawford could do anything, Skorzeny gunned the *Schnellboot*'s diesels, and the E-boat, with us in the dinghy lashed to its side, began to pull away from the embankment. For a few seconds we headed slowly upstream against the current and the tide towards London Bridge before the Colonel put the wheel over and turned the boat through 180 degrees back towards Tower Bridge. With a glance down at us and a wave of his hand, he opened up the engines. Jostling against the E-boat's side as we turned had been bad enough. Now as the boat squatted down on her haunches we were blown about like a leaf in a storm. The oars were dashed overboard, the bitter spray that swept into the bows of the dinghy fast became a cataract, and she began to twist and turn like a thing possessed. It was clear that we would be over in seconds, under the E-boat's hull and into her propellers. As the carriage-ways of Tower Bridge flashed above us, I saw Crawford at the painter with a knife. There was a cry as he severed our tether and the flex attached to the dinghy snapped back like a snake against his wrist. The dinghy, suddenly freed, careered drunkenly away towards the north shore of the Thames, and the E-boat sped off into the night. As it did so there was a chatter of submachine gun fire from its stern and a dull thud as the rounds hit the boat under water. Then a momentary calm settled. I wondered there and then if they had intended to miss.[ii]

---

ii An interesting suggestion. See epilogue.

No longer under tow at fifteen knots, the dinghy quickly lost way. Water was spilling into her bows from under the floorboards where she had been holed beneath the water line. The four of us, though, had escaped injury. It would be an exaggeration to say we took stock. The dinghy was sinking, we had no oars, and the ebb tide was sweeping us inexorably downstream. Kit, Crawford and I had already sampled the water that night. Hawkins would find it chilly.

Kit was ahead of us. Scarcely had the dinghy begun to drift downstream than he was pointing just off her starboard bow at the barge's riding light. 'There she is!' he shouted. 'Paddle with the rudder.' In this there was no place for me. Hawkins unshipped the rudder from the dinghy's stern and passed it up to Crawford. It hardly made a very handy paddle, but at least it gave us some way through the water as we drifted downstream, towards the faithful *Cabby*. At this point we were perhaps three hundred feet upstream of the barge but well to her north in the tideway. In the normal course of events we would drift straight past her. Crawford's job was to somehow drag us south with his paddle across the stream to the barge. At the same time, we were bailing the dinghy furiously with our boots as the water from the bullet-holes rose steadily above the floorboards. Crawford, already knee-deep in water in the bows, battled desperately with the rudder and drew us, ever more slowly, towards the south bank, fighting moment by moment against the stream that threatened to sweep us down to Wapping. A channel buoy, a great black barrel ten or twelve feet high, swept past us perilously close. The water gained on us steadily. When we were about one hundred feet away from *Cabby* and perhaps eighty to her north, I thought we might just make it. Then an unguarded movement from Hawkins did for us. The water in the boat took charge and in a moment all four of us were floundering in the winter Thames.

Thank God we all had the sense to follow Crawford's example and swim back upstream. If we'd tried to swim straight to the *Cabby*, we would have been goners. As it was we were a good five minutes in those filthy freezing waters before we grabbed the bottom rung of the barge's ladder. One by one we clambered up onto her deck, coughing and spluttering with the water streaming off us. I felt done in. In the stateroom the little stove was still glowing as we stripped off our sodden clothes, towelled down, and cast around for dry pairs of trousers and shirts.

I began to feel more human again, but at the same time, I realised how completely we had managed to snatch defeat from the jaws of victory. After the adrenalin high of the escape from the Tower, I was quite flat. I think it was Hawkins — his pale face even paler than usual, his shock of hair looking more than ever like Stan Laurel[i]'s — who expressed what I had supposed we were all feeling. 'What the hell next?'

Kit, who was just pulling on his filthy old trousers, stopped in his tracks. 'After them, of course.' It was as though no other course of action had occurred to him.

'In the *Cabby,* sir? asked Hawkins incredulously. 'Chase an E-boat with an unarmed Thames barge?' Again, Hawkins spoke for me.

'Got a better idea?' asked Kit at his most magisterial. His eyes flashed like thunder. Judging by Hawkins's expression, he had not. Neither, at that moment, had I.

A few moments later, duly stiffened, Hawkins was once again at the capstan, Crawford at the wheel. It was just before midnight on 1 February when we weighed anchor, not much more than six hours since we had arrived. Looking back, I saw the Tower ablaze with light, buzzing like an overturned beehive. No one seemed to be looking our way, which was one thing. Perhaps they thought the whole lot of us had got away in the E-boat. Someone struck a match. It was Kit. Above us, *Cabby*'s great sail flapped momentarily, then caught a light south-westerly that had sprung up. Kit inhaled deeply on his cigarette as the barge swung away from her mooring and headed down-river once again. Then he rubbed his hands. 'Just a couple of watches to see us through the rest of the night, old

---

i Stan Laurel (1895-1965) and Oliver Hardy (1892-1957). The pair of comic geniuses.

man,' he said. 'I'll take the first one with Crawford and wake you about 0300. You take her through to dawn with Hawkins.'

'Assuming that Skorzeny's headed out to sea?' I asked.

Kit nodded. 'I think we have to take that as given. We'll think things through in the morning.'

'You might think just what we're going to tell Ottawa.' I hit the hay and was asleep as soon as my head hit what in the barge went as a pillow.

*

The remains of breakfast had been piled into the tiny sink, the table cleared to make room for a small-scale Admiralty chart of the North Sea and the Channel. A line of pencil crosses marked the barge's passage from the Tower. We were a few miles west of Tilbury, not far from where we'd been yesterday morning. Hawkins the Geordie was at the wheel, and the remaining three of us crowded round the chart. Kit had lit up, I had done the same with my pipe. Crawford, for reasons I never fathomed, didn't smoke. Perhaps he thought it would ruin his peachy complexion. We were speculating on Skorzeny's destination.

'Emden,' suggested Crawford.

Thinking along the same lines, I added, 'Or Wilhelmshaven, Bremerhaven, Cuxhaven. '

Kit inhaled and looked away from the chart for a moment. Crawford, perhaps sensing he was unconvinced, put in: 'Nearest part of the German coast.'

'Very good, Lieutenant,' smiled Kit. 'What have you overlooked?'

'Range and sea-state,' said Crawford promptly.

'Yes,' said Kit, scratching his black thatch and turning round in search of an ash-tray. 'I should put Emden at 300 miles. What do those E-boats do?'

'She'd cover just about 700 nautical miles, so no problem there,' suggested Crawford. 'They do almost forty knots, cruise generally at about half that. She'd make Emden in seventeen hours, twenty at the outside. She left the Tower at about midnight. ETA dusk today.'

'Sea permitting,' put in Kit.

'There's Skorzeny's problem, sir. Westerly's building, maybe Force six to seven in the North Sea. Not very comfortable for the girls.'

'What else?' asked Kit.

'Enemy action,' responded Crawford.

'Quite right, in a sense,' conceded Kit. He stubbed out his cigarette. 'What do we know of the current political situation in Germany, and what do we know of our friend Skorzeny's affiliations? Can we assume that there will be an orderly handover of power to Hitler's successor?'

'No,' I put in. 'We don't even know who that'll be.'

'And we can assume', continued Kit, 'that our good friends Bormann, Heydrich, Kaltenbrunner, Hess, Himmler, Goebbels and Goering[i] are fighting over the succession like ferrets in a sack. As for Skorzeny...' Here Kit again turned away and seemed for a moment lost in thought.

'With Hitler dead, he owes his loyalty to no one,' I suggested.

'Except to himself,' said Kit, looking back at the chart.

I tapped out my pipe into the ash-tray. 'Except to whoever gave him the orders to pick up the princesses. Which cannot have been Hitler.'

'Mmm,' agreed Kit. 'Himmler seems more likely to be our man, doesn't he? Technically Skorzeny's commanding officer.'

'The princesses a useful card in his pack,' I added.

'I wouldn't put it past Skorzeny to be acting on no one's orders but his own,' said Kit, rising to his feet. As he did so the barge rolled rather more than usual. He grabbed the table for support.

Crawford cut in: 'For what it's worth, sir, I wouldn't take the princesses straight across the North Sea in a heavy south-westerly. Not in an E-boat, I wouldn't.'

Kit spun on his heel and seated himself once more at

---

i A handful of the more notorious Nazi leaders.

the chart. 'I believe you're right, Lieutenant. I believe you're right. I think if I was Skorzeny … '. He paused for a second to scrutinise the chart. Then in the tone of someone whose mind is made up, he said: 'I'd get them out of England as fast as I could, and onto another bit of dry land just as quickly. And I'd make damn certain that that land was safely occupied by some good friends of mine. Then I might or might not hand them over to my boss.'

Lieutenant and Admiral were now thinking as one. Crawford traced with his finger the passage of Skorzeny's E-boat out into the Thames estuary, past Canvey Island to Foulness. 'Keeping to the shelter of the coast, agreed Kit. 'Right up to Yarmouth.' Crawford's finger traced the E-boat north past the mouth of the Blackwater to Harwich, Orford Ness, Southwold, Lowestoft and Yarmouth. 'Then a dash across the North Sea to Wilhelmshaven.'

'To the E-boat headquarters,' added Crawford.

'And a collection of entirely loyal friends,' capped Kit.

Kit and Crawford looked very satisfied with themselves at this exchange, like a couple of spinsters who have just solved a knotty little crossword problem in the *Morning Chronicle*. I was less convinced. 'I like *Cabby*. But from what I've seen she only does about nine knots, and that only when the wind's in the right direction. Where does all this wonderful thinking leave us? If you think I'm setting out to Wilhelmshaven in this old tub, you've got another think coming.'

Kit conceded the points quite cheerfully. 'It's simple,' he said. 'We'll call Ottawa. Winston'll be full of bright ideas about fire-ships, floating mines and such-like.'[i]

But before we could suit action to the word, there was a shout from on deck. Crawford was up the companionway before Kit or I could rise from the table. Moments later he was down again. 'Bit blowy, sir. Can you have a look?'

After the drowsy little cabin it was wonderfully brisk on

i Churchill's brain teemed with such hare-brained schemes, much to the horror of professional ser-
vice-men.

deck, and the day was fresh as paint, but it certainly seemed jolly windy. The westerly, sweeping across the Kent marshes, had stirred the muddy estuary into an angry sandy-grey sea, the tops of the waves just breaking. Running downwind with the bellowing sail well out over the starboard gunwale, the barge was beginning to pitch and roll quite unpleasantly. We crowded round Hawkins, who was struggling with the heavy-spoked wheel and — judging by the hue of his face — sea-sickness. 'Barometer's down a tenth since dawn, sir. Need to keep an eye on the rig, too. Some of it's a bit ropey.'

Kit glanced round, then up at the rig. 'I don't suppose we're gaining on Skorzeny quite yet,' he said. 'Still, you'd better shorten sail.'

'Tops'l and stays'l, sir?' asked Hawkins.

'Ask the captain,' responded Kit.

Crawford was looking high up the mast at the triangular topsail set in the 'vee' between the main-mast and the sprit. He glanced behind him at the mizzen. 'It'll freshen. Let's get them off. If it gets worse we'll brail up the main.'

*

For three or four hours *Cabby* moved with slightly greater ease under just jib and mainsail as she ploughed east towards the Goodwins.[ii] Then, as the winter light began to drop, the estuary opened out and the westerly freshened, she began to pitch and yaw appreciably again. Kit and I put up the fiddles on the cabin table, lashed down the loose gear on deck, and fed Hawkins and Crawford, now both at the wheel, with bacon sandwiches and tea. We pulled out the Pye a couple of times but had no luck with Ottawa. In the absence of any other plan we followed Crawford's conjecture and headed north-east in pursuit of Skorzeny's phantom and the putative trail of the princesses. By dusk, we were about ten miles south-west

ii The Goodwin Sands, graveyard of many fine ships and seamen, lie roughly between the North and South Forelands, some 3½ miles east of Deal.

of Foulness,[i] the barometer had dropped another tenth, and the wind had risen to Force five. Kit and I put on some oilskins and ventured on deck.

Aft, behind the wheel, were Hawkins and Crawford, both in their fishermen's jerseys, with hunched shoulders and arms straining at the wheel's spokes, faces set. The halyards beat viciously against the mast and, from time to time, as the *Cabby* punched into the short, sloppy swell, a green sea would come aboard and sluice down the scuppers. The crests of the white horses galloped towards us out of the dusk. Kit and I went forward and, to give us some decent drag, lowered both the lee-boards into the confused waters that rushed past the barge's black hull on their way to the ends of the earth. Aloft, the mainsail and jib were billowing out like great tanned balloons, straining desperately at their bar-taught sheets. To the east pinpricks of light stared down from the heavens, but off our starboard bow I saw steel grey clouds like a jagged wall. Back below, Kit commented, 'We'll be alright. Still, I think we'll tuck into the lee of Foulness once we double the point.'

I left Kit to it and settled down for a doze. It was just 48 hours since we'd been holed up in Queen Anne's Gate, and a lot seemed to have happened since. It was good to be actually doing something, but I have to say that just then the girls and the E-boat seemed about as substantial as the will-o-the-wisp. As I dropped off to sleep the rain began to patter on the deck above my head.

*

A heavy lurch woke me an hour or so later. I grabbed my oilskin, and went back on deck. It still seemed wretchedly windy to me, and the rain was sheeting down. Kit, Hawkins and Crawford were huddled round the wheel, barely distinguishable in their oilskins and sou'westers.

'Want a hand?' I shouted against the gale.

i The largest of an archipelago of islands, bounded by the River Crouch and the River Thames.

'Not from the Army,' responded Kit. 'Three teas, please.'

Just as I was stepping down the companionway there was a sound like a rifle shot and a cry from the wheel. I was back on deck in an instant. From the bows the sound of hell broke loose. The jib had blown out and the canvas and rope were being beaten into oblivion, flogging and twisting like mad things. Kit beckoned me aft. When I was close enough to hear him above the wind, he shouted, 'Give us a hand and the boys'll get it down.'

I had never steered a barge before, let alone in a storm. Without the jib to balance the mainsail, the *Cabby* yawed horribly. Kit and I had quite a job to stop her taking charge. Crawford and Hawkins struggled with the jib halyard, then captured and subdued the huge canvas foresail. When it was safely below, the four of us crowded round the wheel. 'Course, sir?' shouted Crawford, wiping some of the rain off his face.

'We can't do anything to windward in this weather without the jib. Where exactly do you think we are?'

Hawkins chipped in.

'About a mile north-north-east of Foulness point. Heading for Holiwell Point.'

'Tide still on the ebb?' asked Kit.

'Low water more like. Maybe just beginning to flood.'

'What do you say we take her in and ground her?' asked Kit, turning to Crawford.

'Mad not to, sir. Can't muck about in these waters.'

'Very well. She's all yours.' Crawford took the wheel, his cheeks pink in the rain, and began to turn the barge towards the darkened shore. Hawkins went forward with the lead.

'What are we doing?' I asked Kit as we retreated below and shook off our oilskins.

'Beaching her,' said Kit. 'She'll be safe enough on the foreshore, and that's one thing you can do with barges. Flat bottoms. That's what they're there for. There's nothing else we can do for the girls tonight.'

We had a look at the chart. Hawkins had marked our last known position half an hour earlier. It looked as though we were due north-east of some place called Courtsend on Foulness Island. Kit explained in his rather patronising way that if we could make our way gently in we could ground her easily enough. In the morning we might see how the land lay in the village, give Ottawa another try, and see if the gale hadn't blown itself out.

'I'll give them a hand taking her in,' he added.

From time to time I heard Hawkins's voice calling the shortening depths as the barge neared the shore. Half an hour later, I felt the *Cabby* gently grounding. I went up on deck. I could hear rather than see the reeds on the shore. I gave the boys a hand brailing up the mainsail, and they ran out the kedge anchor in the cockleshell of the barge's spare dinghy. It was still raining hard, but the wind had eased a bit. We gave Ottawa another go, quite a long one, before turning in, but they seemed to have left the phone off the hook.

*

The following morning the *Cabby* slept late. When I woke it was well gone nine, and nobody else seemed astir. I pulled on my trousers and shirt and went on deck. It was one of those wonderfully atmospheric winter mornings that you find on the east coast, with a clammy grey mist settled on everything. The wind, though, had gone and with it the rain. Around the barge was a little circle of visibility, bounded to the north by the waters of the Crouch thirty yards away or so, and to the south by a flat, reedy sea-shore. The barge herself sat dry if not entirely high on the foreshore. Occasionally I heard the cries of geese and the high-pitched squeal of a curlew. Then, faintly, across the marshes came the sound of a church clock. I counted ten, and guessed it must have been Courtsend.

I went below, stoked up the stove, and put the kettle on for tea. I thought I'd take a pipe on deck. I wandered up to the foredeck, lit up and — perforce — began wondering about the poor girls. I thought Skorzeny trustworthy up to a point, but it was horrible to think of them out in that gale last night, let alone in the hands of a bunch of E-boat commanders. Sitting there beached on the Essex marshes, it didn't seem as though I could do much to help. The headlong cascade of events that had followed Hitler's death had dried up, and I was left to ruminate on what might have been, and jolly uncomfortable thinking it made.

The whistling of the kettle took me back down to the hold, and I made a good brew of tea. Kit, Crawford and Hawkins were still asleep, and there seemed little point in disturbing them. It was as I clambered back out on deck, nestling a mug of tea, that I saw it. Out of the mist on the river loomed a tiny wooden dinghy, scarcely bigger than a coracle. I stiffened, even though it was difficult to think of anyone tracking us down to such a spot or happening upon us there. This phantom took form, substance and detail. In the boat was a girl in a headscarf, beside her a small milk churn and a newspaper. It was then that I gave a shout that brought Kit and the boys tumbling out of their berths and up on deck.

It was Sergeant Sturridge, all five feet of her. She was dressed as I'd never seen her before, in mufti. Some sort of checked outfit that would have suited a grouse shoot on the Spey. It was the first time I'd seen her as a woman. She sculled right up to the barge and looked up at us all on deck, gaping down at her in surprise, astonishment even. She rested her oars, threw up the dinghy's painter and saluted. 'Morning, sir,' was directed at both Kit and me, Crawford and Hawkins getting a nod.

Kit was the first to find his voice. 'Mornin' Sergeant.'

'What brings you here?' I said, still barely able to believe my eyes, and a dozen other questions teeming in my brain.

'Those girls, the princesses. We've found them.'

There was an actress in Sturridge and maybe she had been practising that line. She allowed no hint of triumph in her voice.

'Wilhelmshaven,' suggested Crawford with his gift for the obvious, looking at his watch. 'Skorzeny could have got there last night.'

'No,' said Sturridge, looking up from the boat and allowing herself a hint of a smile, 'and you'd really never guess.'

This was all getting too much.

'Perhaps you should enlighten us, Sergeant,' I said dryly.

I can still see her in my mind's eye as she looked up at us from her cockleshell and spoke just a single word. She was right. It was just about the last place, the very last place that would have occurred to me.

Part Two

The First Letter

Later, I checked the *Cabby*'s log against the date of the White House minutes. Both documents are quite clear. It was on the morning that the barge was beached at Foulness that discussions were taking place at the White House in Washington DC, seat of the Truman Administration.[i] February 2nd. As these talks had an immediate bearing on the course of events, I must here introduce the reader to the man who now runs the US Central Intelligence Agency, Mr Allen Welsh Dulles.[ii]

He was born — I'm told — in Washington in 1893. His grandfather had been Secretary of State under President Benjamin Harrison and his uncle Secretary of State in the Cabinet of President Woodrow Wilson. After Princeton University — a little like Oxford or Cambridge, but not much — he joined the diplomatic service and served in Vienna, Berne, Paris, Berlin and Istanbul … No. I think that is enough from me about Mr Dulles. He needs to speak for himself. He does that a lot.

After the Rising I visited Allen where he was 'vacationing' — as he put it — in Switzerland. It was the first time I had visited Continental Europe since 1935, and my first time ever in the Alps. I can't say I particularly relish scenery in the normal course of things, but those mountains are another thing. I was awestruck by their scale and grandeur, and by the way they seemed to belittle everything I was doing. Humbling to be reminded of one's own insignificance in a way one doesn't really get in Salisbury or Surrey. It somehow set Hitler's death

---

i Harry S Truman (1884-1972) had succeeded Franklin D Roosevelt (1882-1945) as President of the United States on the latter's death.

ii Allen Welsh Dulles, 1893-1969. First civilian and longest-serving head of the CIA.

and the even more momentous events that followed into context, and made me think about a line from Arnold that had been drilled into me at school, 'Where ignorant armies clash by night'. Either way, I tracked Dulles down in the Bernese Oberland,[iii]1 taking the train up from Interlaken and Lauterbrunnen to Wengernalp in the shadow of the Eiger. There I encountered a man whose mild manners and scholarly appearance belied the role that he played in the affair. He looked like a languages teacher in a minor public school, what with the tweed jacket, the rimless glasses, the greying hair, the slight stoop in the tall frame, and the hint of pedantry in his speech. There, in Wengen, we discussed the whole question of the US involvement in the Rising. There Allen agreed to raise with the President the matter of its public disclosure in this chronicle. He later agreed that this letter and two others that are reproduced in the narrative should be disclosed.

The first was written a few days after our meeting.

Allen Foster Dulles
Director
Central Intelligence Agency
Room 3663
Rockefeller Center
New York, New York

General Sir Max Quick
Chief of Imperial General Staff
The War Office
Whitehall
London West

22 March 1946

Dear Max
(We drop the 'General', don't we?) When we met in

iii The highest part of the canton of Berne in central Switzerland.

Wengen[i] earlier this month, I disclosed to you as much as I felt appropriate about the part played by our great country in the hostages' affair. Given the profound issues that it raised about the national security and defense of the United States, I was in no position to be entirely frank. Nor was I.

That position has been overtaken by the events in the Soviet Union, and the consequent formulation by the principal western democratic states of the Atlantic Alliance. The events that we reviewed can now be seen to form the prologue to a step of capital importance in the protection of democracy and freedom in the West.

It is in these changed circumstances that the Truman Administration has felt it appropriate, at my bidding, to offer a more complete disclosure of its position and the attack on the United States. (Max, we've come clean.)

Our talk at the chalet was couched in generalities (although I'm sure I did nothing to mislead you). I have talked to the President and Secretary of State Byrnes.[ii] We are of one mind that the cause in which we are now all united will best be served by specifics. We have scrutinised with great care the minutes of the critical meetings held on 1 February 1946. I have fleshed out the bare bones of these notes to give you a sense of the personalities involved.

The story, in short, is as follows.

By the beginning of 1946, it was apparent to the new Administration that the fall of Moscow was imminent. I had been heading up the CIA's office in Berne[iii] for more than four years, and I could do no more in that oasis of democracy. At my own request, I was recalled to New York. Before the orders came through, Marshal Zhukov capitulated to Rommel. On

---

i Wengen, 1274 metres. A holiday resort in the Bernese Oberland, Switzerland.

ii James Francis Byrnes, 1897-1977. Secretary of State under Truman 1945-1947. Mother was an Irish dress-maker.

iii Federal capital of Switzerland.

The First Letter

21 January I took the service from Bern to Basle, then the Deutsche Bahn to Wilhelmshaven. The following day I sailed on the *Queen Mary*,[iv] still with much of her old English charm, to New York. We were still a day east of New York when the news of Hitler's death reached us. The event was taken calmly by passengers and crew, a number of whom were German. When I reached New York on the morning of 31 January there was snow on the ground. I went straight to the Rockefeller Plaza and found Bill Donovan, still in his old office where I had left him in 1942.

Bill? Not many soldiers who turned lawyer or lawyers who turned soldier. He picked up the medal of honor in the First War and led his battalion. Guess that's why Roosevelt made him the first head of the CIA. 'Wild Bill' they called him, but that's another story.[v]

I had intended to brief Bill on the situation in Western Europe. Instead, I found myself being briefed by him on the events in England. Through channels I cannot disclose, word had just reached us of your attempt to free the princesses, and its upshot. Donovan had already conceived the idea of the part that we in the United States might play in the affair. It was a notion I entirely endorsed. We worked through that day to formulate a plan. That evening I caught the sleeper from Penn to Washington. On the morning of 1 February I found myself at Union Station, alone in the bustle on a raw morning, hungry for breakfast. An hour later I was being ushered into the Oval Office.

The President was seated at his desk, but rose from behind it as I came into the room, and shook hands. He was dressed in a grey suit and is shorter than the pictures suggest. His pallor suggested the immense strain under which he had been

iv The *Queen Mary* was a 1000ft, 81,000 ton liner that represented the zenith of trans-Atlantic passenger ship building between the wars. She had been seized by the Germans in Hamburg in 1940, and sailed under the Swaztika.

v William Joseph Donovan, 1883-1959. Father of the CIA.

working during the ten months since Roosevelt's death. We took a couple of easy chairs in front of the blaze in the fireplace. He glanced round the office, and then right up at Healy's[i] *The Peacemakers* that hung over the fire. Sherman, Grant, Porter and Lincoln himself. Some peacemakers, I thought.

'Well, Mr Dulles,' he began, 'I don't know if you ever had a load of hay fall on you, but when they told me FDR was dead, I felt like the moon, the stars and all the planets had fallen on me.'

The first version of the remark had of course been widely reported when it was originally made just after Roosevelt's death. I made an appropriate reply, his response to which surprised me. 'Not to what I've heard since. You know, this place is rotten, rotten to the core.'

The President continued. "Whole floor came down last week. Can't use our bedroom. Bess's raising Cain. You married, Mr Dulles?'

'Yes, Mr President,' I said.

He nodded sympathetically, and looked around the office again. 'Changes, Mr Dulles. That's what we're having round here. Not before time.'

Then he resumed his seat behind his desk. 'You've got a scheme for me.'

I won't detail my exposition. In brief, I reminded him that Zhukov's defeat in Moscow three weeks previously had crowned the success of the Axis powers. The United States stood alone as an outpost of democracy. Hitler's death re-opened the question. Britain was a hotbed of revolt, and it was possible that her lead would be followed elsewhere in Europe. I told him of the news coming in from Antwerp, Rotterdam, Lyon and Oslo.[ii]1 I told him of King George's ever more tenuous hold on life in Ottawa, and of the symbolic

i George Peter Alexander Healy, painter, 1808-1894.

ii On 2 February, Antwerp, Rotterdam, Lyon and Oslo were all either in the process of falling or had already fallen.

and constitutional position of the princesses Elizabeth and Margaret. I also told him of the immense affection that they commanded in England. I gave him the gist of what we knew of Churchill's position, of Operation Nonesuch, and your own attempt to seize the hostages. I told him about Skorzeny, and the mysteries of his whereabouts. (This, remember, was the morning of 1 February, when I believe you were east of London.)

'Good yarn, Mr Dulles,' he said when I had finished. 'Nothin' to do with us, though. The United States is neutral' He spoke at some length of the new adherents of the Monroe doctrine, pledged to the isolation of the US from the troubles of the world. He added that he was one himself.

I checked my notes. 'As a Senator, Mr President, you'll remember what you said on 23 June 1941.'

The President scarcely paused. 'The day after the Nazis tiptoed onto Soviet soil? Sure. I said if we see that Germany is winning, we ought to help Russia. If we see Russia winning, we ought to help Germany.'

'Germany is winning,' I put in, quite impressed by his recall.

'Mr Dulles, Germany isn't winning. Germany has won.'

With this, I rose to my feet. 'The Reich is a pack of cards that will fall with its ruler.'

'That so, Mr Dulles?'

I leaned towards him, putting my hands on his desk. 'I've made Nazi Germany my study for fifteen years.'

At this the President himself got to his feet and turned to look out of the window overlooking the Rose Garden. He stood in silence for a couple of minutes.

'Mr Dulles, you've been half-way up a god-dammed mountain for four years. Ain't that right?'

I said it was.

'I don't think you've seen what the war has done to the American people. Okay. FDR didn't choose war. The Japs put it on him. Know how many good American lives ago Pearl Harbor was, Mr Dulles?'

I told him I did. I told him of the friends I had lost at Midway, Iwo Jima and Tokyo Bay. I told him how my nephew died.

'And knowing that, you have the balls to ask me to remember what I said after Barbarossa?'

I stood my ground. 'Yes, Mr President. Knowing that.'

Truman stood quite still, looking out of the window. The snow was now falling heavily, the flakes sparkling in the floodlights. He turned, and for a moment I couldn't tell from his expression which way he was going to jump. Then he said, 'Just tell me what you and Mr Donovan have been cooking up in New York.'

I took my seat again and outlined the plan.

'Who knows about this?' he asked.

I looked carefully at the President. 'You know nothing.'

Truman gave a thin smile. 'What does it matter who runs an island no bigger than Missouri?'

I paused a second to light a cigarette. 'England is the king-pin of Europe.'

The President was on to that one. 'Churchill's a busted flush.'

I inhaled and felt the rush of nicotine though my veins. 'You've spoken to him?'

The President shrugged. 'He's written to me. Can't stop writing to me.'

'Is that your opinion?' I asked.

The President paused and looked down at some papers on his desk. 'Nope.'

There was silence for a few moments. Quite a few moments. I wondered where he would go next. He said: 'Why not just leave it to the Brits?'

This was easy. 'Then you leave it to chance. The British might also have ideas of their own.'

'What would we do with them?'

Assuming he was referring to the princess, I said, 'You would be kingmaker.'

The First Letter

The President stared at this. 'You're like your brother,[i] Mr Dulles, ain't you? You're a clever man.' Then he added. 'I wonder how clever.'

I was saved from having to respond by the entrance of the President's secretary. There was a whispered conversation. The President then turned to me and, consulting his watch, said. 'Gimme three hours, Mr Dulles.'

*

It was half-past eleven when I left the Oval Office. It had gone six when I was asked to return. When I did so the President had been joined by the Secretary of State. Both were in shirtsleeves. Byrnes will be a name to you, Max. I had known James since New Deal[ii] days. He was in London until 1943, and it was he who alerted the Roosevelt Administration to the scale of the Communist threat. Our paths hadn't crossed since the beginning of the war, but Byrnes's way had certainly crossed Bill Donovan's. That's why the CIA was given some facility for covert operations.

I greeted James as an old friend. Square-jawed, thin lips, heavily receding hairline. He was less warm, going straight to the point. 'You've thought this through and through, Allen?'

I knew James sufficiently to respond, 'Tell me what we've missed.'

'Stalin'. He spat out the word.

'Safe behind the Urals. Might as well be bars.'

'Not forever.'

'Moscow's in Rommel's hands. Zhukov is dead,' I said.

Byrnes paused at this. Then he said very clearly and slowly: 'Stalin's three years away from an atom bomb. Maybe two.'

The idea of an atom bomb had been circulating in the press in Berne for years. No one thought it would work. A guy

i John Foster Dulles, Secretary of State 1953-1959 under President Eisenhower.

ii President's Roosevelt's plan to revive the US in the throes of the Great Depression.

called Oppenheimer[i] had run some project called Manhattan in New Mexico for a couple of years. It got nowhere. FDR canned it. The rumours that the Brits had made some progress, circulating in 1940, I'd discounted. We'd picked up on the Nazis' heavy-water work in Norway. It seemed a swell way of wasting money. I said, 'Which works?'

'Nobody knows,' conceded Byrnes.

Here the President interrupted. 'If it does, it means a bomb that takes out a city, not a block.'

Byrnes put in: 'Berlin, London.'

'New York, added the President.

'In a bomber?' I asked, thinking of the practicalities of delivering a weapon to the place where it might be used.

'A bomber would do it. Big one though.'

'I see,' I said, as indeed I did. Even then we had enough of an inkling about what an atom bomb would do. We knew it would change the face of war as much as gunpowder or the machine-gun.

'I hope so, Allen,' said the Secretary of State.

'Where does it leave us?' I asked.

The President took charge. 'It means we're restarting Manhattan and looking to, to… what's the word, James?'

'Contain,' said the Secretary of State, enunciating the word very clearly.

'Contain the Soviets,' echoed the President.

'How are we going to do that?' I asked.

'You just haven't been listening, Allen, have you,' said Byrnes. It was a statement not a question. 'Himmler's[ii] named himself Führer. Just come through on the wires. It's just as the President said. There's every danger of the Russians winning. We're backing Himmler.'

It took a few seconds for the enormity of what Byrnes had just said to sink in.

i J. Robert Oppenheimer, 1904-1967. American particle physicist, 'father of the atom bomb.'

ii Heinrich Himmler, 1900-1946. The second most dangerous man in the Third Reich.

The First Letter

'Heinrich Himmler,' I said. 'Head of the SS. Man behind the Night of the Long Knives. Creator of the concentration camps. Man who thinks Jews are sub-human. Strange little fellow with glasses. Are we talking about the same man?'

Byrnes had a good poker face and appeared unmoved. 'We believe we have no choice.'

'The hostages?' I asked, wondering how they figured in Byrnes's thinking.

'It's a toss-up between the Brits and the Nazis. You're right about your plan. We're going to send a commando over to make sure the right guys win,' said Byrnes.

'The Brits,' I said, though without much conviction.

'The Nazis,' corrected Byrnes. 'Not Skorzeny, Himmler. Skorzeny's a loose cannon. Himmler's our man.'

I turned away, scarcely able to believe my ears. I mastered myself before turning to Truman. 'Mr President, you endorse this madness? You know what's happening in Europe? You've heard what the Nazis are doing in Poland? Sending Jews to the gas chamber.'

'Rumours,' interrupted Byrnes.

'I'm sorry, Mr Dulles,' said the President. 'It goes against the grain. But I believe America will be a stronger place with the Soviets under pressure. I believe Germany's the country to do that.'

'You're declaring war?'

'Not war, Mr Dulles. I thought we'd discussed that. I might have to square Congress if I did. We think your plans for some behind-the-scenes support for Himmler will work very well.'

(Max, I felt I'd been hung by my own braces.) It was some moments before I managed the only response possible. 'Very well, Mr President.'

Byrnes grinned. 'I thought you'd see it that way, Allen.'

'Coffee, boys?' asked the President.

*

We took a break. I wired Bill Donovan to break the news that the President was backing the wrong horse. By then it was nearly 8.00, and the House night staff had come on. Someone ran out for some bagels. It was snowing again. The three of us spent the next couple of hours fleshing out the plan Bill and I had put together. Intelligence was coming in all the time but — like you — we didn't know one critical thing. Just where Skorzeny had gotten to. Until we knew that, we fixed what we could. We had a frigate, the *Boston*,[i] in the east Atlantic. We ordered her to Dublin, where, we argued, she'd be well placed in all sorts of eventualities. The commandos would have to fly if there was any chance of grabbing the hostages before Skorzeny — or you — squirrelled them away. There was a squadron of Catalina[ii] flying-boats up at Newark with the Army Air Corps. They'd fly up to Gander to refuel, then across to Shannon. From there they could cover most of Western Europe.

The President called de Valera's[iii] office in Dublin to square the Irish on all this. It was good timing. The Taoiseach had just come back from presenting his condolences on Hitler's death to the German ambassador Eduard Hempel. Dev was tactful enough not to ask what the *Boston* and the Cats were for. Maybe he knew, or at least surmised. He'd heard about the hostages. Anyway, said Byrnes, he'd be calling in a favour later. Handily enough, there was a Marine Raiders unit based on the Hamptons. Much the same outfit as your SBS. These ones were veterans of Tokyo Bay. They were pulled off exercise and ordered to Newark for first light. Everything was coming together. In spite of myself, I have to say I felt pleased. It must have been just after 10.00 p.m. when the three of us left the President's desk and gathered round the fire. As Truman pointed out, the whole of the White House was

i A Tacoma Class vessel, 1264 tons, 303 feet.

ii A twin-engined patrol bomber developed in the US in the '30s.

iii Eamon de Valera, 1882-1975, the dominant 20th century Irish politician.

abominably heated. Someone came in with rye. We knocked glasses together.

'Just about covered off,' said the President. He sounded satisfied.

Byrnes was staring into his glass as though he'd discovered a foreign object in his rye. 'Who is our Skorzeny?' he asked, looking up.

I thought it an interesting question that, somehow, in the onward rush of events, we'd parked.

Byrnes continued. 'Skorzeny's a big hitter and General Quick and Admiral Conway aren't entirely fools. Who's going to trump them?'

'No Paton,' I said, thinking about the distinguished Lieutenant-Colonel who had been killed in Tokyo Bay.

'No MacArthur,'[iv] added the President.

'Any case,' said Byrnes, 'we need a young guy into irregular ops, commando. Remember the Brits had someone before Teheran collapsed? Dennis Stirling? David? Made something of a name for himself. Someone like that.'

'Guess you're right,' I said.

'There's Joe Kennedy junior,' suggested Byrnes.

'Joe's son?' asked the President, referring to our former ambassador in London.

'That one,' replied Byrnes. 'Commander. Best of four brothers. Joe, John, Bobby, Teddy. Good Irish American stock. We all know Joe's a bit of a chancer, but his heart's in the right place. Teddy's still at Fessenden. Bobby's rising 20 and in the navy. John was quite badly hurt when his MTB was rammed by a Jap destroyer near the Solomon Islands in '43.'

'Joe's the one who was walking out with Little Edie before he went to London in '39,' said the President. 'Lucky boy. Navy flyer. Sister married some Brit aristo. Still lives in England.'

The President seemed to have been very well briefed. I wondered there and then what lobbying Byrnes had done behind the scenes.

'That's the guy,' said Byrnes casually.

iv Field Marshal Douglas MacArthur (1880-1945) was killed in Tokyo Bay.

'Joe Kennedy's a Nazi sympathiser, a womaniser, antisemitic and on the take,' I said.

'We're hiring his son,' responded Byrnes tartly.

'Like father, like son,' I said. 'Does the Commander root for Himmler?'

'Joe junior follows orders,' responded Byrnes.

'You know him?'

'I do,' said Byrnes shortly.

The President was nursing his rye. 'I guess we'd better see Commander Kennedy.'

'He's on his way,' said Byrnes.

'Very prescient,' I said.

There was nothing else we could do that evening. Byrnes was staying across the road in the Capitol Hotel in Pennsylvania Avenue. The Trumans were putting me up in one of the guest rooms. The President was right. The place was falling down. As I was washing the basin almost came off the wall. I turned in just before midnight. The snow had stopped. I slept poorly, hardly dozed. I couldn't get Himmler out of my head. I dropped off at some stage, for at just gone 03.00 I was woken by someone at my shoulder. It was the night steward. 'They're after you, Mr Dulles, sir,'

I looked at my watch and struggled into my clothes, splashed my face and wandered out into the corridor. The steward was waiting. 'I'll take you to the map room, sir,' It seemed the dead of night, and the old house was eerie, full of long shadows. The map room was somewhere in the basement. The President was in his dressing-gown and slippers, looking every bit his sixty-two years. I guess I didn't look much myself. Byrnes, five years older than the President, looked tousled, pinched and drawn, like a visitor from the grave. 'We've got 'em,' he said.

Open on the map chest was one of the whole of the British Isles.

'How come?' I asked.

'The Brits have been broadcasting,' said the President.

The First Letter

'Why would they do that?'[i]

'Doesn't matter,' said the Secretary of State dismissively.

'Well …' I began.

'Doesn't matter,' Byrnes interrupted. 'We picked up an SOE signal. They're at some crappy little place on the Wash. Near where the invasion was.'

We looked at the map and in eastern England found the watery quadrilateral that divides County Lincoln from County Norfolk. 'Where precisely?' I asked.

Byrnes put his finger on a spot four or five miles from the south-eastern coast of the inlet.

Sandringham. I had never heard of it.

'Belongs to the King,' offered the President. 'Bit like Camp David, I guess.'

'The princesses'll feel at home then,' I suggested.

'Not for long,' said Byrnes.

*

That was the first letter I received from Mr Dulles.

---

i A very good question. See epilogue.

To Holkham

The 1.34 snorted into Shenfield station in a lather of sparks and steam at just before two o'clock. I like trains. When I was a child living in Bath my father used to get a private carriage attached to the GWR[i] express to take us down to Teignmouth. There we used to spend the golden summers up until the Great War. The whiff of smoke, the thundering roar of the great engine, the quiet clackety-clack of the rails, the white napery of the restaurant car, the gorgeous chocolate and cream carriages of God's Wonderful Railway. All so much more civilised than an oily old motor car forever breaking down and frightening the horses. This particular train was more modest. It comprised an old saddle-tank coupled to three carriages that dated back to well before the turn of the century. I made out the old Great Eastern coat of arms, much faded but still just recognisable, on some of the ancient wooden doors. A pale imitation of the Great Western, indeed a parody, but still a *railway*.

Sergeant Sturridge and I bundled ourselves into a Third Class compartment and threw our traps onto the rack. There was a lumpen mass of field grey in one corner, an elderly and bespectacled *Feldwebel*[ii] from the 14th Landwehr,[iii] who didn't spare us a glance. The other couple were in their dotage, stiff emaciated figures whose clothes, faces and very skin bore witness to the privations of five years of Occupation. A faint odour of urine, tempered with horse hair, permeated the compartment. Above the seats, posters advertised the pleasures of an age long gone. The beach at Skegness, Cromer Pier and the Norfolk

i Great Western Railway, known by its many adherents as God's Wonderful Railway.

ii Deputy platoon leader.

iii A militia force of older soldiers, the 14th was raised in Bavaria.

To Holkham

Broads, the Harwich Boat Train for the Continent. Outside, as we drew out of the town, the flat Essex landscape, punctuated with silver birch and willow. The storm had blown itself out, but the sky was still hard and leaden. It looked like snow.

There had been time only for decisions on the barge. Sturridge and I were to form the land party and make our way with all dispatch to Holkham. Twenty miles to the east of Sandringham, this was the seat of the local Resistance — indeed, the place where I'd first met the princesses. I knew Tommy Coke of old from the Scots Guards and Vimy Ridge,[iv] where we'd both been wounded. Scion of the Coke family, present proprietor of Holkham estate on Norfolk's north coast, talented violinist, he would put himself at our disposal. Kit and the boys would throw themselves on the mercy of Neptune and bring the *Cabby* round to the Wash as quickly as they could. There was no question of abandoning the barge, for she might prove a boon at Sandringham. Equally there was no question of the five of us travelling as a party to North Norfolk. According to Sturridge, warrants — *Haftbefehl* — were out for the arrest of me and Kit, and it had to be assumed that dear Haupsturmführer Brunner would eventually turn his mind more actively to the issue of our whereabouts and recent activities. Travelling around as a posse would be good for no one's health. Sturridge and I had only to row a mile or so upstream to Burnham-on-Crouch to pick up the train for the main line up from Liverpool Street at Shenfield. We left Kit waiting for the tide at Foulness. The question on everyone's mind was whether we would reach Sandringham in time. Skorzeny and the princesses were there now but how long would they remain?

The train pushed north with all the punctilio of a stopping service, through Ingatestone, Chelmsford, Hatfield Peverel, Witham, Kevedon and Marks Tey. It was gone three before we reached Colchester, saw the silver flash of the Stour at Manningtree and a distant glimpse of the cranes at Harwich.

iv The victorious Allied action of April 1917 on the battlefield north of Arras.

It was past the half hour when we crawled through the tunnel into Ipswich. Here we spent forty minutes kicking our heels before changing trains. The station buffet had made modest concessions to the occupying forces by adding some German sausages, cakes and the like to the menu. They served us watery tea. *Careless Talk Costs Lives,*[i] one of the old posters, much stained with condensation, was still up on the buffet's grimy brown walls. We took heed. Sturridge read her novel. I busied myself in the *Englische Zeitung*. The coverage was all about Himmler. You would have thought that there was nothing good to say about the head of the SS, creator of the concentration camps, and much else besides. Still, Goebbels had done his best. Himmler appeared as a kindly family man, dedicated to his daughter Gudrun, and a fine upholder of the Aryan ideal. The other news was that Goering was under house arrest at Karinhall.[ii] There was no word of the princesses, which was interesting. It was hardly that they had not been missed. Goebbels had clearly decided to conceal the escape. Whether this all meant he was in cahoots with Skorzeny, God knew.

As an afterthought, I dashed out to the Post Office just round the corner from the Station Hotel and scribbled a telegram to Tommy at Holkham. The 4.18 drew in just as dusk fell, only ten minutes or so late. We found an empty compartment, pulled down the blinds and turned up the gas. Our route was across the Anglian Breckland and fens to Dereham, then up to Wells right on the eastern invasion coast. According to the *Cabby*'s copy of Bradshaw,[iii]there was a local service of sorts from Wells to Holkham, right across the top of North Norfolk. Tommy Coke used to keep a good table, and

i One of a series of poster produced by the Ministry of Information in February 1940. Two and a half million were distributed to places of public assembly.

ii Goering's great manor house in Prussia, dedicated to the memory of his first wife.

iii The railway timetable, the Whittaker's Almanac to the Via Ferrovia.

he possessed one of the finest cellars in Norfolk. It crossed my mind that we might get there just in time for dinner.

Sturridge, now, was full of talk. I had half guessed she had tracked us down through the Pye. The Jerries had no monopoly on radio direction finders and of course Nancy — as I had now better call her — knew what she was looking for. As early as '42 the SOE had established a network of radio hams all over the country. Nancy and Sir Hugh---, her godfather, were party to Operation Nonesuch and had picked up the *Cabby* every time we tried to call Ottawa. In a sense it was a blessing that it had been impossible for us to get through, but it did make me wonder just who else knew the whereabouts of the barge. A lot of smart staff work at the covert Admiralty in Chatham[iv] had established the weather conditions the *Cabby* was likely to be meeting off Foulness. Of course, no one knew what had happened to the barge's jib, but it was a natural supposition that an operator like Kit would have sheltered in the lee of Foulness Island on a night like that. The rest was down to Nancy's initiative, Sir Hugh's blessing and a good deal of luck. Nancy might have spent all day trying to find us. As it was, fortune had favoured the brave. I was beginning to admire her gumption. 'How did you find out about Sandringham?' I asked, glancing at my watch. It had gone five and we were getting on for Dereham.

This, too, was as much luck as judgement. For all Nancy and Sir Hugh knew the previous night, Nonesuch might have been a complete success. By midnight they knew the princesses had been taken from the Tower. Then, just before 2a.m., a couple of stray reports came in from passers-by on the Embankment close to the Tower, and on Tower Bridge itself. These witnesses had seen nothing of our apprehension by Skorzeny. They had, though, seen the E-boat making its get-away. They had also seen what had happened to the *Cabby*'s dinghy. This gave them the first inkling that something had

---

iv The famous naval dockyard Kent. Here parts of the Admiralty continued to function secretly throughout the Occupation.

gone wrong. It was no great leap of logic for them to conclude that the princesses might be on board the E-boat rather than the barge. It was a horrible supposition, in some ways even worse than their incarceration in the Tower. In one there was at least certainty; in the other the unknown. Beyond that, on the night of the kidnapping, they could see no further.

'Hugh was beside himself,' said Nancy, turning towards me in the dim light of the carriage.

'And you?' I asked, sensing something more.

'Lady Julia's my first cousin,' she said, turning away again. It was a relationship of which I had not been aware.

Dereham came and went before I got the rest of the story. The following day was Friday and Nancy was expected as usual in Room 504. Brunner was already sniffing around asking where I was. Fortunately, he was sufficiently distracted by the aftermath of Hitler's assassination and the furore over the succession to trouble himself much beyond issuing a warrant for my arrest. Kit's absence from Fareham[i] had also been finally discovered by the Abwehr, and Brunner added his name to the wanted list for good measure. As we knew, no public announcement had been made about the princesses, and it was certainly not the talk of the War Office — at least in the circles in which Nancy moved. Goebbels had been quite clever to bottle the story up for so long. There are some advantages to a Police State.

Slipping away at about five, Nancy made her way to Sir Hugh's offices in Cambridge Circus. These were innocuous in the extreme, and seemed to be part of the Home Office department that managed the ration-card system — the *Bezuggscheine*. Set up by Sir Hugh in 1942, the department necessarily had an office in every town. It was an admirable cover for the Resistance.

By this time Sir Hugh had more or less puzzled out what had happened the previous night, and had made a pretty shrewd guess as to the identity of the commander of the

i Where the General believed Admiral Conway was being held under house arrest.

E-boat. He was no better informed, though, as to where that particular party might be found. Indeed, his speculations on the destination of the *Schnellboot* were no more accurate than our own. He imagined a cross-Channel dash for Ostend, Calais or Dieppe, and that the princesses were on their way to Berlin.

It was with these discouraging speculations that Nancy was greeted by Sir Hugh that Friday evening. They were tempered only by his views on the whereabouts of the *Cabby* — news that I suspect provided little comfort for Nancy. Frustrated in their pursuit of the hostages, the pair could do no more that evening than pass the time following our movements as we battled through the gale in the Thames Estuary. One of Sir Hugh's factotums brought in some cheese sandwiches and couple of bottles of Bass, these forming the basis of a cheerless supper. Then, just when Nancy was thinking of returning to her rooms in Dolphin Square,[ii] a call came through on the telephone. The line was not secure, and Sir Hugh was quite often the recipient of enigmatic telephone communications.

'That Sir Hugh?' The voice was cultured but provincial, distinctly provincial.

'Speaking.'

'How's the ankle?'

Sir Hugh had suffered a bad twist when shooting at Sandringham in the last winter before the war. 'Not bad. Gives me a bit of gyp on very cold days.'

'Poultices,' said his interlocutor. 'You can't beat them.'

Sir Hugh had now identified the speaker as the Sandringham GP who had treated the sprain, George Gurney by name, one of the Norfolk resistance stalwarts. Clearly he had a story to tell. Sir Hugh prompted, 'Good season?'

'Spanking. Not much doing on the estate here, but Tommy Coke had a couple of hundred-brace days. You should try and run up. There've been a couple of cracking hens squawking round the House lately. Just your line.'

---

ii The monstrous 1930s apartment block on the Chelsea Embankment, then as now infested with politicians.

'Surprised they haven't been snaffled up by your fox,' commented Sir Hugh.

At this there was a snuffle of suppressed laughter. 'Seems the fox has been winged.'

At which point Sir Hugh realised he had his story. 'I'll get up when I can.'

'You're always welcome, Sir Hugh, always welcome.'

Sir Hugh put down the receiver with a smile of relief on his face. He turned once again to the map. 'Well,' he said to Nancy, 'we don't know why they're in Sandringham, but in Sandringham they are. And if they're in the hands of Skorzeny, he's been injured.'

*

I glanced at my watch and then drew up the blind of the window. The train slowed and pulled into a station that proved to be Walsingham. Here, in 1012 it is said that Our Lady appeared to a widow called Richeldis de Faverches and desired her there to build a replica of the Holy House of the Annunciation. De Faverches had fulfilled her pledge, and in that place created England's Nazareth. Although the original shrine had been destroyed during the Reformation, there one still alights from the train into the Christian fervour of the High Middle Ages, into a medieval town of almshouses, chapels, a ruined priory and travellers' inns.

In the corner of the compartment Nancy had dozed off. Outside, the gently undulating North Norfolk landscape was lit by the winter moon, a line of poplars standing out starkly on the banks of the little river Stiffkey. Here and there blinked the lights of remote cottages. It was strange to think of Guderian's Panzers[i] rolling through this peaceful English landscape, but so they had five years ago. It was just as Erskine Childers had prophesied in *The Riddle of the Sands*: an armada of German

---

i Heinz Guderian commanded the 2nd Panzer Group that led the East Coast invasion. His account of the operation in *Panzer Leader* (1952) is excellent.

troop barges falling on a largely undefended coast. A signal box flashed past. I guessed we were close to Wells-next-the-Sea, right up on the coast and no more than two or three miles from Holkham. I woke Nancy and leaned out of the window as the train eased into the platform.

The night now was bitter, the wind easterly, the air flecked with snow. The station's feeble gas lamps provided little puddles of light. At the end of the platform a man stood ready to take our tickets. Flanking him were two grim figures in the unmistakable black uniform of the SS.

*

'Some of Brunner's friends waiting,' I said to Nancy.

'Not for us,' she said stoutly. I doubted she meant it. If she did, I thought she was wrong.

I cast around the compartment. There was no chance of getting out on the rail side because our train had drawn up next to another on the adjoining line. We could make a run for it to the far end of the platform and onto the tracks beyond, but the platform was short and the SS were close. Alone, I might have tried. With Nancy the best hope seemed to be to brazen things out.

I grabbed our bags and threw open the door to the cry of 'Arll change, arll change.' It was an injunction which the broad Norfolk dialect stripped of all its urgency. There were a dozen other passengers getting off the train: an elderly man, a couple of lads who looked — and smelled — like fishermen, the rest women of motherly appearance in the drab austerity clothing that seems the norm for the working classes. We could hardly corral them into rushing the gate. The fishermen were already having their *Ausweise*[ii] scrutinised in the light of the porter's station lantern. The SS were taking some care. The women in front of us stood with the resignation of the defeated. The fisherman were waved away, and I saw one of

ii Identity cards.

the SS men glance up the platform with some interest at us. He turned to speak to his colleague, embroiled with one of the old women. The second man glanced up.

Just at that moment, I saw — beyond the gate — a large Riley draw up outside. This was an event in itself in Norfolk, where cars have always been a rarity. A ramshackle shooting brake drew up alongside, and out jumped the ramrod figure of Tommy Coke. I could have shouted for joy. Up he strode, flanked by half a dozen toughs of the gamekeeper type, Tommy playing lord of the manor to the hilt. He looked as if he owned station, town and countryside all around rolled into one. Now I came to think of it, he was Lord Lieutenant of Norfolk so in a sense he did. By comparison the local Gauleiter, installed by the Boche in 1940, was nobody. The porter doffed his cap, the SS johnnies were just shouldered aside and then Tommy, all six foot of him, was kissing me on both cheeks. It was a form of salutation we'd adopted at Vimy in homage to Joffre.[i] I introduced Nancy as my ADC, Tommy's men collected our traps and, a couple of minutes later, we were on our way to Holkham. The SS had vanished. I wondered at the time, though, whether we had seen the last of them.

'Another time,' shouted Tommy over the noise of his horrible diesel, 'let me know more precisely the time of your train.'

'Where are we going?' asked Nancy in my ear.

'Whose was Holkham, Tommy?' I shouted. 'Your great-great uncle's?'

'I'm not that old, my dear fellow,' he replied. 'Add a few more greats. Coke of Holkham, 1754 to 1842. The great agricultural reformer, Turnip Townsend and all that rot. Built the pile to keep his descendants in perpetual penury. There's a whacking great monument to him just up the hill from the house. I've got it by heart. Says his was "a life devoted to the welfare of his friends, neighbours and tenants, pre-eminently combining public service with private worth, and affording an illustrious example of birth and station activated by duty

i Marshall Joseph Joffre, one of the architects of the Allied success at Vimy Ridge.

98

and inspired by benevolence". Shouldn't credit it myself. Absolute rot, I dare say.'

We had come in from Wells past the east lodge, through the open parkland and a scattering of oak, beech and larch to the back of the house. Under the thin moon and sullen grey clouds you got little sense of the neo-Palladian Hall other than its scale. The north frontage must have been a good three hundred feet long, and the façade perhaps seventy-five feet high. The great doors into the Marble Hall were shut, and we entered through a modest door that led through the servants' quarters into the west wing. The Third Earl had shut up most of the house in 1939, and when Tommy inherited in 1941 he, his wife Marion and his violins retreated to the private quarters in which he claimed himself much reduced. A brace of Gainsboroughs, a Titian spirited out of Lombardy by one of Tommy's illustrious ancestors, and half a dozen Whistlers gave lie to this, though his domestic retinue was reduced to the butler Rayner and the cook Mrs Scoles. The maids lived out. When Tommy had been stuck in London during the invasion, Guderian had seized the place and used it as his forward headquarters. He and his staff had treated the Hall with surprising respect, and made perfectly presentable arrangements for Tommy's people on the estate itself.

This Tommy recounted over dinner in his gorgeous little terracotta dining-room, where we were served by a now elderly Rayner. Marion was away visiting friends, but nevertheless we fed like kings. The estate was virtually self-sufficient, and the Boche in Fakenham — the local market town a dozen miles south — were bamboozled by Tommy's agent and so denied the tithe that they tried to impose. We had some of the local mussels and then venison from the herd of roe deer. Tommy gave us Chinon and a couple of bottles of Crozes-Hermitage. Over a port that had been laid down the year Hitler came to power, we mulled over our plans.

Like Sir Hugh----, Tommy had been apprised of the guests at Sandringham by the good doctor, George Gurney. Indeed, it transpired that it was Tommy who had prompted the call to

Sir Hugh. Tommy had sent his scouts out to see how the land lay. This was yesterday. There was certainly a Boche force of some nature at the House, but of indeterminate size. A skeleton staff lived in, and had been in place for years. No one had succeeded in contacting them as yet, and the postman and the milkman reported 'Nowt amiss'. Some of the circumstances in which the hostages had arrived had nevertheless emerged. Skorzeny's E-boat had been wrecked on the bar at a tiny drying harbour called Thornham. This was eight or nine miles north-east of Sandringham, on the North Sea coast rather than the Wash. Tommy dug out the Ordnance to show us. 'Nasty entrance. Shifting sands. Not properly buoyed since 1940. They must have had very good reasons for wanting to get in.'

'Engine trouble,' I speculated.

'We don't know', declared Tommy. 'Any more than we know why they were here in the first place. There's hardly a decent harbour on this coast between Lynn and Yarmouth and I certainly wouldn't count Wells. Not very close to the wonderful Fatherland, either.'

'They were lucky to get off the boat,' I hazarded.

'We know they all did?' asked Nancy, who had said little over dinner.

By way of an answer, Tommy returned to the map of Thornham. 'The wreck of the *Schnellboot*'s about here. Here's the pub and here's the church. They waved down a car just here on the main road. The District Nurse, Mrs Gent. All very polite. Said they'd had an accident and could she take a couple of them to Sandringham. She's an obliging sort and did just that. She was going to Anmer and dropped them at the gates. What they didn't know is that she'd spotted the girls sheltering in the porch of the church and of course recognised them at once. Everyone knows them round here. The princesses and Lady Julia. All safe and sound.'

'Good show,' said Nancy.

'Now Mrs Gent isn't much of a hand at languages and hadn't seen much of Jerry,' Tommy continued. 'They whipped through this coast like a dose of salts on their way to

100

the Midlands in 1940 and they haven't been seen much since. Whole county's very lightly garrisoned. Except Norwich and Lynn, of course,' he said, naming Norfolk's two main towns. 'But she nursed a couple of Jerry invasion casualties in the Cottage Hospital here who'd parachuted in too low. Heinz and Franz or Fritz or something. The long and short of it was that in the course of the trip to Sandringham, she thought they said several times, 'The Colonel's leg'. *Der Obersts Bein.* Again we don't know, but it sounds like the dear Colonel hurt himself legging it from the boat — as well he might. If you get stuck on the bar, you can walk off. But only if you're damn lucky.'

'Man like Skorzeny makes his own luck,' I remarked.

'Might well,' agreed Tommy. 'But it certainly seems he didn't get off Scot free. And he's lost his boat.'

'And now they're all holed up in the House,' I added.

Tommy seemed to take this as a reproach. He said, 'Perimeter's staked.'

My mind was racing ahead. 'Why haven't they sent for reinforcements?'

'May well have,' countered Tommy. 'How would we know?'

'Or Skorzeny may be playing his own game,' I suggested. I explained to Tommy our speculations about Skorzeny and his loyalties.

'Do we need the hostages?' Tommy asked.

It was a reasonable enough question, and I couldn't reproach Tommy for asking it. Somehow, though, at the stage we had now reached, it seemed like heresy. I blurted out, 'Can you ask?'

As for Tommy, he passed round the port again and placed his fingers together like a church. It was a habit I remembered of old, and it brought back the day of our briefing by Byng[i] at Vimy, with Tommy scraping away at his violin. Can't have been many men who brought violins to the trenches. I fumbled for my pipe.

'We're in unknown territory,' he began. 'A Thousand Year

i 1st Viscount Byng commanded the Canadian Army Corps at the capture of Vimy Ridge.

Reich presupposes a fairly orderly transition from Führer to Führer, and that National Socialism is here to stay. Like Communism in the Soviet Union. The people may not like it but, in a Police State, they'd adopt the line of least resistance and tolerate it. That's one line. The other way of looking at it is that the Reich's vassal states have strong national identities and are merely biding their time before overturning their oppressors.'

'There'll be a rising,' declared Nancy. 'There is already.'

'It'll be suppressed,' said Tommy. 'Brutally.'

There was something in Tommy's tone that gave me pause for thought. 'Do you know?' I asked.

There was a pause, and I felt rather than saw Tommy's shoulders droop in the low light of the dining-room. He was well the wrong side of sixty and, at that moment, looked it.

'Yes,' he said, more quietly. 'I'm afraid I do. I'm sorry to have to tell you that they shot Alec and Wingate[i] today. Stewart-Richardson[ii] and Hore-Belisha[iii]. Dozens of others besides.'

'Good God!' I cried, though I suppose at least part of me had long expected this news. Nancy buried her head in her hands. She had been very fond of Alec.

'Many of them are perfectly civilised,' Tommy commented. 'A handful are barely human.'

One of the candles guttered and Tommy pinched it out. Then he continued.

'Leeds is more or less in our hands. Ditto Liverpool. Newcastle's in the balance. Leicester, Coventry and Nottingham may be going our way. Birmingham, Bristol, Plymouth all under the heel. Things are very iffy for Jerry in

---

i Orde Wingate (1903-1946), who made his name as a soldier in the Middle East.

ii Douglas Alexander Stewart-Richardson (1899-1946), the Afghan specialist.

iii Leslie Hore-Belisha (1893-1946), politician and secretary of state for war 1937-1940.

To Holkham

Paris, of all places, I hear.[iv] What did you see on your way up?'

'Not much,' I conceded.

'No,' said Tommy, 'and there's very little doing in London.'

'They're soft,' said Nancy. She had recovered herself.

'They're scared,' corrected Tommy. Then he continued in his more jocular vein, 'That, my dear, is why we do need the hostages. Those girls are much loved. They might just tip the balance.'

The tension relaxed in the room and Tommy returned to the Ordnance. 'Here we are and here's Sandringham.' His finger followed the line of the railway through the little settlements of Burnham Market, Docking, Sedgeford, Heacham and Wolferton. 'No distance at all. Twenty miles.'

'And we have the advantage of surprise,' added Nancy.

'Well,' said Tommy lightly, 'I don't suppose the good Colonel feels himself entirely invulnerable.'

'Alright,' I conceded. 'He's prepared for an attack but doesn't know when or if it's coming.'

'Agreed,' said Tommy. 'Now, Sergeant,' he continued, 'your plan.'

This was patronising, and to my surprise I found myself getting angry. Nancy was no fool, nor was her rank nominal. It was to her meticulous arrangements for Queen Anne's Gate that I owed my life. I opened my mouth before thinking better of it. For her part, Nancy took the suggestion in all seriousness. After a few moments thought, she asked, 'He's got a dozen men?'

Tommy shrugged his shoulders. 'We presume no more than the crew of the E-boat. Dozen at most.'

'Covered lines of advance?'

This was more in his territory. 'Flattish heathland round there. Fair number of trees around the house.'

'Who have we got?' asked Nancy.

'Jerries have cut them to the bone. In 1939 we had a couple

iv A moderately accurate summary of the extent of the Rising on this date: 3 February. General Model temporarily regained control of Paris on the 4th and the 5th.

of hundred on the estate. It's about a quarter now. Most of them are in one of Sauckel's[i] munitions factories in Leipzig.'

'What about Admiral Conway?' She turned to me.

'Well, he said he'd see us when he saw us. Tomorrow evening at the earliest, I'd guess.'

'Arms?' Nancy asked of Tommy.

'Not exactly Karabiner 98K,'[ii] conceded our host.

'Shotguns in fact?' I asked.

'Yes,' said Tommy. 'Mainly Hollands[iii] belonging to my father.'

I don't suppose any of us looked particularly bright at this intelligence. Nancy asked: 'Margin for error?'

'None, given who we're dealing with. I don't think Winston would relish an accident, particularly with the King breathing down his neck.' Such was Tommy's judgement.

I looked at both of them and concluded, 'Not very good, is it?'

'No, it's not,' admitted Tommy. 'We can't go in through the front. We might' — and here he indicated a group of outbuildings a few yards to the south-east of the main house close to the stables — 'get this far without being noticed. Woodcock Copse.'

'Diversion,' put in Nancy.

'Precisely,' agreed Tommy, although without much enthusiasm, I thought. I remembered from Vimy that he preferred his own ideas.

We laid our plans in some detail. Rayner had long gone to bed when we turned in a little before midnight. Long after I heard the sombre airs of Tommy's violin.

---

i Ernst 'Fritz' Sauckel 1894-1946. Generalbevollmächtigter für den Arbeitseinsatz — General Plenipotentiary of Labour - for the Reich from 1942 to its collapse in 1946. Oversaw the importation of 5 million foreign labourers into Germany.

ii The German precision arms manufacturer.

iii Traditional English shot-guns.

What Happened at Sandringham

I slept badly. After the thin comforts of the *Cabby* I should have luxuriated in one of Holkham's feather beds, but the face of Alec as I had last seen him barely left me all night. He was not a warm man, but beyond his frosty exterior lay someone of sympathetic imagination, intelligence and intense loyalty. It was a bitter sacrifice. I thought how easily I myself might have drawn the short straw in the Cabinet War Rooms, and ended up in Vine Street en route to Prince Albrechtstrasse[iv] in Berlin and the gallows or the firing squad. Wingate, too, I had known; some of the others fleetingly met. They were fine men who had died doing their duty. God help them.

I rose with the sun, washed, shaved and went down to the breakfast room with its views over the deer park. No one was about, but Rayner or Mrs Scoles had already been about their business. Breakfast was in chafing dishes on the sideboard. Eggs, bacon, sausages, mushrooms and black pudding. I remembered Tommy's weakness for black pudding. I hadn't had a breakfast like it since the beginning of the war. Afterwards I lit my pipe, and thought I'd have a poke around the stables with which — I'd remembered — Holkham was pretty well furnished. The raid was set for dusk, and we had most of the day to kill. There were a couple of fillies in the yard, one of which I quite liked the look of. Piebald, sixteen or seventeen hands, and a very easy carriage. I was just about to return to the house when Tommy came round the corner from the park at the double.

'Trouble,' he said shortly.

'What's up?'

'Don't know. Just had a call in from Lynn,' he said.

This was King's Lynn, the old Roman port on the Wash, the railhead from London and Cambridge, and the Wehrmacht's

iv The Gestapo HQs at Vine Street in the West End and Prince Albrecht Strasse in Berlin.

western county headquarters in Norfolk. 'Armoured column's just left heading north.'

'Routine patrol,' I suggested. Tommy had a tendency to panic, I sometimes thought. Perhaps it came more with age.

'Never on a Sunday,' he countered. 'They've got a bunch of Bavarians down there barracked in the Duke's Head and the Corn Exchange. Strict Catholics. Very observant.'

Well, it was his call, I supposed. 'Well we'd better get on.'

The men had originally been told to foregather after lunch. Tommy said he needed to spend an hour on the radio-telephone and he detailed me and Nancy to dig out the men. It took a good two hours to round them up from all over the estate: some from the Model Farm, some in the old almshouses and most of them out in the fields. There was a bitter easterly and the park was at its bleakest. Not a bud was to be seen on the oak and chestnut in which the estate abounded, the winter wheat had barely sprouted, and the great lake — according to Tommy excavated by Napoleonic prisoners-of-war — was as grey as the sky it mirrored. The deer seemed huddled together for warmth, the lapwings cried forlornly and even the Brent geese looked cold.

Nancy saw it through quite different eyes. 'What a place to live in', she said as she took in the splendour of the great Hall in its setting of rolling parkland. Here and there was a spinney or a copse, and up the hill beyond the old ice-house a Doric temple to ease the eye. On balmier days the place was certainly Arcadian. I'd forgotten she hadn't seen it in the light.

'England,' I said, setting out for Nancy's benefit my late father's views on the Regency as the highest expression of English genius, the age of enlightenment, progress, hope, elegance and empire. These achievements were tempered by the less agreeable and subsequent developments of the Great Reform Act, emancipation, socialism and the motor car. All of these seemed to him, indeed to all men of reason, retrograde steps.

Nancy considered the statement. Then she turned to me with a smile that left me moved. 'Yes, England.' She took my

What Happened at Sandringham

hand and for the first time since the deaths of Dorothy and the children I felt the weight of bereavement shift from my shoulders, and the future colour with something more than resignation.[i]

*

We took the men, only a couple of dozen, in the shooting brakes up the drive to the north lodge and through the village itself to Holkham's station. It was simple red brick building to the north of the Hall set in the sombre winter salt marsh that had been reclaimed by the Second Earl: nothing more than a single platform, a tiny ticket office and a waiting-room. Tommy was already there, dressed in plus fours of what seemed to me a very vulgar check. God knows why he couldn't have stuck to a salt-and-pepper tweed. Goes with all that nonsense about being an artist, I suppose. As we drew up he glanced at his watch. It was already nearly noon.

'Shouldn't be long,' he said.

The men, some in Norfolk jackets and a couple in Ulsters, were a weather-beaten lot. A couple were fresh-faced lads. Most were the wrong side of sixty. I guessed they were deemed either too old or too young to be at work in the munitions factories of the Reich. They were solid Norfolk types who looked as much concerned with the day's prospects as they would of a day's beating for partridge or pheasant: phlegmatic sorts, uncritical and uncomplaining of their lot in life; slow to anger, easy to please, infrequent to wash. The waiting-room was normally reserved for the Coke family. The men were clearly amused to find themselves promoted. We were there for only a few minutes, crowded round the fire, the men chattering ten to a dozen, when a whistle brought us out onto the platform. To the east, on the embankment and bridge that carried the train from Wells over the coast road a mile

---

i A development about which the General tells the contemporary reader perhaps less than they would like to know.

107

or so away, there was a spurt of smoke just visible against the leaden sky. Within a couple of minutes the steam had materialised into some sort of train. It took a few seconds for the men to realise quite what it was, then they gave a ragged cheer.

'What on earth is that?' asked Nancy, as a formidable assemblage pulled into the station, drawn by a dirty little black six-wheeler that might have pre-dated the Boer War.[i] The leading car behind the locomotive sprouted the unmistakable barrel of a 4-pounder, shrouded in a gun-metal casing.

'That, my dear,' said Tommy, proudly as if he had himself conjured it up out of thin air, 'is our armoured train.'

I have to say that I had entirely forgotten about Tommy's train. The previous night he had promised transport to get us to Sandringham, but more than that he had not specified. Tommy, though — I suppose fifteen years my senior — was a veteran of Bloemfontein. Here the Scots Guards, aided and abetted by the Royal Engineers, had used these trains to great effect against de Wet's republicans. When the shadows gathered over Europe in the aftermath of Munich, it was Tommy who had made the case for the vulnerability of the east coast with vehemence. He argued that a German armada would make its way straight across the North Sea from the mouths of the Weser and the Elbe, and fall upon the negligibly defended coast of East Anglia. I remembered the correspondence in *The Times* and the *Morning Chronicle*. At his behest pillboxes, AA guns and anti-tank traps began to spring up all over the Norfolk countryside, and the component parts of the great train were procured: a couple of artillery wagons, an infantry assault wagon, a command wagon, an ammunition car and a lightly armoured E4 locomotive. In 1939, with much ceremony, the train was patrolled up and down the coast between Heacham on the Wash and Wells — much to the gratification of the locals, especially the small boys. If Tommy had had his way it would doubtless have played its part on

i Seemingly the second Boer War, 1899-1902.

What Happened at Sandringham

15 July 1940, when Guderian's[ii] transports were spotted in the Boston Deeps in the mouth of the Wash, not much more than a mile from the Lincolnshire coast. Tommy, though, had been with the remains of the BEF[iii] in London on Lord Gort[iv]'s staff, and General Ironside[v] thought poorly of such trains. Its chance of glory passed by as it sat neglected in a siding in Melton Constable, the railway junction a dozen miles inland where the cross country route from Lynn to Norwich met the line from the South. Come the Occupation, on the initiative of one of the engineering staff at Melton, the gun carriage was spirited to some remote siding in the empty countryside, as was its ammunition, and the more innocent rolling stock was returned to everyday use. At Tommy's behest the train had now been reassembled and he was clearly determined to give it another chance.

We got the men into the infantry wagon, and I ushered Nancy into the saloon that passed as the command car.

'Good lord!'

I turned as quickly as Tommy. It was the Hall cook in an apron as white as Noah's, waving a piece of paper. She was so out of breath she couldn't speak, her face the colour of beetroot, her ample breasts almost heaving themselves out of her dress. She thrust the paper into Tommy's hand.

'What's this, Mrs Scoles?' asked Tommy.

The cook caught her breath. She must have run all the way from the Hall. 'Adm'ral Conway on the radio, M'lord. Terrible hurry. In his barge by Wolferton he said. Said you'd be pleased. Then he said, especial, that, there's aircraft in t'bay. Flying

ii See page 102.

iii British Expeditionary Force.

iv Whom General Quick replaced. See p 18.

v William Edmund Ironside, 1880-1943. Commanded the home defence forces from 1940 until the surrender.

boats, he said. Flying boats. Lord I'm glad I caught thee.'

Tommy had a gift with his servants, indeed the working classes in general. I always used to think he put them at their ease while ensuring that they knew their place. 'Mrs Scoles, you're a wonder.'

'Did he say anything else?' I asked.

Mrs Scoles, still recovering her breath, thought for a moment, screwing up her eyes with effort. 'Yes, my lord,' she said eventually, replying to Tommy rather than to me.'Said he'd see you at the 'ouse.'

'At the house?' I asked, presuming Kit had meant Sandringham. 'At Sandringham?'

''e just said "the 'ouse,"' she responded.

There seemed little point in further interrogation. Tommy must have felt similarly. 'Very good, Mrs Scoles,' said he.' Now be off with you.'

Tommy went off in the direction of the engine driver. I joined Nancy in the train's saloon, followed a moment later by Tommy himself.

'Flying boats,' he said, as the train pulled slowly out of Holkham heading west for Sandringham. 'Who in the hell's got flying boats?'

It was a question that took me back four years to something that Alec had said about long-distance seaplanes. What was it? No, it had gone.

*

The saloon was quite a comfortable affair, with a couple of leather-covered seats, a sideboard, a green baize table and a small library. Nancy, Tommy and I crowded round the Ordnance map, trying to puzzle out what on earth was going on. 'Here's Wolferton,' said Tommy. 'We'll be there in about half an hour. The village and the station's between Sandringham House itself and the coast. We go through the village to the house, approaching from the west. Couple of miles.'

Nancy fingered the map. 'Where are the Jerries?'

110

What Happened at Sandringham

'They're coming up from Lynn, so they'd normally approach from the east, on the Anmer side of the house. May be there already. May still be on their way. We don't know quite when they left. Don't even know they're heading for Sandringham.'

'Yes, and Skorzeny? I asked.

Tommy stared out of the window at the thin winter wheat in the fields approaching the village of Burnham Market, the next station on the line. He thought out loud. 'Called for reinforcements.'

'Or Brunner and his boys might have concluded Skorzeny's rowing his own boat, and decided to put a stop to it,' suggested Nancy.

My own mind was elsewhere. 'Has the Luftwaffe got flying boats here?'

'Don't know,' said Tommy, turning back to the map. 'I rather lost interest in that heavier-than-air stuff when they did away with the RFC. Met Trenchard[i] more than once. Dreadful man.' Tommy had been a great admirer of the Royal Flying Corps, particularly at the stage when it was more interested in lighter-than-air machines — balloons, dirigibles and so on. He was aghast when it was detached from the army and set up as a Service in its own right under Hugh Trenchard, a man whom he loathed for reasons I now forget.

'Must belong to someone,' I said, trying to keep him engaged on the subject of the seaplanes.

'If Kit's got any sense,' said Tommy, ignoring my attempts, 'he'll have beached that barge of yours at the south end of Peter Black Sand. That's about as close as he can get to the house. Bit above a mile to the station. Three in all to the house.'

'Planes can't be far from there,' I said, persisting.

'Handy for the house,' commented Nancy.

'Just so,' remarked Tommy ruminatively. He was clearly thinking about something else.

i Hugh Trenchard, (1873-1956). Father of the RAF.

111

The engine began to labour as it pulled up the long chalky hill from Burnham Market to Stanhoe, a tiny station lost in the fields, more than a mile from the village it was supposed to serve. It seemed to be taking us inexorably into a situation of confusion. I said as much to Tommy. He just mentioned Vimy. Here it was true things hadn't been quite as organised as they might have been, what with one thing and another.

From Stanhoe we toiled up to Docking, through the Norfolk that nobody knows, of big skies, fields that stretch to the horizon, and cottages of chalk, brick and flint. At Heacham the Wells branch joins the line to Lynn. Here, after some banter with a signalman, we turned south. As we did so, above the grunts of the old E4, I heard the crackle of gunfire. The driver did what Tommy had told him to do in such circumstances and closed down the regulator. We crawled into Wolferton station and drew to a halt in front of the exquisite carstone station buildings that had been built for the Prince of Wales.[i] Out popped the station-master, a wizened little man who looked as though he'd been there since the place opened in 1898. (I checked with Tommy later. He had.) He greeted Tommy as an old friend, and nodded respectfully to me and Nancy, but he was more interested in the train.

'Heard talk you'd had her out.' He cast his eye over the artillery wagons on which the men were busily at work loading ammunition. 'She's a real beauty'.

Tommy was proud of his train but, at least at that moment, he seemed to be thinking more about the matter in hand. 'Quiet morning, Ray?' he asked.

The station-master eyed him knowingly, and looked as though he would have preferred to pursue the matter of the train. 'There's a right lot of loose talk,' he said with an air of reproof. 'From folks as should know better.'

'Yes, Ray,' said Tommy.

'Hard times,' began the station-master. 'Why, I was just … '

i The eldest son of Queen Victoria and Prince Albert (b1841), who became King Edward V11 on the death of his mother in 1901.

112

What Happened at Sandringham

But before he could continue, Tommy cut in with another, 'Yes, Ray.'

The station-master, clearly prepared to make a story out of his day and his troubles, sensed Tommy's urgency. 'Long and short is that the girls are back in the house, boy, guests of a *Chairman* gentleman they say.'

'That right,' said Tommy.

The station-master nodded sagely. 'Planes on t'beach, too,' he said. 'Aeroplanes,' he added, as though he might not have made himself clear.

'Yes?' said Tommy encouragingly.

'Land on the water, they say. Mrs Buttle saw 'em. Never seen nowt like it. Planes that land on water.' There was real wonder in his voice.

We had got the drift.

'Are they German planes, Ray?' asked Tommy.

'*Chairman*?' repeated the station-master, correcting Tommy's pronunciation.

'Yes.'

The station-master nodded as though appreciating the sagacity of the question. 'Funny thing,' he said. 'No markin's, roundels, swastikas, crosses, hooplahs, whatever you call'em.'

'None at all?' I asked.

He shook his head slowly and definitively, looking from one to the other of us, then back at the men. With that he retired to his office, albeit with a parting shot for Tommy. 'Go careful, boy.'

We divided our party into two. One, led by Tommy, was tasked to circle the house from the north. I was to take the other from the south. I had half a mind to leave Nancy in safety with the train. Of course she would have none of it. What with the girl and a dozen grandfathers with shotguns, I thought we were a bit of a scratch crew. Tommy and I synchronised our watches. It had just gone 2.20 and the light was already beginning to drop quite markedly. We agreed to regroup in an hour.

As it turned out the whole thing took less than half that. Tommy knew his job, I knew mine, and the grandfathers and the greenhorns were admirable. They were a good deal lighter on their feet than I was myself, and they had a far better eye for the country. I suppose they weren't gamekeepers for nothing. As for Nancy, she had the agility of a cat.

Regrouping at the train, we exchanged notes. The house was besieged alright. There were half a dozen not very good positions right round it, just within the surrounding woods, three or four to a post. Who they were we couldn't see. Skorzeny — assuming it was him — had a couple of men posted on the roof, and from time to time there was a bit of desultory fire. It was stalemate, Tommy and I agreed. No one would do anything before dusk. Under the cover of darkness anything could be done. We made our plans accordingly and acted at once.

In a sense, the timing was good. For, as we later discovered, the column from Lynn that we had been expecting was actually just about to arrive.

*

We left half a dozen of the men with the train. The remainder of us set off for the house. We scouted from the station through Woodcock Wood to the Anmer road. We met no one. The road was deserted. Like a crooked arm it embraced the west-facing house from the north and the east, and led round to Wood-cock Copse. There we planned to make our base. Once, before the house was built in 1870 the whole area had been largely cleared, so creating the West Lawns in front of the house and the North Garden. Conveniently enough, a strip of wood had been left edging the road right round to the stables at the back of the house. Within its cover we could work our way right round the quadrant formed by the road to within a few yards of Woodcock Copse and its sheltering outbuildings.

We crossed the road close to the glade and made our way without incident to the stables. They had been a particular passion of the Queen, and were a legend in equine circles. When I saw them my heart fell. Every single box was empty and the gates were ajar, a couple of them banging in the wind. Not a soul was in sight, but now and then came the odd rifle shot. Between the stables of Woodcock Wood lay a track in perhaps seventy-five feet of open ground. I checked my watch. It was now 4.12. We had three minutes. Tommy and I divided the party into three groups. We hoped to slip across unnoticed by the units in the wood. At 4.15 sharp there were two gratifying explosions as the four-pounders on the armoured train were let loose. The shots were ranged well over the house and fell harmlessly a couple of hundred yards to the east. It wasn't quite the bombardment before the Somme, but it would give Skorzeny a bit of a turn. Nancy grinned, the excitement coupled with fear that comes from being under fire and that I knew only too well.

We left it precisely a minute before the first group of four scuttled across the road. There was no response from the woods where the units we had failed to identify were set up. The remaining two groups crossed at one-minute intervals. By 4.20 we were safely in the corner of the copse and at the doors of a tumbledown old summerhouse, the back of which had collapsed. Tommy said he remembered playing there a child. We crowded into the old summerhouse with its faded deck-chairs and parasols, archery targets and croquet sets while outside the bombardment continued as planned. We now divided our forces further.

The men waited in the summerhouse, while Tommy, Nancy and I crept north to the corner of the copse and peered out of the trees. It was now dusk. We were just a stone's throw from the back of the house, a three-storey edifice of no great distinction constructed of red brick garnished with the local brown carstone. It was the sort of place that might have constructed to the order, and possibly even the design, of a minor railway magnate. At first glance, it was unguarded. Nancy, though, looking up, spotted the two men on the roof whom we had seen earlier, silhouetted against the darkening sky. They seemed to be looking east over our position into the ribbon of trees by which we had made our way to the copse. It crossed my mind then that perhaps another unit was moving up behind us. From the roof came a blast of fire and, just as suddenly, the four-pounders fell silent. I glanced at my watch. They should have continued for at least another five minutes. I think Tommy drew the same inference. Something was up. With a nod the three of us sprinted across the grass towards the old scullery back door at the rear of the house. There was a shot from the roof. It went well wide. Then we were through the door and into the main kitchen. On the range a kettle was gently simmering; a dozen loaves sat cooling above the oven; and on the table lay four brace of neatly trussed partridges. Of the cook and the scullery maids there was not a sign. Tommy put his hand to his lips. The house seemed strangely empty.

By comparison with Holkham, Sandringham was really not much more than a shooting lodge. From the door of the kitchen one corridor ran to the main dining-room, another via a dog-leg to the larger of the two drawing-rooms. We crept along the first to the dining-room. Nancy put her ear to the door. She shrugged her shoulders. We retraced our steps and tried the drawing-room. There, too, the door was closed. Within, though, I could hear the murmur of voices. I grasped the door handle, turned it gently and eased the door open a couple of inches.

At once the murmur coalesced into identifiable voices. One was just declaiming, 'I'm bored.' It sounded damned like Princess Margaret. I opened the door further. The voice was unmistakable. There was someone else there too. I nodded to Tommy and Nancy, took a deep breath, and pushed open the door.

*

A curious scene confronted us. One element was reassuringly domestic. Princess Margaret was lying in front of a blazing log fire kicking her legs in the air and — it seemed — demanding the attention of anyone prepared to give it. Next to her, seated at a pretty little mahogany occasional table, sat Lady Julia and

116

What Happened at Sandringham

Princess Elizabeth. They had been playing mah-jong,[i] the tiles piled high higgledy-piggledy all over the table. Above the fire the princesses' parents looked down, giving their blessing to the scene in so far as their manifestation in oil paint permitted. The other element struck a frankly discordant note. There were half a dozen men in uniform standing round the room, several of whom carried machine-guns of a type I didn't immediately recognise. They looked most surprised to see us and expressed their consternation by raising their guns. We were surprised, too. The uniforms were not the dark blue of the Kriegsmarine but olive green. Colonel Skorzeny was nowhere to be seen.

Princess Margaret was more hospitable than the soldiers. She seemed to regard our arrival as a welcome diversion from the tedium of the afternoon. She jumped to her feet, ran over to Tommy and embraced him. I was granted a peck on the cheek and Nancy a hug. Her sister Elizabeth, with greater reserve, also seemed pleased to see us. She smiled in the manner of one whose expectations had been pleasantly fulfilled, although I have to say she looked twice at Tommy's plus fours. Julia and Nancy, the kissing cousins, were momentarily in tears. Our captors, if so they were, seemed entirely bemused by the situation. Tommy, ever gracious, sought to set them at their ease. One of the men had shoulder flashes that seemed to indicate primacy. He looked about thirty, had dark hair and a finely chiselled face with small eyes. I thought he seemed vaguely familiar. Tommy offered him his hand. 'Tommy Coke,' he said.

'The Fourth Earl of Leicester,' added Julia, freeing herself from Nancy's embrace. The officer took Tommy's gesture in the spirit it was clearly intended, and shook hands. What he said, though, did surprise me a good deal. I had expected Germans. Now a man dressed in a uniform I didn't recognise spoke clearly and confidently: 'Commander Joe Kennedy Junior of the United States Navy.'

'Kick Cavendish's brother,' added Julia, in a manner I

i A game of chance and skill originating in China. Enjoyed a great vogue before the war.

thought perhaps more mischievous than helpful. While I was trying to digest this information and all its ramifications, the simplest elements of the story came back to me. 'Kick' — Kathleen — Kennedy was the girl who had come over with her father, the appalling Ambassador,[i] in 1938. She was what the illustrated papers carefully called a 'spirited beauty'. Dorothy had another word for it. I remember reading in *Picture Post*[ii] that she was 'widely regarded as the most exciting débutante of the year', for the idiots interested in such things. Her name was 'linked' with all sorts of men. Linked indeed. Eventually, in May 1944, she married Bill Cavendish: heir of the 10th Duke of Devonshire. Caught might be a better word.

And in some curious way it was this story of Anglo-American liaison that reminded me of poor Alec's comments about a pre-war Anglo-American initiative to develop long-range seaplanes. Seaplanes! The penny dropped. Clearly, this was how the precious Commander had got himself to Sandringham. That was one thing. How on earth he knew the princesses were there and what he was up to with them remained to be seen.

It was time to introduce myself to Kennedy. I did so, adding that I had served with his brother-in-law. Then, not intending to let him off the hook entirely, I added, 'Met your father, too.'

'General Quick,' was his response. He looked me straight in the eye, doubtless aware of the opinion I was likely to hold of the former Ambassador to the Court of St James and notorious Nazi apologist.

I turned towards Tommy, taking in with my glance the guns still levelled at us. It was time to come to the point.

'We were expecting Colonel Skorzeny,' I said.

Princess Elizabeth and Lady Julia had resumed their game of mah-jong. Lady Julia chipped in from the table. 'In the cellar.'

i Joseph Patrick Kennedy, 1888-1969. Ambassador to Britain 1938-1941.

ii An illustrated magazine. Fore-runner of *OK!* and *Hello!*

What Happened at Sandringham

The Commander frowned at this interruption and I have to say that Nancy laughed.

'We have Sandringham House secured. Colonel Skorzeny and his men are under arrest,' said Kennedy.

Tommy butted in. 'Those are your men in the woods outside?'

'Sure,' said Kennedy. He seemed surprised by the question.

Tommy glanced at me and I nodded. He continued. 'I think you should know, Commander, that I was told earlier today that there is a Wehrmacht armoured column heading north from King's Lynn. We assumed those were the troops surrounding the house.'

'The hell there is,' said Kennedy.

I wasn't quite sure what to make of this. Was it an expression of surprise or if did he think we were bluffing?

'This is an Occupied country, Commander. Skorzeny's a resourceful man,' I said.

Kennedy turned to what I took to be his second-in-command, a stockier figure who looked as though he might have a touch of native Indian blood. 'Check it out, Lieutenant.'

Conversation languished. I'm not much of a man for small-talk, and even Tommy seemed to think the situation beyond the normal bounds of etiquette. Kennedy's men were watchful. In any case, it was only a few moments later that Kennedy's second-in-command returned.

'Wehrmacht unit at the main gates,' he said. 'Got a couple of mortars.'

'And the rest'll be working their way round to the back,' I volunteered.

This was cheap, and Kennedy knew it. 'Thank you, General Quick. I know my job.' He snapped to the Lieutenant, 'Get the girls and go to the garage.'

'A question, Commander.' The voice from the table was quiet, but it had about it the breath of winter. Kennedy turned to Princess Elizabeth.

'Ma'am.'

'On whose orders are you acting?'

Kennedy paused before responding. 'I'm not a liberty to say.'

'The Commander-in-Chief of the US military forces,' I suggested.

To this Kennedy said nothing.

'President Truman, I believe,' said Princess Elizabeth, evidently taking silence for assent. 'May I ask you why he believes I and my sister Margaret are any business of his?'

To give Kennedy credit I have to record that he coloured at this question. 'Ma'am, it's not my job to question the orders of the C-in-C.'

'Really, Commander,' I intervened. 'I'd have thought the kidnapping of the heirs to our throne amounted to a declaration of war between the United States and Great Britain. I should check your manual of military law if I were you.'

At that moment the door of the drawing-room was flung open and in marched Kit with Hawkins and Crawford in tow. They sported three days' growth of beard and heavily soiled dungarees. Kennedy's men wheeled round to cover the new arrivals. 'Sound recommendation, Max,' said Kit lightly, picking up a fag-end of conversation in that annoying manner of his.

'Commander,' I said. 'This is the First Sea Lord, Admiral Sir Christopher Conway. Kit, meet Commander Joseph Kennedy Junior of the US Navy.'

'Delighted,' said Kit, offering his hand to the Commander and ignoring the guns levelled at him. 'Max's right,' he continued in an avuncular manner. 'You take those girls and anything — but anything — happens to them and you'll be court-martialled sooner than you can say Uncle Sam. They'll just hang you out to dry. Who's behind this? Jimmy Byrnes,[i] I shouldn't wonder. Wouldn't trust him further than I could throw him.'

It will be one of the unanswered questions of my life whether at this moment Kennedy would have faltered. He

---

i One of the occasions in the narrative when Admiral Conway seems far better informed than General Quick seems to realise and far more so than he might reasonably have been expected to be.

What Happened at Sandringham

held the aces in so far as his men still had their guns on us. Yet had he the will to counter the forces of institution and personality represented by the young princesses, together with Kit and myself? I wonder. By the look of him, so did Kennedy. Just for those few seconds in the drawing-room at Sandringham I thought we'd retrieved the girls.

Then there was a roar of explosive from outside, a flash as bright as noon, a shower of glass as the windows blew in, and a Pentecostal wind that threw me off my feet.

In the ensuing seconds, the Commander seized the initiative. His men bundled the princesses and Lady Manners out of the room almost before Kit, Nancy and I were back on our feet. The lights had gone but there was enough daylight in the sky to see them backing out of the room through the west doors. There was time only for Lady Julia to shout: 'The *Schnellboot*,' and they were gone.

'The men,' shouted Tommy.

We swept up Crawford and Hawkins and rushed out of the east doors just as another mortar round fell close to the house. We dashed back down the corridor to the kitchen and out through the scullery door. To the men in the summerhouse Tommy said no more than, 'Cut 'em off at the beach.' It seemed a forlorn hope. At the double we forged back through the ribbon of wood along the road. Careless now, we must have sounded like a herd of buffaloes. Kennedy had drawn off his men, but what of the Wehrmacht? The sound of the mortar receded into the distance as we struggled through the woods towards the station. The younger gamekeepers, together with Crawford and Hawkins, led the pack. Nancy wasn't far behind. The rest of us found the pace desperately hard going. As the woods thinned, the mortar finally fell silent, and — quite suddenly — we found ourselves on a low ridge.

Immediately in front of us the ground fell away. No more than half a mile away lay the Wash, its waters glinting under a moon peeping from behind scudding clouds. We all stopped, most of us desperate to catch our breath. Kit and Tommy, a couple of yards in front of us, were scanning the shore trying to get their bearings. 'Peter Black Sand,' said Tommy.

Kit turned to me and Nancy, pointing a little way off to the north, and said, '*Cabby*.'

I followed his line of sight. The moon shone thinly, and I found it impossible to make out her tarred hull against the dark shore. 'The sprit,' said Nancy. I looked again. Yes. There was her great mast and sprit piercing the sky no more than a couple of hundred yards away.

'We can't have got here before them,' said Tommy. It was more question than statement. It had taken us three-quarters of an hour at the double to cover the three miles from the house. Kennedy's men were young and fit. They should have been a good fifteen minutes in front of us. Kit glanced over his shoulder back into the Sandringham woods. 'Don't know their way. Plenty of paths going nowhere round the House,' I said.

'Where were the planes?' Tommy asked of Kit.

I knew what a difficult question it was. A landscape recognisable by day is rarely so by night except to those quite familiar with it. I knew Sandringham in passing; Kit — to my knowledge — not at all. I remembered without much relish how often I had been mistaken in the Picardy trenches, occasionally at the cost of the limbs and lives of my men. Kit didn't need to answer, for in that moment I think we all heard the gentle throb of aero-engines. The sound seemed to be coming from more or less straight out to sea. There we all stared, but I for one could see nothing. Then Kit shouted and pointed at once. 'Dead ahead. Bow waves.'

At first, perhaps a mile from us, all you could see were half a dozen splashes in the water. Then the splashes became streaks, and I saw the float-planes cutting, skimming the water as they raced almost straight towards us, into the easterly wind. There were five or six high-winged, twin-engined machines, grey or white against the black sea. Their hulls were kissing the water and then kissed no more as they rose smoothly above the light swell of the Wash, with all the grace of a flight of swans. They roared no more than a hundred feet above us.

Then they were gone.

The Secrets of the Schnellboot

'This is the Prime Minister.'

The tones — sonorous, grandiloquent, rhetorical — were unmistakable, even over the ether from Ottawa. He sounded as though he was addressing a public meeting.

'Mr Churchill,' I said, trying to make myself comfortable in front of the *Cabby*'s Pye.

'You have been the victim of misfortune, General. Despite your great endeavours, we find ourselves in a parlous position. Our princesses are in the hands of the Americans. The revolt against Himmler and the evils of the Reich hangs in the balance. It is a most solemn hour for our country.'

I could only agree.

'I have spoken to their poor father, the King. He accepts with great reluctance that it is necessary to take a step that he finds most painful. We must appeal to his brother, the Duke.'

It is public knowledge that relations between the King and the Duke of Windsor had been poor ever since the Abdication in 1936,[i] and they worsened after the Duke and Duchess mooted leaving the French Riviera for England in the early summer of 1940. The Duke felt that the King was less enthusiastic than he should have been about the return of the native in the brief weeks before the invasion and the King's trans-Atlantic voyage into exile. Careless of — or blind to — the political, constitutional and ethical problems posed by his return to the country the throne of which he had abdicated only four years previously, the Duke clearly expected better treatment. With the British Expeditionary Force in retreat in France, a faltering Prime Minister in Chamberlain, much talk

---

i An understatement. King George V1 (1895-1946) was precipitated onto the throne by the abdication in 1936 of his brother, Edward V111 (1894-1972). The new monarch abhorred a duty to which he felt unequal. It is widely believed that it materially shortened his life.

and some substance in a Fifth Column, and an invasion on the horizon, the King had other matters to occupy his mind. This consideration clearly didn't cross the Duke's mind.

I asked the Prime Minister what end such an appeal would serve.

'We must bring to bear all the forces at our command on the sensibilities of the leaders of the United States. The Duchess is the most powerful American in England.'

It was an interesting point of view, one that had not occurred to me. I asked, 'Has she the ear of the President?'

His reply left me in no doubt. 'If I know the Duchess, she will relentlessly beat a path to the White House. She is a most formidable woman.'

I thought back to the Abdication Crisis, and Mr Churchill's counsel to King Edward, as the Duke then was; and of Mr Churchill's well-publicised visits to the Windsors in the south of France[i] in the years that followed. Everyone had seen the Windsors and Churchill on the newsreels. The Prime Minister knew the American divorcée who had so enamoured the once and future king.

'We should approach the Duchess directly,' I said.

'We have no avenue for so doing. The court at Blenheim is open to few other than Herr Himmler's flunkeys.'

'In that case we have no means to cajole the Duke,' I observed.

'General,' said Mr Churchill in his most purposeful tone, 'we have you. You must go to Blenheim.'

It was true that I had served with the Prince of Wales — as the Duke then was — immediately after the Armistice, and had known him moderately well. He and I had both been caught by the flying bug in the trenches and were thrown together with another dozen tyros at Boscombe Down[ii] in the early weeks of 1919. I had shot with the Prince at Sandringham

i The Windsors settled in the Villa la Croe in Antibes, dividing their time between the Riviera and Paris.

ii The military aircraft testing and training station in Wiltshire.

124

when his father was still alive, and visited him with Dorothy once or twice at Fort Belvedere[iii] when Mrs Simpson was merely one of a number of female companions. I remembered that Dorothy had been uncharacteristically tart about Mrs Simpson, who she was far from alone in seeing as a hard-hearted gold-digger. I had not supposed the Prime Minister was so well informed. At the same time, it was hardly the sort of role for which I had been trained.

'I am a soldier, not a diplomat,' I objected.

The reply came back very promptly over the airwaves.

'A soldier who knows his duty, and who has done the state some service.'

There was no reply to this, or at least none that I could think of. The Prime Minister continued: 'President Truman will be receiving the benefit of my counsel this evening. In the meantime we are endeavouring to find the princesses.'

*

With this, the interview was at an end. I threw the Pye's switches and rose from my seat with a sense of relief mixed with apprehension. I made my way through the hold, where Tommy's men had settled down to gin rummy. Up on deck it was a bright morning, warmer than the previous day, with patchy cloud driven by a light easterly. I found Kit lounging round the wheel talking to Nancy and idling through the newspapers. He didn't seem to have changed his clothes overnight or indeed washed. Still, that's the Navy for you.

'Did you get the job?' he asked.

I was irritated by Kit and thought I knew who had told Churchill about my friendship with the Duke.

'Need you ask?' I countered.

Nancy's eyes were on me, green-grey eyes beneath her blonde fringe.

'No,' said Kit, smiling.

iii A country house in Windsor Park, once the home of Edward V111.

He was very good at disarming people. I wondered, though, if he had quite disarmed Nancy. He of course knew nothing of the changing relationship between Nancy and myself, but he was too observant not to suspect something was afoot.

'Still,' he continued with his usual calm, handing me the papers, 'there may be a small problem. Goebbels has papered us.'

The front page of the *Englische Zeitung* bore a single word: *Verräter* — Traitors.[i] Below it, artistically arranged, were pictures of Alec, Kit and me. The thrust of the article beneath appeared to be that the three of us had masterminded the assassination of the Führer. That Alec had already paid the price for his crime. And that Kit and I would soon follow him to the gallows or whatever more unpleasant demise could be arranged. The other papers carried a very similar story. Hauptsturmführer Brunner was credited with uncovering the plot, and was said to be leading the operation to seize Kit and me.

Nancy ran her hands through her hair and looked across at me. 'How does it feel to be a fugitive?'

'Better than a hostage,' I said, in the absence of anything closer to the truth.

Kit, with a tact I'd rarely have expected of him, drifted off. I took Nancy up to the foredeck, where we sat in the shadow of the *Cabby*'s jib as she clawed her way up that remote coast.

*

After the misadventures of the previous evening, the *Cabby* had been turned into a dormitory for the motley crew that had raided Sandringham House. The men had dossed down in the hold. Tommy, Kit, Nancy and I got such rest as we could in the stateroom. Tommy snored badly. At first light, Hawkins and Crawford had set off for the village of Wolferton.

---

i These yellowing pages lie before me as I write. They are dated 4 February 1946.

The Secrets of the Schnellboot

Avoiding the house itself, they picked up the essentials for providing breakfast for nigh-on twenty. There did not seem to be much rationing in the village and the day's papers had already arrived. Tommy said the Nazis rarely got much of a hold in these out-of-the-way places, and I can believe him.[ii] As to the train, Tommy said it would look after itself. He and his men would sail with us on the *Cabby* round to Wells. By 0900 we were under way. We had had an easy reach up to Hunstanton on the north-eastern corner of the Wash. Here the easterly headed us just as we passed the squat white lighthouse high up on the polychrome cliffs that eased the Wash into the North Sea. We tacked laboriously in a light wind up the coast in the direction of Wells, pushed along by the end of the ebb tide. By noon I had concluded the w/t interview with the Prime Minister and I was turning my mind to the implications of Truman's strategy in seizing the girls, of Goebbels's little publicity drive, and of falling in love at the age of 52 with a girl nineteen years my junior.

*

When we returned from the foredeck Kit was sitting with Tommy at the top of the companion steps. He had the glasses out and the chart on his lap, and he was scanning the shore. Hawkins, a sturdy figure in bargeman's dungarees, his freckled face peeling from the attention of sun and sea, was behind him at the wheel.

'Where are we?' asked Nancy.

Kit threw the chart in her direction. We were on the starboard tack heading inshore towards a strip of sand above which the corduroy winter fields rose gently to an azure sky.

'That's Holme,' he said.

This settlement amounted to no more than a cluster of

ii Largely true. The Nazis concerned themselves with the major population centres and were content to leave the countryside to its own devices providing it was not openly in revolt. The exception lay where the local *Gauleiter* had a particular interest in the country. Hugh Kingsmill ruled Cannock Chase with a will of iron.

houses huddled round a church in the dunes. I glanced at the chart. Holme, Thornham, Brancaster, Overy Staithe, Wells. Twelve miles to cover against the wind.

'We'll make it this evening,' continued Kit. 'Not much before.'

'Cocktails?' asked Nancy.

'Have to wait for the tide at Wells,' said Kit. 'Hawkins, when's the tide?'

'2053,' shouted the Lieutenant promptly from the wheel. He at least had bothered to shave and might just have passed muster as a naval officer. It seemed some time since I had last seen him at Foulness.

'Very good,' Kit nodded. To do him justice, he was a better disciplinarian than some supposed.

'Why wait?' asked Nancy.

'Neaps,' said Kit. 'Low tides. Not much water over the harbour bar. Even for the *Cabby*.'

I looked at my watch, then up at the great tan mainsail, slack and barely drawing in the breeze. 'Don't go in for speed, do you?'

This Kit ignored.

'Give us the glasses,' said Nancy abruptly.

At this moment Hawkins shouted, 'Ready about.' I thought how strangely the scene contrasted with my last voyage on the *Cabby*, culminating in the storm off Foulness, when going about was attended by frenetic activity. Now Kit barely bothered to move, merely glancing up to ensure the sheets were free and handing over the glasses to Nancy. A moment later came, 'Lee-oh.' I heard the clank of the steering gear and the squeaking and groaning of the blocks as the barge swung very slowly though the eye of the wind. With a flap of heavy canvas the great sprit swung over our heads, and we found ourselves on the port tack heading out again to sea.

Nancy seemed captivated by something on the shore. She handed me the glasses and pointed. 'See what you think.'

I focused the glasses and ran them along the littoral. Holme church was now abeam. Not much more than a mile further east was another grey squat tower, a church I knew to be Thornham. I had fished there once with Tommy, maybe in '35 or '36, and caught a couple of whiting.

'On the bar,' added Nancy.

Between Holme and Thornham the strip of dunes that run from the Hunstanton cliffs to Holme give way to salt marsh, crowned with a riot of sedges, plantains and sea lavender, in the low light of that day a delicate yellowy green. Somewhere was the creek that wound its way through the marsh towards the church. There was the old black tarred Lifeboat Inn. Once it had been a haven for smugglers. Now it was the purveyor of the watery beer the authorities permitted. At least it wasn't 'lager' or whatever they drink in Munich and Berlin.[i]

'The bar,' said Nancy impatiently.

I followed what I imagined to be the course of the creek seawards away from the Lifeboat. Sure enough, there, where the bar at the north of the harbour must be, was a wreck. Certainly not a fishing boat. Too large. More of a small ship or a patrol boat.

'The *Schnellboot*,' said Nancy.

I looked more closely without reaching any particular conclusion. 'Could be,' I said, handing the binoculars to Kit.

'Dozens of wrecks on a coast like this,' he remarked after a few moments. 'Right size, though.'

'Julia's last words,' said Nancy.

For a moment I was nonplussed. 'What do you mean?' I asked.

'At Sandringham,' she added.

I cast my mind back to the moments after the mortar had shattered the windows of the drawing-room and handed the advantage to young Kennedy. Now what had Julia said?

'"The *Schnellboot*,"' recalled Kit, taking up the glasses and having another look at the wreck. 'Could have meant anything.'

---

i The German authorities were energetic in restricting the use of raw materials throughout the lands they occupied, despatching large quantities of barley and hops back to the Reich for their own use. They did not concern themselves with the brews produced from the ingredients that remained.

'Or something,' said Nancy doggedly.

Kit handed the glasses back to Nancy.

'Julia doesn't always mean what she says.'

'That right?' I put in.

Kit was rising to nothing that morning. He just seized the chart. Then he glanced again at the wreck, now off the *Cabby*'s starboard quarter as we pulled away from the shore. He looked at his watch. 'When was that tide, Hawkins?'

'20.53, sir,' came the bellow from the wheel.

'Put her about,' ordered Kit testily. 'You are about to become His Majesty's Receiver of wrecks.'

It was now just about slack water, so we beached the *Cabby* on the sands just to the east of where the creek disgorged its clear waters into the North Sea. The wreck was now clearly enough the E-boat, but it was remarkable how thoroughly the sea had already done its work. She was barely recognisable as the smart little warship that had nearly cost us our lives under Tower Bridge. The craft was canted over at an angle of 30 degrees with its gunwales already settling into the sand. The deckhouse was in ruins, the cannons and the torpedoes had collapsed through the foredeck, and to the stern the transom lay open to the sea. Thirty or forty feet of sea around the boat was stained with diesel, the emulsion of water and oil making a liquid rainbow in the sand. I supposed that all this damage had been caused after her beaching.

A thought crossed my mind. There might be something on board to show why the boat had ended up in Thornham of all places — rather than Wilhelmshaven. Maybe there was a log-book or something. Tommy and his men all jumped off the barge to stretch their legs. I followed them with Nancy and Kit. Our admiral wouldn't let anyone within a hundred feet.

'Death trap,' he said. 'She'd have cannon shells, depth charges and God knows what else. Unstable as hell. Disposal job.'

'What are we looking for?' asked Tommy.

'Can't think,' said Kit.

Nancy folded her arms.

130

The Secrets of the Schnellboot

Tommy was always something of a diplomat. 'I think I'll have a poke around.'

So, ignoring Kit's strictures, the pair of us clambered very gingerly onto the starboard gunwale close to the step in the deck, getting very wet in the process. We doubled ourselves up and stooped through an open hatchway into what proved to be the engine-room. We stood ankle-deep in a vinaigrette of diesel oil and water, seasoned with empty cannon shell-cases. The diesels had been wrenched free from their mountings and the anti-aircraft gun had burst through the deck above and was lying precariously across a generator housing. On the firewall was pinned a shift rota together with a couple of pictures from illustrated magazines: one of Leni Riefenstahl,[i] the other Mae West.[ii] From the engine room a serviceable door led forward to what proved to be the wheelhouse. The windows were smashed, and there were oilskins and the sodden remains of a chart all over the floor. Tommy expressed my own thoughts. 'What *were* they doing here?'

'Can't think.'[iii]

We pushed forward towards the ship's bows. Originally there had been a couple of tiny cabins, a mess quite nicely tricked out with wood panelling, and half a dozen bunks. Now there was only the mounting and firing mechanism and part of the barrel of the anti-aircraft guns. In an alcove we found the radio, about the only thing that seemed more or less intact. Of the naval code-books the E-boat must have carried — and which were of some interest to us — there was no sign. Nor could I see the log-book, which might also offer an explanation of her presence here. In what we took to be the CO's cabin there was a bunk that can't have been very comfortable for a man the

---

i Leni Riefenstahl (1902-2003). German actress and filmmaker, best known for her record of the Nazi rally at Nuremberg, *Triumph of the Will*.

ii Mae West (1893-1980), American film actress.

iii See epilogue.

size of Skorzeny, and a tiny bar that caught Tommy's attention. He likes his drink, does Tommy — particularly *eau de vie*. Other than that nothing caught my eye aside from a pack of rather dog-eared playing cards lying scattered on the bunk.

Back in the engine room I poked my head out of the hatch. Kit had disobeyed his own orders and was examining the wreck from close quarters, kicking a shell-case along the sand.

'Dead loss,' I said.

'No bullion?'

'I didn't think Lady Julia was a gold-digger.'

'Been thinking,' said Kit ruminatively. 'Must have meant something.'

'You said not.'

'Found any ship's papers, orders, such-like? Navies like that sort of thing.'

'No,' I said, ignoring this feeble slight.

'What about a safe?'

'No safe.'

'Must be a safe,' asserted Kit. 'Otherwise the ratings would get to know the orders. Never does.'

Tommy was still rooting around the control room in search of schnapps, like a pig after truffles. I told him what Kit wanted. He shrugged and said: 'Nothing like that here.'

'Skorzeny's cabin?' I suggested.

We returned to the ruined fore-quarters of the E-boat. There wasn't much to search in the cabin and we looked everywhere; under the bunk, in the tiny wardrobe. There was nothing. Tommy shrugged his shoulders. We had a final look round. The whole fore-end was as we'd first seen it, but something seemed ever so slightly different. Perhaps it smelt different. I put this to Tommy. 'Cordite? Petrol? Oil? Flares?' Kit was right. There were certainly plenty of combustibles. At which point, apropos of nothing, Tommy said: 'Code books.' He wound his way across the slanting deck to the radio alcove. It wasn't dissimilar to the set-up in the *Cabby*: a cased unit at eye-level, a tiny metal desk and a steel stool for the operator. At knee level there was a small cupboard. Tommy pulled it open. Inside was a bottle of schnapps and a safe. '*Voilà!*'.

I put my nose out of the broken porthole and shouted to Kit. 'Open?' he asked.

I sometimes wonder what they do by way of intelligence in Dartmouth.[i] 'Of course not.'

'Probably cleared by Skorzeny,' said Kit.

'Most likely,' I remarked.

Another thought crossed my mind. 'Do you think the whole thing's likely to explode?'

Kit raised his black eyebrows in the manner of one speaking to the sub-normal. 'Very likely.'

At this he trotted off to the *Cabby* at an impressive pace for a First Sea Lord. He returned with a crowbar and a sledgehammer. These were tools without which, he said, no self-respecting barge-master would think of setting sail. The Boche, being a careful lot, had embedded the safe very securely in the E-boat. What with the topsy-turvy deck, the impossibility of wielding the crowbar or the sledgehammer in such a tiny space, it was the devil's own job. Eventually we had to cut away the light aluminium hull with a cold chisel to extract the safe — along with a couple of feet of plating to which it was bolted and welded.

'Hope it's worth it,' said Kit as we finally heaved the assembly onto the *Cabby*'s deck.

'Worth a King's ransom,' I assured him.

The young flood had now crept up the beach and the *Cabby* was afloat. Tommy rounded up his men and got them aboard. They hadn't had anything to eat since breakfast and were beginning to get bored. With the tide had come a freshening wind, and we beat steadily down to Brancaster with the gentle February sun on our backs. The wreck was well out of sight when we heard the thick dull sound of a distant explosion, for me like an echo of the trenches. I said nothing and neither did Nancy. Kit merely smiled the smile of one whose prophecies have been fulfilled. Think they know it all, the Navy.

i The Britannia Royal Naval College in Dartmouth, where naval officers receive their initial training.

*

'Blenheim,' said Kit, drawing on his cigarette. 'Rather you than me. The Windsors are awfully dull and the food's worse than Tommy's.'

The *Cabby* was floating in a fathom or so of water a few hundred yards to the north of Wells harbour bar, waiting for the tide to rise sufficiently to get her safely into the port, and Kit was giving us the benefit of his views on my mission to the Duke of Windsor. What with the stove, my pipe and Kit's horrible Capstan Navy Cut,[i] we'd worked up a wonderful fug in the little stateroom. Tommy was sampling the schnapps he'd won from the E-boat, and Kit was matching him glass for glass. Nancy pronounced it undrinkable.

Tommy was more constructive. In front of us on the table lay a jumble of newspapers, the charts and the Ordnance we'd used the previous day for Sandringham. He pulled out the *Englische Zeitung* that bore our pictures.

'Doesn't make your job easier, does it?' he remarked.

'Rules out trains,' I agreed.

'Why?' asked Nancy.

'Brunner's sufficiently organised to have the main stations watched,' responded Tommy. 'Your route would take you through Lynn, Ely, March, Peterborough, Northampton and Buckingham to Oxford. Then it's what, ten miles to Blenheim? Of those I certainly think he'd certainly have Peterborough watched. Maybe others too.'

'Ports as well?' asked Nancy.

'Point,' said Tommy, nodding.

'Car,' suggested Kit.

'My old jalopy will get you to Lynn. Not much further,' said Tommy. 'Shouldn't think you'd get any petrol on the road, either. Especially now. I think things are cooking up a bit. Something planned for London this evening, I hear.'

'Long way to walk,' said Nancy.

i A popular brand of tobacco, particularly among naval officers.

The Secrets of the Schnellboot

'Or cycle,' said Kit.

We seemed to have reached a dead end. Tommy pulled out the Ordnance as though seeking inspiration. It was an inch to a mile, covering Wells down to Lynn. The railway, a thin black sinew, ran down through Wolferton to Lynn. The coast road did the same. You could also cut across country to Stanhoe and pick up the Midland and Great Northern line at Hillington, then go on to Lynn. Neither were realistic routes, given the extent to which we thought the railways would be watched.

There were also a couple of lightly sketched crosses. One at Docking and one at Bircham Newton. Airstrips.

'What about these airfields?' I asked Tommy.

'All my doing.' I supposed he was thinking about his pre-war efforts to get the coast fortified.

'Surely not,' said Kit.

'Date from 1917,' said Tommy firmly. 'I persuaded the powers-that-be to locate a couple of squadrons at Boulton Pauls[ii] at Bircham. One at Coltishall, one at Norwich and a couple at Manningtree. That was all the east coast got.'

'Still operational?' I asked.

'Luftwaffe runs a shuttle between Bircham and Norwich for the Wehrmacht brass. Possibly the odd sea patrol,' remarked Tommy.

'Planes?'

'Little Fieselers, I think. I've seen a Junkers transport at Bircham once. Short strip. Bit of a handful. Sometimes a Focke-Wulf.'

'You can't fly,' said Nancy to me.

'Used to with Alec,' I retorted. 'Got my wings in '36, on a Hawker Cygnet, I'll have you know.'

'Right-hand drive,' said Kit.

Tommy was more constructive. He took the Ordnance from my hands. 'If I got you into the cockpit of one of the

ii Boulton Paul: a less than distinguished British aircraft manufacturer, known at this time for the *Defiant fighter.*

135

Fieselers, could you get yourself to Blenheim?'

'Try me,' I said, wondering in fact whether I could.

There was a knock on the door and Hawkins walked in, clutching half a dozen little notebooks and some papers neatly bundled by a rubber band. Somehow he looked less than his usual confident self. 'Jemmied the safe. Got the code books. Log book. This stuff too.' He handed the pile to Kit. 'One for you, chief, I should say.'

Kit set the notebooks aside and slipped the rubber band off the papers. These he leafed through. The bundle was about half an inch thick, and it took him some minutes. He glanced up. 'Thanks, Hawkins.' He watched the door close before handing the papers over to me. 'Your German's much better than mine. I'll have a look at the log.'

I glanced through the papers. It was not difficult to see what they were. The papers comprised a series of minutes of bi-monthly meetings that had taken place since 1941 at a place called Faslane, a name that chimed somewhere. The language was spare, bureaucratic and — for me — largely opaque. These days my German's fine for reading newspapers but not for this sort of highly technical stuff. The attendees seemed to be monitoring the progress of a scientific project. Some of the people were German, some English.

'Not really Julia's taste, is it?' I said, handing the papers on to Nancy. 'Do you think this is what she meant? I can't see how she'd know what Skorzeny kept in the safe, one way or another.'

'Well,' said Kit, 'there is the log, too.'

'Anything in it?' I asked.

Kit was leafing through a small grey book puzzling out the entries. After a few moments he said, 'Looks as though they hit something off Cromer.'

'That'd be just as they were about to head east across to Wilhelmshaven,' I commented.

'If that was the intention,' countered Kit. 'Either way, they were taking in quite a lot of water and headed for shelter. Pumps weren't holding her.'

The Secrets of the Schnellboot

Tommy chipped in. 'They wouldn't try to head south again. Yarmouth's a horrible harbour at the best of times.'

'Where then?' I asked.

'I'd have made for Lynn. Tricky entrance but pretty sheltered.'

'So why did they settle for Thornham?' asked Kit.

'You tell us,' said Tommy. 'You've got the log.'

Kit consulted the log. 'Doesn't say.'

'My best guess is that they were making for Lynn and just didn't get that far. Thornham was any port in a storm,' said Tommy.

I shrugged my shoulders. At this stage of the game the puzzle seemed less how those girls had got to Thornham or Sandringham than where they were now.

Nancy, meanwhile, was utterly absorbed by the technical papers or whatever they were. 'Who are all these people?' she asked. 'Elbogen, Braun, Huber, Kline, Cockcroft, Wheatfield, Lethermann.'

'Say it again,' said Tommy, leaning forward in his seat.

'Elbogen, Braun, Huber, Kline, Cockcroft, Wheatfield, Lethermann,' repeated Nancy.

'I know one. Cockcroft,'[i] said Tommy very deliberately. He put down his glass of schnapps. 'Or know of him. Used to stay at an hotel up here before the war. Moorings at Overy Staithe. Came up from Cambridge.'

'What is he?' I asked.

'Particle physicist,' said Tommy, shortly.

'What's that?' said Nancy, her voice cutting brightly through the saloon. Even Kit seemed taken aback by this intelligence. I'd rarely seen him so serious.

'Nuclear scientist to you and me. Atoms and such-like.'

Nancy shoved the minutes back on the table as though they were infectious. I picked them up again.

'What use are these to anybody?' I said, thinking aloud. 'Why were they locked up in that safe?'

i Sir John Cockroft, 1897-1967. Physicist and first director of the Atomic Energy Research Establishment.

There was complete silence for several moments.

'They're evidence,' said Kit slowly.

'Evidence of what?'

It was Tommy who ventured to state what had now become obvious to us all. 'Of progress on Anglo-German collaboration on atomic fission.'

'Big deal,' I said. 'Those funny chaps in white coats have been working on it for years. Public knowledge.'

Kit shrugged his shoulders. 'Never know with the Jerries. They like records. If I was a betting man and could actually read this sort of German, I'd make a guess.'

'Yes?'

'Not so much progress as success. Otherwise, why would they be here?' He glanced round the stuffy little stateroom. Nobody said a word.

*

I have to say that I count that morning at Bircham Newton — according to my notes it was the 4 February — as the lowest of the whole affair.

Hitherto, the march of events since the Führer's death had provided sufficient distraction. Now, for the first time, I had the opportunity to reflect upon the situation in which we found ourselves. One of our close number was dead. The remaining two had been publicly accused of treason and were fugitives from Nazi 'justice'. The prospects of freeing the princesses seemed utterly negligible. Their lives seemed in greater jeopardy than ever before — even if the Americans were unlikely to kill them. I had thoughts — still too vague to be called suspicions — about the train of coincidences, mischances and odd occurrences that had led us to North Norfolk. To cap it all some wretched scientists had thrown in their lot with the Boche and supposedly made some frightful bomb. I would execute the Prime Minister's orders to the utmost of my ability, but I was sceptical as to the influence I could bring to bear on the Duke, he in turn on the Duchess,

138

The Secrets of the Schnellboot

and she in turn on the President and his entourage. Never before, on that windy morning with the leaden clouds racing over the wide Norfolk skies, had I been so sceptical of the success of our mission. I half wished I was back in Picardy, leading my division over the top.

The immediate task seemed no more promising. There is a sense of desolation peculiar to an airfield, an empty stage on which, it seems, no actors will ever again appear. After an all-too-brief night at Holkham, the morning brought nothing but rain. We had a brief discussion over a painfully early breakfast. Having lost track of the princesses, Kit had suggested making for Faslane, where the atom bomb people were — or had been — based. His argument was that the presence of the papers on the *Schnellboot* suggested that Faslane was in some way bound up with Skorzeny. I pointed out that this was hardly likely to help us with the princesses. Kit reminded me that Nancy and I could not very well turn up at the War Office and ask for our old jobs back. Brunner might have something to say about that. I found myself without the energy or sense of purpose to disagree. In the end it was settled that Kit and Nancy were to make their way their up north as best they could. Tommy would square the PM and tell him about the bomb. Doubtless he — Churchill — would have an opinion on that. Tommy also said he'd try and track down his chum Cockroft and get the inside track on the story of the bomb. Despite his lineage, Tommy was an artillery man at heart, and he had a passion for explosives of all sorts. He talked of the difficulties of keeping what must be a big-scale operation secret, and of the tell-tale signs of something he called radioactivity in the vicinity of the bomb. He said there was even a machine that measured or detected it. A Geiger-counter he called it, and said he'd try and find us one.[i] Nancy also had her task. She would talk to her godfather Sir Hugh. He'd tracked the girls down at Sandringham. If they were still this side of the Atlantic — and in the land of the living — he had as good a chance as any of

---

i Invented by the physicists Hans Geiger and Ernest Rutherford in 1908.

finding them, wherever they might now be.

Regretfully, we said goodbye to Hawkins and Crawford, who would take the *Cabby* back to London. I had no more than five minutes with Nancy. Then Tommy plumped me in the shooting brake and deposited me on the perimeter of Bircham Newton airfield not long after eight. Half an hour later I had wormed my way up to one of the two large hangars on the eastern side of the main strip. At its side stood a bin half full of sand used to clear up petrol and oil spillages on the concrete apron. It was the size of a couple of domestic dustbins. Here I secreted myself. The ensuing three hours were characterised by the complete absence of what the RAF calls 'air movements'. Nothing had taken off and nothing had landed. It had just rained.

From time to time I had crept out of the bin and worked my way right up to the hangar. It sheltered half a dozen artificers[i] in Luftwaffe fatigues going about their duties in a desultory way. One was dismantling the engine of a tatty Junkers 52 transport, vintage Spanish Civil War. A couple of others had got the wings off an elderly Focke-Wulf. The remainder seemed to restrict themselves to making tea or whatever it is the Boche drink. There was nothing that was airworthy. The second hangar lay across a stretch of ground so open and so overlooked by the accommodation blocks and control tower that I dared not risk a recce. I could not go forwards. Nor could I return to Holkham, for fear of further compromising Tommy's position. The Abwehr had long-standing suspicions about him, and the incident at Wells station would not have endeared him to the local SS. The bin was degrading. By noon on the morning of 4 February I felt I had reached an impasse.

*

It was a little after half-past twelve when the first signs of movement began. I heard the grumble of a starting-motor

i A soldier or airman mechanic.

and cough of an engine firing. A couple of minutes later an old grey-green Skoda field-car lumbered slowly into and then out of the field of vision afforded by the bin. Nothing further happened for at least a quarter of an hour. Then the Skoda returned, trailing in its wake an equally dilapidated troop-carrier and a small black Humber staff car. The drivers carefully stationed their vehicles just within the hangar, so sheltering from the still steady rain. Then they lit up, evidently awaiting events.

Ten minutes later there was the hum of an aero-engine. I scanned the lowering sky. The cloud base can't have been more than 500 feet. I could see nothing. The drivers in the hangar stubbed out their cigarettes and started their motors, drowning the gentle hum of the approaching plane. I stared into the gloom and after a few moments saw a plane crystallise close and low, a big ungainly transport, head-up, battling into the headwind and the rain, now a hundred, now fifty, now twenty feet above the rough grass strip. She touched down heavily on her main wheels, ran a couple of hundred yards, then settled into her tail wheel at the far end of the strip. Then she turned, and began to taxi slowly back up the strip. The Skoda and the troop carrier trundled off to meet her. The three engines wound down, the rear door was thrown open, a dozen figures in grey stepped down the aluminium steps. As they did so, a couple of them glanced up and back over the strip.

A little high-winged monoplane with legs like a spider was just touching down at the far end of the field. In scarcely more than a hundred feet it rolled virtually to a stop. I recognised it at once. It was a useful aircraft. It was a Fieseler Storch[ii].

Here, at last, was a plane I could fly.

*

The pilot pulled up the Fieseler alongside the Junkers. As he did so the Humber drew up, and the rear door of the Fieseler

ii Small reconnaissance and liaison aircraft built in large numbers of the Luftwaffe.

was thrown open. A figure emerged and slipped into the car. I was less than a hundred feet away and could not conceivably have been mistaken. A squat figure with a face too large for its features. It was my old friend, Hauptsturmführer Brunner.

Ten minutes later, all was quiet. Brunner and the troops had been spirited away. The two pilots of the aircraft had disappeared, presumably to the mess. My only concern were the artificers in the hangar. Cautiously, I lifted the lid of my prison.

The rain had now more or less stopped and the cloud-base had lifted slightly. I took this as a good omen. The eye is attracted by rapid movement. I acted accordingly. I walked slowly and steadily from the corner of the hangar around the back of the Fieseler, opened the door and climbed up into the pilot's seat. I was clearly visible from the hangar, but only to someone who happened to be looking. I assured myself that they wouldn't look until I started the motor. A map was tucked into one of the door-pockets. I saw at a glance that it would get me to Blenheim. Petrol. The gauge would be driven by generator, so I'd have to hope for the best until I'd started the motor. I checked the controls: rudder bar, ailerons, throttle — all more or less the same as things I'd flown before. The flap control was a bit of a puzzle, and I'd no idea how much I'd need to get off. Ignition — yes. Starter.

Yes. I was going to do it. Quietly, I closed the pilot's door and strapped myself in. I had a good look round. The accommodation blocks, the control tower, the hangars, the strip, the windsock. Everything seemed in order. With the pilots in the mess, the artificers would presumably wish to satisfy their curiosity as to who was starting the Fieseler. Very well. I had a last look round. No one was in sight. I flicked on the ignition and punched the starter. The prop turned a couple of times, and the engine caught. I grabbed the throttle and eased it forward.

Nothing happened.

I pushed it further and felt the tail lift slightly. It flashed through my head that there might be a lock of some sort. I eased back the throttle and felt the tail settle again. I glanced at the hangar. Its mouth was still empty. As I did so, I caught sight of the Fieseler's left wheel. It was chocked. Like a fool, I hadn't thought to check. I tore off the seat-belt, jumped out of the cockpit and kicked the two chocks away from under the wheels. As I did so, I saw out of the corner of my eye the grey fatigues of an artificer dashing across the concrete apron. I was back in my seat in an instant, but now he was half-way across from the hangar. In his hand was a hammer. I eased the throttle forward and felt the plane come to life under my feet. It was going to be a damned close-run thing.

In the Court of the Puppet King

It wasn't a landing to be proud of. The light had dropped
suddenly at the end of the short winter's day and, in an
unfamiliar craft, I found it extremely difficult to judge my
approach. There was Vanbrugh[i]'s baroque masterpiece, all
porticos and columns, ochre in the gloaming, with its two
great wings stretching forward in welcome. A windsock
and a couple of other light planes gave me a sense of where
the airstrip was. At first, perhaps a mile off, I had convinced
myself I was too high and would fly straight into the house.
I over-corrected, and then found myself too low, skimming
the rough parkland and — to all appearances — just clearing
a couple of fences. Petrified of stalling, I hastily cranked on
some more flap, giving the tiny plane a hint more lift. Right at
the extreme end of the grass strip the port wheel touched, then
the starboard, then the port again. At last both more or less
touched together. I eased back the stick and felt the tail settle
slowly onto the ground. I was awash with sweat, but I was
down. The palace was still a couple of hundred yards away.
I opened the throttle slightly and the little Fieseler jolted over
the turf towards the other planes. These, I now saw, were also
Fieselers or something very similar. The nearest had its nose
cover up and a man in some sort of uniform — field-grey as
far as I could see — was at work on the engine. As I taxied
towards him he glanced up, broke off his work and suddenly
set off at a run towards me.

All the horrors of my departure from Bircham Newton
came back to me. As I had suddenly swung the little plane
away from the hangar, the fool of an artificer had run straight
into the whirling propeller. Whatever happened, I couldn't go

---

i Sir John Vanbrugh, 1664-1726. Combined the careers of playwright and architect. As the latter designed both Blenheim and Castle Howard.

through that again, seeing a man sliced in two in front of me, the two halves collapsing neatly on either side of the propeller in a waterfall of blood and intestines. I had seen such sights often enough in trenches, and thought I had become inured to them. I was getting old.

I flipped off the ignition, and the blades swiftly slowed their wild gyrations and stopped. No sooner had they done so than my door was pulled open and a sharp little face under a dirty grey cap thrust his head into the cockpit. As he did so he saluted smartly and identified himself in tones that were reassuringly English. 'I'll park her up, sir. Very particular round here. Queen likes 'em all lined up neat.'

I recovered myself sufficiently to say, 'Very good, Corporal.'

'Fuel her up too?'

I saw a petrol bowser behind the second Fieseler. 'By all means.'

Now I had arrived at Blenheim I had no idea how — or indeed if — I would get away again. The little Fieseler might just be the ace up my sleeve. I loosed the straps, slipped out of the cockpit and jumped down on to the turf. It was good to get out of that tin and glass prison. The Corporal jumped into my seat. Just as I was setting off to the house he called, 'Know your way, sir?'

'Of course.'

I could hardly say otherwise. I had in fact visited the Marlboroughs a couple of times before the SS seized Blenheim. John, the 10th Duke, was a Lieutenant-Colonel in the Life Guards,[ii] and my junior by a couple of years. He and I had met from time to time on the courses the Royal Military Academy arranges for its more promising officers. He was a good sort, though an amateur soldier at heart. Dorothy and I had been to a garden party at the Palace just before the Munich crisis and I remembered a discussion we'd had then about the viability of a German invasion. That thought put another in my mind.

ii John Albert William Spencer-Churchill, 1897-1972.

Besides the man who loyal Englishmen still regarded as the Duke of Windsor rather than their King, there was another figure in the household whom I knew quite well. This was the Duke's long-standing private secretary, Edward Ferris — Teddy to his friends, of whom I was not really one. I added, 'Mr Ferris about?'

'Works all hours, that one,' said the Corporal, looking down at me with a grin from the Fieseler's cockpit. 'Has to. Five o'clock is it? You'll find him in his office. West wing, first floor.'

I could hardly burst in on the Duke unannounced, and Ferris was the only person likely to provide me with access to the man with whom I'd once been friends. Whether Ferris would actually perform this office was a very different question. His loyalties certainly lay with the Duke rather than the regime but I thought he might baulk at introducing a man marked by Goebbels and plastered all over the *Englische Zeitung*. He would have to be persuaded.

I followed the directions I had been given, making my way through the grandiose corridors of the palace, and soon found myself outside Ferris's office. At the door I paused and listened. I had to see Ferris alone. I had no wish to encounter anyone else who might recognise and denounce me. There was no sound from within. I knocked sharply and at once thrust the door open. Ferris had done himself well. The room must have been forty or fifty feet square, amply furnished and lavishly decorated, with windows commanding the water garden. Everywhere were pictures of the Duke. As a child in a sailor suit, as a lieutenant in the Grenadier Guards, canoeing in Canada in 1919, the notorious one of him with Mrs Simpson on the yacht *Nahlin* in the Mediterranean in 1934, Landseer's official Coronation portrait, meeting Hitler at Berchtesgaden in 1937, and being welcomed to Blenheim by Mosley and Goebbels in September 1940. Seated at the desk with the water garden behind him and facing the door was the figure I remembered well. The grey hair cut *en brosse*, the pudgy nose, tortoiseshell glasses, unimpeachable grey suit.

In the Court of the Puppet King

Judging by his desk he had been reading the papers. I saw that they included the *Englische Zeitung*. I also noticed the scroll of a telex message among the jumble of papers around one of those new-fangled intercoms. Ferris half rose, then subsided into his seat. 'What the hell are you doing here?'

I had never liked Ferris. He was too much his master's creature. His past cordialities to me had patently been hollow. Now they were entirely abandoned. 'Not pleased to see me?'

'I'll give you five minutes before calling the guard.' He fumbled for his watch in his waistcoat pocket, and placed a golden circle in front of him.

I had considered with some care what my opening card should be. Now I played it. 'The princesses have been kidnapped.'

Kit, Tommy and I had long discussed the extent to which this information had circulated, given that it had been excluded from the newspapers and the official pronouncements of the BBC. Ferris's response was in a sense disappointing. 'Hardly news,' he said, without expression.

Now we knew. I played the second card. 'By the Yanks.'

'*What*?' He got to his feet.

'The descendants of the colonists,' I added, waiting for the disclosure to sink in.

'How do you know this?' he demanded.

'I was there.'

'Where's there?' shot back Ferris.

'Sandringham.'

'Good God!' he exclaimed, sitting down and taking off his glasses. He looked genuinely shocked. As he recovered himself, I gave him a brief summary of the circumstances of the capture of the princesses by the Marine Raiders or whatever Kennedy's lot were called, and how I came to be at Blenheim. I had at least got Ferris interested.

He digested this information for a few moments before asking, 'Where are they now?'

'Well, old boy,' I replied,' I think this is one of those rare occasions on which your guess is as good as mine.'

Ferris glared at this. 'Where do you think?'

I had in fact been giving a very considerable amount of thought to this as I'd flown the wretched little tin can down from Bircham. Indeed, I'd thought of little else. If Kennedy had flown the girls straight back to the United States, I thought them gone for ever. He would hardly fly them elsewhere in an occupied country. The one hope I harboured was that he might have flown them to somewhere like Shannon on the west coast of Ireland en route for the US. A flying-boat might have the range to get from the east coast of England to the east coast of the US, but I doubted it. Shannon to Gander was the route of the Pan Am transatlantic passenger flights that had got going just before the war, and there was a chance that this was just what Kennedy would do. I wondered, too, whether Kennedy would risk flying his charges further than he possibly could. However, I hardly thought that Ferris should have the benefit of all of my thoughts. I hazarded, 'Washington DC, I should say, wouldn't you?'

'You don't think Kennedy's acting alone?'

'I think he's acting directly under Truman's orders,' I said, forbearing to add that Kennedy had virtually said as much. 'That's why I'm here to see the Duke.'

'The King,' he corrected severely. 'What do you want from him?'

I temporised. 'I think he'd like to know.'

Ferris smiled at this. He was too wily a courtier to forget that knowledge is power. 'How very well meaning of you.'

I decided to cut to the chase. 'We want him to use his influence.'

Ferris smiled again. 'On the Queen? I shouldn't overrate that, if I were you.'

This was one thing I had also considered with some care.

'The Duchess is a sufficiently intelligent woman to realise how delicate her position — and that of the Duke — has become. The sands are shifting, Teddy. They say Paris has fallen. I wouldn't regard Himmler as a permanent feature, would you? What's he done with all those Jews? Nothing very nice. I shouldn't be surprised if it didn't all come out at some stage. I think the Windsors might be well advised to hedge their bets and use their influence on Truman. Along with the Kennedys, the Duchess is just about the only thing approaching Royalty the States has got. I believe that even in America, royalty counts.'

Ferris considered this for a moment. He looked at me with some scepticism. 'You're the honest broker?'

This was easy. 'I see no advantage in the Americans holding the princesses.'

Ferris picked up his watch and replaced it in his pocket. In front of him was the intercom with its half dozen buttons. He pressed the one at the top. 'Have you a moment, sir?' The affirmative reply was audible to me. Ferris flicked the switch down again. 'He'll see me. I'll raise it with him.'

'I'll join you,' I said.

'You'll do no such thing,' said Ferris sharply, touching another button on the intercom. 'I should think things over for a bit if I were you. The facilities here are very good, managed by our friends in black.'

I don't know if Ferris had thought through my likely reaction to his pronouncement. I had had quite enough of the SS over the last five and a half years and I wasn't going to spend any more time in their company if I could help it. Perhaps Ferris didn't see it that way. He certainly seemed surprised to find himself straddled over his own desk. I put my finger to my lips and then drew it right across my neck. I think he got the message.

At that moment the intercom came to life. 'Mr Ferris, sir,' it spouted.

I raised my eyebrows.

The intercom repeated its enquiry, the tones of the speaker indicating concern. 'Mr Ferris, sir. Are you there?'

I drew my finger once again across my neck. At last Ferris managed, 'No calls for half an hour. I'll be with the King.'

'Sir,' came the reply.

I released him. 'We'll do this in a civilised way, Teddy.' I ushered him to the door and took his arm.

'You're compromising the King. Me too, dammit,' said Ferris. Not necessarily, I thought, in that order of importance. He continued,' It's the gallows for you. Or worse.'

'Sure?' I said.

Ferris managed a smile as we walked down the corridor. I wondered why. Then he continued: 'Unusual to get in to see the King with so little notice.'

'Yes', I said conversationally. 'I suppose it is.'

'Fact is he had a cancellation. Or at least a postponement.'

'Ah yes.' Ferris clearly had a rabbit. No doubt he would pop it out of its hat.

'Haupsturmführer Alois Brunner.'

I nodded, not wishing to commit myself. I presumed Ferris had read the papers and knew what Brunner was up to. 'Apparently he's been visiting Norfolk. Interesting, given your tale about Sandringham.'

I thought so too. It hardly seemed worth mentioning to Ferris that I had seen Brunner at Bircham Newton. 'I hope he hasn't met with an accident,' I said.

'No,' said Ferris. 'Not yet, anyway. Just delayed. On his way here by car, according to the telex. I mistrust this new-fangled gadgetry, don't you?'

'The Resistance permitting,' I said.[i] With the country falling into chaos, I thought Brunner was putting his life in his hands driving cross-country from Norfolk.

Ferris ignored my comment and straightened his tie. Again, he allowed himself a smile. 'Not in the best of moods, I hear. You might even stoop to a cliché. On the warpath. Some reckless and foolish person had stolen his plane.'

So that was his rabbit. It was not particularly surprising. Merely awkward. I would have to work quickly. We had reached the Long Library. A couple of footmen flanked the doors that led within. Ferris gave them a nod, and they flung the doors open.

i It is difficult to pin down the precise march of events at this distance in time. It was certainly true that by now the Wehrmacht was losing its grip on the province, but the order to withdraw from the islands was as yet some days away.

In the Court of the Puppet King

'Brunner has some intelligence for the King,' continued Ferris as we entered the ante-room. 'Who knows what that may be? Our friends are a diligent lot and are very good at tracing stolen property.' At this he knocked at the inner doors. From within, I heard the once familiar tones of the Duke. 'Come in!'

*

Given the extent to which he's been pilloried recently in the Press, it's worth restating what a topsy-turvy life the Duke has led.

King George's eldest son and heir, the Prince of Wales had the looks and manners to dazzle both his peers and his subjects. He took every opportunity to do so. As a lieutenant in the Grenadier Guards and a man about town in the early '20s, his name and photograph were never out of the press. Balls, hunts, shooting parties, race-meetings, passing-out parades, skiing in the Tyrol: all the glittering cavalcade of royalty. He had good looks and a delightfully easy manner, and I believe it right to say he was widely and sincerely loved. Ever anxious for an outcome, the press portrayed quite discreetly the liaisons that peppered his late twenties, particularly those with Freda Dudley Ward, Mildred Harman and Lady Furness. Like the Prince's father, the press wished for marriage and progeny. They make good 'copy'. The desire became a clamour as the King's health deteriorated and, unbeknownst to the general public, the Duke's association with Mrs Simpson began. Public sympathy on the occasion of his father's death and his own Coronation in 1935 could not have been greater. When the press finally broke its self-imposed embargo on the Simpson affair, many of our countrymen were genuinely appalled. The Abdication crisis was a stab to the heart of this country that no one will ever be able to forget. It is said that Mr Churchill himself was in tears during the course of the King's Abdication address on the wireless.[ii]

ii 11 December 1936.

151

Thereafter, it has to be remembered that the public abruptly transferred its affection to the new King, his redoubtable wife Elizabeth (the Bowes-Lyon girl),[i] and of course the princesses. The Duke of Windsor, as he became after the Abdication in 1936, would scarcely have been human if he had not envied the paeans of praise, once visited upon him, that were now heaped on Princess Elizabeth and Princess Margaret. The girls, respectively ten and six, suddenly became the objects of attention everywhere — in the newspapers, in illustrated magazines and on cinema newsreels. Once again the country was dazzled. The Duke and Duchess, in their exile in Antibes in the south of France, found themselves in a penumbra. It was not to their liking. The couple's flirtation with fascism, not least the well-documented visit to Hitler in Berchtesgarten in 1937, deepened their disgrace. It seemed the nadir of their fortunes. Yet the outbreak of war in 1939 and King George's refusal to countenance their presence on British soil when they sought to flee the south of France ahead of the Nazi invasion saw them regain a level of public sympathy. From King of England to homeless refugee in barely four years was a story to excite the Englishman's penchant for the underdog.

The Duke was no doubt as horrified as his former subjects by the invasion and the overrunning by Nazi forces of the land of his birth.[ii] It will be remembered the extent to which the establishment of the King's court and Churchill's administration in exile in Canada divided the country.[iii] It was said to have been Goebbels who suggested to Hitler the stratagem of representing the Duke to the English people as their rightful monarch, the Duchess as his consort. 'The monarchy', Goebbels supposedly remarked, 'is the opium

i Better known as the late Queen Elizabeth, the Queen Mother (1900- 2002).

ii A generous interpretation, given the Duke's notorious sympathy for the Nazi movement.

iii There were those who thought that Cabinet and King should have stayed and fought and died. See AJP Taylor, *England 1914-1946*.

of this people.' Not quite original, someone told me once. In August 1940 von Ribbentrop flew to Nice as Hitler's personal envoy to put the proposal to the Duke. This was of course the former Ambassador to the Court of St James's and — more importantly — the former salesman of fine wines and champagnes. It was the limitations of his grasp of English mores and etiquette — not to mention politics — that had led to the nickname 'Herr Brickendrop'. To do the Duke credit, he is said to have at once seen the notion of his 'reinstatement' — as von Ribbentrop put it — as the sham it was. Immoral, illegal, unconstitutional. The Duke equivocated for far longer than the public has been led to believe. In any case the Duke, though as partial to champagne as any other man, didn't really like the people who sold it. He believed they should be restricted to below stairs.

The Duchess saw things in a different light. Wallis Simpson had seen the cup of happiness snatched from her lips all too often. She was outraged by her treatment by the British establishment during the Abdication crisis. She had been charmed less by Hitler than by the corpulent Herman Goering in his excruciating sky-blue uniform, who ferried her around in his own aeroplane. She bore nothing but ill-will for King George and Queen Elizabeth. She had no scruples about being called 'Queen'. Von Ribbentrop was an astute salesman who had done his homework. He knew of the Duchesss' weakness for grand houses. As the Duke was wavering, von Ribbentrop mentioned Goebbels' idea that Blenheim Palace was the only fitting place for the couple to establish their court. It was a thought designed to appeal to the illegitimate child of a couple of Maryland labourers. That night the Duke's resistance collapsed and, as we all remember, the news was flashed by the Nazi propagandist around the world. It was a masterstroke, snuffing out the dying embers of resistance in the west of the country and in the Highlands. By the time the Duke and Duchess, now publicly proclaimed King Edward VIII and Queen Wallis, were flown back to Hendon by the Luftwaffe, the country had accepted the yoke of the Nazis.

Or so, to many, it seemed. Mosley was proclaimed deputy Reichskommisar of the new province of the Greater Reich the next day, Heydrich his master a couple of days later.

*

Ferris pushed open the door and we entered the library. It had been conceived by Vanbrugh on a scale that would later appeal to the Nazi ideal of grandiosity, all of a couple of hundred feet long and eighty or so wide. Not exactly cosy. Perhaps it had once been decorated with taste and discretion. I remembered it from the days of the 10th Duke, my friend Johnny, whose father had brought much-needed wealth into the family by marrying the American railroad heiress Consuelo Vanderbilt. Their work to enhance the beauty of Blenheim began on their honeymoon, and the collection of tapestries, statues and paintings that adorned the library was one of the results of their efforts. You can't really expect the owners of the Beech Creek Railway Company to have much taste, can you? If you did you'd be jolly disappointed. Still, I imagine the Duchess found the style rather sympathetic.

The Duke himself sat on a chesterfield in the far corner of the room in front of the fire, leafing through an illustrated magazine. At the table by his side stood an intercom and a drink. In the five years or so since I had last seen him, he had aged ten. He had lost the smooth, pink-faced boyishness for which he is remembered. His face was lined, with crows-feet around the eyes. His hair was now grey and thinning. His bearing had lost its former tone and command, and his grey suit hung limply on a frame which had become too thin. The Duke has spent much of his lifetime concealing his emotions, but I read in his blue eyes consternation at my presence. I presumed he read papers other than the illustrated ones — or at least had their contents brought to his attention. He must have known — or at least should have known — what I was supposed to have done. His tone was brisk in the extreme.

'Who is this you have brought, Ferris?'

In the Court of the Puppet King

Ferris was hardly likely to take responsibility. 'The General came at his own insistence.'

The Duke put his paper down, saying, 'Call the guard.'

I flung myself down on the sofa. 'Wait till you hear what I have to say.'

'Ferris?' questioned the Duke sharply.

I wondered what line he would take. Perhaps the Duke wondered, too. It was several moments before Ferris came out with, 'I believe you should, sir.'

With no great show of enthusiasm, the Duke said, 'Lock the doors.'

Ferris did as he was bidden.

'Your nieces, the princesses,' I began. Though childless himself, I believed that the Duke was very fond of his brother's daughters.

'In the care of the SS in the Tower,' he interrupted. It was interesting that our rescue and subsequent surprise by Skorzeny had been kept from him.

I raised my eyes at Ferris and nodded. He knew what was required and spoke to the brief. 'There have been developments,' he said, following with a quite accurate account of my adventure at the Tower and the subsequent appearance of Colonel Skorzeny. I wondered if he had got it from Brunner. I have very rarely seen the Duke angry except with the Press. In the course of Ferris's narrative he became almost uncontrollably so, the colour rising in his face and his hand shaking so much that he almost spilled his drink. 'Why was I not told?'

'I felt … 'began Ferris.

'Why was I not told?'

Ferris's face was now as puce as his master's. He managed to get out: 'Goebbels' orders.'

The Duke rose to his feet and threw his glass into the fire. I had never seen him lose control before.

I interrupted. 'That's not all.' I gave him the briefest account of the events at Sandringham.

'Those poor girls.' He sat down next to me and stared

into the middle distance, away over the lake that mirrored the darkening skies.

'Lady Julia Manners is with them. I thought they were holding up very well,' I said.

For some moments, no one spoke.

'Why have you come, Max?' the Duke asked eventually.

'I think you know,' I replied.

Again, there was a pause. Then, quite slowly and emphatically, the Duke said, 'It will be the Duchess's decision.' I noticed that he did not refer to her as 'Queen'.

I said, 'They're your nieces.'

Ferris began: 'Your Majesty, if I might ...'

I thought this was enough from Ferris. 'How do you serve two masters, Teddy? Do you get double wages, or does Goebbels pay you in kind?' Rumours of Ferris's predilections for small boys had been rife for years.

'Bastard.'

I turned to the Duke. 'I wonder if Mr Ferris has much to contribute to your discussion with the Duchess.'

The Duke glanced at his secretary, rather as one does at a pair of old brogues in the last stages of repair. 'Probably not.'

'Is there somewhere here safe to keep him?'

The Duke thought for a moment. 'There's an old privy off one of the guest bedrooms in the next wing.' He glanced in the direction of the far end of the library.

'Ideal,' I said, rising to my feet. I took a couple of steps towards Ferris and then the intercom buzzed. He was much quicker than I. Before I could do or say anything he had replied to the enquiry. He turned to the Duke and me with a smile playing around his lips.

'Hauptsturmführer Brunner has made excellent time from Sandringham. He's on his way up.'

The Duke, I have to say, was calmness itself. He nodded in the direction of one of the doors that led off the library. 'The privy.'

*

In the Court of the Puppet King

In practice, there seemed little danger of Brunner penetrating the Windsors' inner apartments. The Duke was a puppet king who ruled by courtesy of Hitler. Goebbels was far too clever to fail to appreciate that the illusion of the British monarchy was best maintained if the puppeteer was kept offstage. The court of Blenheim was constituted not so very differently from King George's at St James's, albeit with a cadre of senior SS staff at the Feathers in Blenheim village itself, at the gates of the Palace, and one of the Model Farms turned over to form a barracks for the men. The domestic staff was largely British, and the atmosphere remained that of an English country house rather than a *Schloss* in Bavaria. By Nazi standards the use of swastikas in the village and the palace itself was restrained, even tasteful if you like that sort of thing. I didn't suppose that Ferris and I would be surprised by a German footman or maid, and denounced. Judging by his expression, Ferris seemed to have drawn similar conclusions. We found the room with the privy. I locked the door behind us, pulled out my pipe and settled down to wait. Ferris had nothing to say for himself. I had nothing to say to him. If things turned out in our favour, his destination was the gallows. If things turned out in his, then they beckoned for me. For the present, we could only serve our different masters by standing and waiting. I ruminated on Brunner, Skorzeny and Kennedy, and the curious sense I had of unseen hands manipulating events.

At about eight o'clock, a sharp knock on the door brought me out of my reverie. It was the Duke himself. We returned with him to the library. He had sent Brunner packing, so he said. On the chesterfield sat the Duchess. She looked very much the part, indeed radiant. I have no eye for women's clothing, but even I could see she had patronised the best couturier. She wore some sort of sequinned tulle gown with a plunging neckline that Dorothy would have considered grossly immodest. Her face was in bloom, her eyes danced, and not a hair was out of place. Her smile was brief, thin and professional. It would have been eleven years since I had last met her, I thought. She remembered my name, and she clearly intended to make no concession to sentiment. 'Can't help you, General,' she began in her most distant manner. 'Wouldn't if I could.'

'You understand the princesses' position?' I asked.

'I have been told your story.' It was a bleak little statement.

I didn't think the Duchess would respond to blandishment. Attack seemed the best approach. I raised my voice a couple of notches. 'You have reason to doubt it?'

The Duke, taking a seat next to her on the sofa, took her hand. He said, 'Brunner has much the same story.'

The Duchess took her hand away. Her colour rose slightly. 'Do you know what the King and I have suffered under that pair's parents?'

I tried diplomacy. 'I know that King George was in a position that forced him to make some very difficult decisions about you and your husband.'

The Duchess's eyes glinted. 'She hates me.'

It seemed necessary to be more direct. 'The Queen holds you responsible for forcing the monarchy on her husband. She thought his health wouldn't stand it. You know he's dying, don't you?'

The Duchess glanced at the Duke. It was impossible to tell what the Duke made of this, whether it was news to him, and if so whether good or bad. She said: 'When will Princess Elizabeth become Queen?'

I had in fact no precise information on this point. I considered what answer would best forward my position. 'Weeks or days. He's on his death-bed.'[i]

Ferris thus far had had the sense to keep his mouth shut. 'Under Himmler, never.'

The Duchess silenced him with a glance. She looked at her hands, folded neatly on her lap, adorned by wedding and engagement rings. Probably not paste, I thought, though you never knew these days. 'The British love Elizabeth, don't they Max?'

i In fact this was accurate.

158

In the Court of the Puppet King

'They loved your husband,' I countered.

'What will happen to him?' she asked, curiously referring to her husband sitting next to her as though he was a chattel.

'Oh, I should think Antibes.'

'Not the Tower?' cut in Ferris.

This was utter nonsense, and Ferris knew it.

'I shouldn't think so under Churchill, would you, Teddy?' I said.

The Duke interposed. 'We were happy at Antibes.'

The Duchess's thoughts were elsewhere. 'What use are they to Truman?' she asked.

I pitched it as high as I dared. 'They are the means by which he may be able to control the future of Europe. They may win the States the war without fighting a battle.'

'You want me to stop that?' she asked.

'What other choice have you?'

'To remain.' It was said quite quietly.

'With all that that means?' I countered.

'Is that a choice, dear?' asked the Duke.

It was the first time that her composure faltered. She stared into the fire for a long time. Then, 'We barely know Truman. He's from Kentucky. Sells shirts.'[ii]

'We know Kennedy,' said the Duke. 'You know Kick. Between them they know everyone.'

There was silence for a few moments. I thought of the colourful reputation that Kennedy's sister — for reasons I've never fathomed, always known as Kick — had acquired when Joe Kennedy senior had introduced her to London society in 1938. She had something in common with the Duchess, I felt. The Duchess said more lightly, 'Yes, Kick. There is Kick. Something might be done with Kick.'

Sensing victory, I asked, 'She can find out where the princesses are?'

The Duchess gave a wry smile. 'Kick knows everyone and everything. Think she's not going to be able to wheedle that out of her own brother?'

ii The President was indeed a former shirt salesman.

The Second Letter

I won't trouble the reader with a detailed account of the next few days as I made my way across England and the Scottish borders on my way to the intended meeting with Kit and Nancy at Faslane.

I had half thought of taking the Fieseler. The Duke dissuaded me. With a clear course of action ahead of him, his spirits revived and I saw once again something of the man I had liked, and the king-in-waiting the nation had loved. As he pointed out, the Boche would now be on the lookout for the plane. My luck had held on the run down from Norfolk. A venture into the Scottish Highlands was a very different matter. Moreover, he had, he said, a better plan. I was to assume the guise of a chauffeur and take one of his own cars north. My cover was that the Rolls was needed in Balmoral.[i] I would travel under the protection of the Royal laissez-passer. From Blenheim I could perfectly plausibly drive north through Coventry, Stoke, Preston and Carlisle. Only from there would my route become questionable. For Balmoral in Deeside I would head for Edinburgh; for Faslane I would take the westerly route over the Borders towards Glasgow. As the Duke pointed out, other than in the townships the Scots were pleased to call cities, the Nazis' writ barely ran. Neither the terrain nor the people were susceptible to such control, as others had discovered before Mosley's Gauleiters. I might well be stopped by the Abwehr or the *Geheime Feldpolizei* in Preston, my papers checked and my movement orders scrutinised, but beyond Carlisle it was bandit country, where at least in some respects I would be safe.

So it was that, shortly after dawn on 6 February, I found myself in an ill-fitting and noisome black suit at the wheel

i Scottish home of the Royal family.

of the Duke's old grey Continental tourer. It was a journey I remember only as a series of snapshots, for my mind was on other things. Being waved out of the lodge gates at Blenheim with barely a glance from an unshaven SS guard. The ruins of Coventry, where what was left of the Cathedral still stood in dumb witness to the terrible blitz on the night of 14 June 1940. The road-block outside Stafford where I saw a German staff officer, a plump fellow with glasses and a stammer, fall into the hands of the mob to be publicly lynched. Lancaster and the commercial hotel where the rumour first reached me of the fall of Antwerp.[ii] Changing a wheel in the blinding Cumbrian rain on the roadside south of Penrith as a column of Werhmacht armour fled south. My spirits lifting with the road as I climbed out of Moffat and into those great bare rolling hills that seem as timeless as man. Dusk on the outskirts of Glasgow illuminated by what I assumed were looters' fires.[iii] Suspicion in the tiny inn at Arden on the shores of Loch Lomond, where Sassenachs are rarely welcome unless bearing gold. Whisky. Bed. Struggling with the Rolls on the rutted winter track up to Auchenvennel on the saddle that divides the Loch Lomond from Loch Gare. The spring breeze on the fresh hillside of Glen Fruin and a glimpse of the Gareloch below. Journey's end with the sight of the tiny loch-side settlement of Faslane.

I glanced at my watch that morning on the hillside. It was nearly ten. And as I did so I felt a hand on my shoulder.

*

Given the events that were to follow, I now need to turn again to the evidence presented to me by Mr Allen Dulles of the CIA. I must record here that I am not entirely satisfied with Mr Dulles's account of the machinations of the Truman administration in the preceding days. They seem to me,

ii1 Antwerp actually fell on the 4th.

iii This was the preliminary to the Glasgow rising of the 8th.

simple soldier though I may be, incomplete. Far be it from me to suggest that the head of the Central Intelligence Agency would be guilty of dissimulation or fabrication. Rather, as he himself implies, he is not being quite frank. With regard to my own political ambitions he is, of course, utterly mistaken.[i]

General Sir Max Quick
Chief of Imperial General Staff
The War Office
Whitehall
London West

Allen Foster Dulles
Director
Central Intelligence Agency
Room 3663
Rockefeller Center
New York, New York

22 March 1946

I'm sorry, Max, I simply don't know where we go on this. I understand what you're doing. I appreciate its importance. I really do. The whole Administration does. There are sensitivities, though, huge sensitivities. They don't simply affect us. They affect you, too, yourself, your fine country. Intimately. Yes. That's the word. Aren't there some things that are better left unknown? I — we — cannot conceivably answer all of your questions. The following goes far further than I would personally be happy to go. As to the rest, you must draw your own conclusions.

You will recall my account of my return to the United States, my meeting with Bill Donovan in New York, and my subsequent mission to the White House. The President and Secretary of State Byrnes failed to appreciate the position of

i A point on which the reader will have her or his own views.

The Second Letter

the CIA. Operation Holystone was conceived as a buttress to our friend Himmler. I left the White House in the small hours of 2 February. Sixty miles north in the chapel in Newark, Commander Kennedy was — I was later told — at Mass, praying for the success of his mission.

At this stage, we could not affect its immediate outcome. There was much else I could do, though, to ensure that the President was more appropriately informed and advised.

I took a room at the Willard in Pennsylvania Avenue. You don't know Washington. Anyone who is anyone was there. The place was alive with rumour, speculation and indiscretion. I loved it. I saw Daladier,[ii] Ciano,[iii] Halifax[iv] and Ribbentrop. Everyone who was anyone. I saw those less official and less — the term is relative — discreet. I cannot say that there was a clear consensus on the way in which events in Europe would turn out. Few, least of all Ribbentrop, manifested much confidence in Herr Himmler. You know he used to farm pigs. There was some regret expressed on the passing of Hitler. Some saw Mussolini[v] taking the opportunity to seize Switzerland and the north Tyrol. Others saw a renaissance of France under a military junta led by Darlan. Some even whispered, Max, of your own political ambitions, an aspiration to unite a shattered country, and to usher in a new Elizabethan age.

Yet there was an absolute belief that we had reached a turning-point in world history. It was a moment akin to Hitler's accession to the Chancellorship in 1933, to the invasion of Poland in 1939, to the fall of Great Britain in 1940, to Pearl Harbor, to the calamity in Tokyo Bay. All these were matters

ii Edouard Deladier, 1884-1979, French PM.

iii Galeazzo Ciano, 1903-1949, Italian minister of foreign affairs.

iv Edward Wood, First Lord Halifax 1881-1959, Foreign Secretary of the British government in exile.

v Benito Mussolini, 1883-1946, Italian dictator.

that merited the attention of the President — if not necessarily of Secretary of State Byrnes. As I gleaned even the smallest kernel of intelligence, Commander Kennedy flew east into the rising sun and to his own strange destiny.

In the next seventy-two hours I mooched around the Willard and diplomatic Washington. The news from Germany and the Greater Reich grew from bad to worse or — according to your taste — from good to better. Quisling[i] was murdered in Narvik on 3 February, and the Danes managed to bundle their occupiers off their peninsula with scarcely a fight. King Leopold returned to Belgium on the 5th after Antwerp was liberated, and Mussolini was shot in Perugia that same day. Then, on the 6th I was having dinner with Vice-Admiral------- in the Constitution Club when I was paged by the bellboy. It was the Oval Office. I abandoned my guest and took a cab through the snow to the White House.

In the Oval Office the President and the Secretary of State awaited me. Both were in shirtsleeves. The rye was on the table. Truman had a five o'clock shadow and Byrnes looked as though he hadn't slept for a week. Ignoring me, Byrnes said to the President: 'Still can't see what the CIA can do for us.'

Truman had the air and tone of a man whose patience is wearing thin. 'Give it a try, James.'

It was time I intervened. 'Where are we?' I asked.

The President swivelled himself round in his chair to face Byrnes. 'Secretary of State, your story.'

With no great evidence of enthusiasm, Byrnes recounted the unfolding of Operation Holystone at Sandringham. He contrived to suggest that everything had gone as planned. Maybe he thought I was born yesterday or that I didn't have my own sources of intelligence. When he had finished his account, I commented: 'Except the Brits are in the know.'

'Yes,' said the President. 'That's exactly the point, Mr Dulles. The British are aware that a US commando has seized the heirs to their throne. This has diplomatic consequences

i Vidkun Abraham Quisling, 1887-1946, Norwegian politician who betrayed his people to the Nazis.

that Secretary of State Byrnes is reluctant to grasp. Goddamit, James, the fox is in the hen-house.'

The argument had clearly been well rehearsed. Byrnes seemed to lack the energy to reply. Eventually he said: 'It was a risk we were aware of, Mr President.' He turned to me. 'The CIA told us.'

'As did the Secretary of State, I believe,' rejoined Truman, looking straight at Byrnes.

'Where's Kennedy now?' I countered. 'Where are the princesses?'

'Dublin,' said Byrnes shortly. 'Supposedly.'

'Supposedly?' I said. I wondered what they would be doing in Ireland. Then I remembered the plan to fly Kennedy's Catalinas from Gander to Shannon en route for Sandringham.

The President said, 'We've lost them.'

I was dumbstruck, Max, dumbstruck.

'*Lost* them? How do you mean lost them?'

The President raised his eyebrows in the way he had. 'Kennedy's been out of radio contact for seventy-two hours. Remember the orders? He was supposed to fly straight from Sandringham to Dublin, then put them aboard the *Boston* for onward transit to the US. He got as far as Dublin. Then we lost him.'

'Yes?' I could think of half a dozen reasons for this, none particularly sinister.

'Secretary of State?' prompted the President.

'We have concerns,' conceded Byrnes, fingering his chin.

'Yes?' I said.

The President had clearly had enough of Byrnes. 'For Chrissake, James.'

'US agents in Dublin,' said Byrnes testily. '*My* agents. Useful agents. They report the princesses are out and about with Kennedy consorting with the British — I use the word advisedly — aristocracy. Kennedy's been mixing it with his sister. Kick or whatever she calls herself. Her husband, too. Calls himself the Duke of Devonshire, if you will.' James is a republican in an old-fashioned sense of the word.

'Nice for them,' I said.

Byrnes didn't seem to like this. He broadened his front of attack. 'Does the CIA work for the Administration or the Administration for the CIA?'

I was tempted to say that it was too early to tell. I thought better of it. 'The CIA is the servant of the President and the American people.'

Byrnes laughed, but without much humour in his voice.

'And the other matter, James,' prompted the President.

Byrnes made an effort to get a grip on himself. 'You remember Project Manhattan?'

I did as a matter of fact. 'Yes,' I said. 'I think you told me about it being restarted. Atomic bombs.'

'Yes,' said the President. 'Damn right. Atomic bombs.'

'We have some news,' continued Byrnes.

I wondered what was coming. 'Yes? Good?'

'Not quite,' said the President.

I cast my mind back to what had been said in the great room ten days earlier. 'You said the Soviets might be a couple of years away from making a viable bomb.'

'That's what we heard,' said Byrnes. 'May still be true'.

'So?' I asked.

'The Nazis,' began the President.

'I thought they were behind the Soviets,' I said.

'So did we,' said Byrnes. It was not the habit of his department to share intelligence.

The President took a little walk around his desk. He touched the standard of the Stars and Stripes. Then, quite quietly, he said: 'We've been told the Nazis have the bomb.'

I could see now why poor James had been quite so exercised. I asked, 'By whom?'

James was very quick on this, Max, very quick. You may know the reasons. 'We're not at liberty to say.' [i]

The President, who, I have to say, looked distinctly

---

i The evidence for this is now quite clear; so, too, the way in which the bomb was used as a bait. See epilogue.

166

embarrassed by this, said: 'Point is they have it.'

'We're *told* they have,' I countered.

'We have to *assume* they have,' said Byrnes, with equal emphasis.

I tried another tack: 'How?'

'A few collaborators among your friends the Brits,' said Byrnes. 'Some place called Rutherford Laboratories in Cambridge. All co-opted for work for the Reich in the noble cause. Did very well, it seems.'

'I doubt they had much option,' I said.

'For Chrissake, what's the difference?' said the President, clearly riled. 'They've got it.'

I looked at Byrnes. I recalled being bested by him when we had last met. I hadn't enjoyed the experience. Here was my opportunity. An opportunity not to be missed, I thought.

I said: 'Seems to me this affects the desirability and eligibility of the Nazis as allies, wouldn't you agree, Secretary of State? If they regain their mastery over Europe and have the power of the atom at their fingertips, I wouldn't call them a great power any longer.'

'What'd you call 'em?' asked the President with a note of surprise in his voice.

'A super-power,' I said. 'Rather, *the* super-power.' I thought it was a good phrase.

Byrnes shook his head. 'A proposition based on ifs, buts and maybes, hypotheses, suggestions and speculation.'

The President eased himself out of his chair, took the rye and emptied the remainder of the bottle into three glasses. He put on his jacket, and took his place behind his desk. 'That's enough, boys. Quite enough. I've heard what you've got to say. Fine. Fine and dandy.'

He smiled brightly and briefly at us both. 'I'm not going to knock your heads together. I am going to charge you both to agree, co-operate, work together and do whatever it takes to crack this. Please.

We were admonished, I and the Secretary of State.

'What can we agree on?' asked Byrnes.

He had folded his arms across his chest.

This was easy. 'Help find Kennedy,' I said. As doubtless Byrnes knew, his were not the only US agents operating in Dublin.

His reply surprised me. He unfolded his arms and sat up. 'Done,' he said — so quickly I thought the idea was already in his head.

' "Bomb" sounds kinda *abstract*','I continued, warming to my theme. 'Do we know what it's like, how big it is, who's got it. Are there lots of them?'

'What do we know, James?' asked the President. It sounded more like an order than a question.

The Secretary of State numbered off the items on his fingers. 'High explosives can be mass-produced. These things can't be. Very slow scientific process. Called uranium enrichment. I won't bore you with the science. You wouldn't understand it. Uranium's the raw material for the bomb. Quite a lot of it about. Places like the Rockies. Give me a sample of the stuff, the ore. Out of every shed-load of the ore all bar a plank's Uranium 238. No more use than lead. The plank's Uranium 235.That's the real McCoy. That'll make you a dandy bomb. Lot of sheds to give you the planks they need. They might have half a dozen, if that. Maybe two or three. They don't have an arsenal. Next question?'

'Size?' I asked.

'Quite a bulky piece of ordnance,' said Byrnes. 'Bit like a thousand-pounder, we think.'

'Fit in a Catalina?' I asked.

Byrnes paused, considering the implications of the question. 'Not quite, I guess.'

The President nodded. He was following my line of thought.

'Condor?' I was thinking of the Germans' bomber,[i]1 deployed with some success at Kursk, Stalingrad and Moscow.

---

i Focke-Wulf Condor, an all-metal four-engined monoplane. First flew in 1937.

'Got the size, maybe not the range,' said Byrnes.

I tried another tack. 'Lancaster? Didn't I hear that the Brits had been developing the four-engine version of the Manchester at the end of the war?'

James raised his eyebrows. 'Interesting idea.'

'Germans are full of them,' I said. 'Ideas.'

'Another Pearl Harbor', said Byrnes, and returned to look at the blazing fire. It was some moments before anyone spoke.

'Can't rule it out, Mr President,' I said.

'Damned sight worse,' said Truman. 'Pearl Harbor, Iwo Jima and Tokyo Bay all rolled into one. Maybe here. Maybe Chicago. Maybe New York. Who knows? Himmler's another lunatic. Know what he's doing in Poland, Mr Dulles? Gassing Jews. That's what we hear. '

Byrnes raised his eyebrows a little at this but made no comment. He returned to his fingers and his briefing. 'Location. That's an interesting one, isn't it? Take Manhattan. New Mexico. That's where it is. Miles away from anywhere. Neat from a security point of view. Not a bad idea if it all goes up in flames or whatever atom bombs do. Shouldn't be surprised if the Brits took a similar view. Allen, you know England. Where do you put it?'

I thought for a moment. 'West Country, Wales, Scotland,' I said. 'Three otherwise useless pieces of real estate.'

'There again,' said Byrnes, 'you don't have to leave it where you make it.'

'You're playing games again, James,' said the President.

The Secretary of State threw up his arms. 'Okay, okay. We're told they've got some of these things in a place called Faslane.'

The name meant nothing to me. Absolutely nothing. James added: 'On a loch on the west coast of Scotland.'

'Very scenic,' I said. I had once been taken on a yachting cruise up that coast. It had rained without remission. 'Why a loch, I wonder?'

'Coolant, I guess,' said Byrnes. 'Don't think you'd want one of those things far from water.'

'Sure,' I said. 'Good for Catalinas, too.'

'If you were thinking of borrowing one of these things,' said Byrnes, 'I told you you'd have to think bigger than a Catalina.'

I had been turning the problem over in my mind as I spoke. 'In the first instance I was thinking of the borrower.'

The President got up from behind his desk. 'Kennedy's got his hands full. Or he should have anyway.'

'I didn't think we had a superfluity of commandos in Britain,' I observed.

'Nope,' agreed the President.

'What about the *Boston*, Mr President?' asked Byrnes.

I had forgotten about the frigate dispatched to Dublin in support of Operation Holystone.

The President turned to Byrnes. 'Your call, James.'

'Not far from Dublin to Faslane,' was his comment.

We walked over to a table on which was lying a map of the Western Approaches to Britain. Byrnes was right. North from Dublin, past Belfast and you're in a stretch of water called the Firth of Clyde. Funny name. Loch Gare leads north from the Clyde, Faslane's towards the head of the loch on the eastern shore. Not that far from Glasgow.

The President resumed his seat behind his desk and consulted his watch. 'It's 1.38. Guess you have till breakfast to fix things. James, what time do you think? For the rendezvous at Faslane of Commander Kennedy and the *Boston*.'

'The orders?' I asked.

'Just to bring back the princesses and the bomb. We'll — no — I'll decide then what to do next.'

'A double aim,' I said.

'Put it any way you want, Allen. Provided you come up with the goods. A double aim if you want.'

*

So ended Mr Dulles's second letter. Make of it what you will.

Part Three

Faslane

I glanced at my watch on the hillside of Glen Fruin, and as I did so I felt a hand on my shoulder. I turned and got the surprise of my life. If I'd had to guess who might apprehend me that February morning, Commander Kennedy was just about the last on my list. Still, it doesn't do to seem too discomposed. 'This is unexpected,' I grunted.

'Hope so,' said Kennedy, who sounded tiresomely pleased with himself. 'I rather pride myself on my scout-work. Didn't think you'd hear me.'

I was in no mood for exchanging pleasantries with the Commander, wherever he had sprung from. My mind that morning was on a little other than the princesses. 'You've got some of my belongings.'

Kennedy allowed a smile to play across his face. 'Thought you might not have been told, General. '

'Told what?' I asked tersely.

'New orders,' said the Commander pleasantly. 'Talk of strategic alliances, whatever that may mean. I have them in writing. Long and short is that I'm instructed to work in close co-operation with the SOE. I believe that's you and the Admiral, as far as I'm concerned.'

I now felt simply bemused by the turn of events. 'What's brought this about?' I asked.

Kennedy shrugged his shoulders. 'Circumstances change, I guess. Seems to me the Reich's falling round Himmler's ears.'

'And the States wants to back the winner,' I said.

Kennedy bridled at this suggestion. 'I'm a sailor, General, I follow orders.'

Seeing I was still puzzled, he added: 'Admiral Conway was given the inside track. Has he reached you?'

'I've been on the move,' I replied.' He's on his way here, I believe. May be here already.'

'Explains it,' said Kennedy.

I could hardly agree with that. It seemed to me to explain remarkably little. However, I now became conscious of behaving gracelessly. Something would have to be done with Kennedy. I thrust out my hand. 'How can we help?'

Kennedy relaxed. 'We heard we might find you here,' he said. 'I believe we're both looking for the same thing.'

We were high on the hillside above the base at Faslane. It was a beautiful late winter's morning, and the great waters of the Gare Loch below scintillated in the sunshine. Above and around rose the Trossachs, a deep green round the noble shores of the great waters, shading into purple as they stretched towards the heavens. Perhaps a couple of thousand yards away towards the mouth of the loch lay half a dozen of seaplanes with the black cross of the Luftwaffe, lifting and falling, ducking and yawing at their anchors in the light westerly breeze. Closer, sheltering in the little bay on the eastern side of the loch in which the base nestled, a Kriegsmarine frigate was basking in the sun. At first I thought she, too, was at anchor. I now saw she was steaming in gently towards the base.

The base didn't seem to amount to much. Judging by the disembowelled carcasses of ships that littered the shore, it had once been a breakers' yard. A rough, semi-circular fence of timber posts and barbed wire had been thrown up around three or four acres of scrubby foreshore. A mole, clearly of recent construction, had been cast out from three tumbledown corrugated iron sheds that seemed to constitute the port buildings. The breakwater sheltered half a dozen small Jerry patrol boats, a couple of trawlers and a similar number of spindly tubes I recognised as small U-boats. On the inner wall of the harbour lay a larger submarine, its casing topped with a squat conning tower carrying the designation *U-511* in white letters the height of a man. A light railway line ran round the harbour and on it I could make out a couple of oil-wagons, three or four flat-bed trucks and a mobile crane. A dozen or so men were milling around the U-boat. Behind it appeared to be

174

another altogether smaller submarine.

Before I had time to respond to Kennedy's remark, he asked, 'What do you make of it, General?'

I assumed he was after my professional opinion of the military situation. It was a reasonable question. Indeed, it was one I had been asking myself before Kennedy had materialised. 'My appreciation? Seems pretty well set up, to me, Commander. Air and sea cover, and crawling with Jerries. They may object to a visit.'

Kennedy then sprang the second of his surprises. Quite laconically he said: 'Fact is, General, the whole base is in my hands.'

This seemed utterly contrary to the evidence of my own eyes. 'What about the frigate?' I asked.

He offered me his binoculars. 'Try my glasses.'

I did so. I'd seen enough of the Jerry *Flottenbegleiters*[i] at Newhaven to last me a lifetime. More a miniature battleship than a frigate, she had a couple of stacks, two small hooded turrets on the foredeck, and the usual assemblage of depth-charge throwers, anti-aircraft guns and torpedo tubes on the quarterdeck. The hands were fallen in for and aft, and she was flying pennant numbers and what looked like a brand new swastika. There seemed nothing odd about this particular ship. 'Surprising what you can do with a bit of plywood and paint,' explained Kennedy. 'That's the USS *Boston*.'

'Is it now?' I said wonderingly.

I looked again. Come to think of it, there was something about the frigate's prow that was a bit odd, not quite the sheer of the *Flottenbegleiter*. Maybe she was a bit on the big side, too. A thought occurred to me. I had another look at the seaplanes gently nodding at their anchors in the sun. 'Those your flying-boats?'

Kennedy nodded. 'Yep.'

'Your men,' I suggested, looking down at the congregation round *U-511*.

i Frigates.

'In at dawn,' confirmed Kennedy. 'Four platoons.'

'Quite an operation.' I don't think I managed to squeeze the admiration out of my voice.

'Glad you like it.' There was pride — justifiable pride — in his voice.

This certainly put a different perspective on the whole situation. I began to think things through. 'Where's the Boche area command? Glasgow?'

'Glasgow,' echoed Kennedy. 'Detachment of the 914 Grenadiers.'[i]

'Will they have heard?' I asked.

'We cut communications before we went in.'

'They'll notice,' I pointed out.

'They will,' agreed Kennedy, sounding quite relaxed. 'But maybe not quite yet. I hear they've a lot on their hands.'

He was right, of course. I told him about the disturbances I had seen on my way through Glasgow the previous night. I wondered how much grace he thought we had. 'Twenty-four hours?'

'If that, I'm advised,' said the Commander.

'And our job?' I asked.

'Find a piece of ordnance,' said Kennedy.' Around here somewhere, I'm told.'

I had half suspected this. If Kit was on the case, I saw no reason for discretion. 'A bomb,' I said.

'Yes,' said Kennedy, with greater weight in his voice. 'A bomb.'

So that was it. How Kennedy had come by this information and how he knew about Faslane were questions that could wait. The principal issue remained the girls. 'Where are the princesses?' I asked.

'On the *Boston*. President wouldn't have them flown back.'

*

i Part of the 352 Infanterie Division.

Faslane

Nothing would now keep me from Elizabeth and Margaret. After abandoning the Rolls I had worked my way down that steep hillside with some care. Now we doubled down the remainder in less than fifteen minutes. As we did so, I heard something from the Commander of his movements after Sandringham and how he'd ended up in Dublin. It seemed that my conversations in Blenheim had born fruit, for Kennedy divulged that he had seen his sister and her husband, Billy Cavendish, there. A reception at the United States Embassy. I wondered if this was the work of the Duchess. If it was, she had been diligent. Not necessarily a quality one would associate with the former Mrs Simpson, but perhaps on this occasion she felt her own interests were at stake.

Kennedy and I came to the base of the hill about four hundred yards from the perimeter fence. As we dropped down I saw that the *Boston* was closing the mole and entering the small harbour. I could just about make out seamen on the deck hauling out berthing wires and ropes. As we watched, the frigate drew very slowly closer to the quay and seemed to come to a complete halt a few feet off the harbour wall. Heaving lines shot out, the bow and stern lines were secured, the spring wires followed. There was a rumble from the engines and the steel grey ship — all 300 or so feet of her — edged sideways towards her mooring against the backdrop of the loch and the hills beyond. As she did so, I was near enough to spot the princesses on the flag-deck by the bridge, right by the ALDIS lamps glinting in the sun. A few moments later, just as we approached the corrugated iron sheds, I heard the *Boston*'s engines die away to a murmur.

Out from behind one of the sheds stepped a soldier, in the olive green drill I remembered from Sandringham. He had his rifle in the rabbiting position and looked ready for trouble. As he saw Kennedy he relaxed and saluted smartly. Kennedy responded in kind. 'All secure, Sergeant?'

'Sure thing, Commander. Jerries were a bunch of pussycats.' He spoke in that slow easy drawl of the American East Coast.

'Where are they?' asked Kennedy.

'Under guard in their own barracks'. He thumbed towards one of the bigger sheds by the dock.

'Casualties?' I asked.

The sergeant looked at me uncertainly. I was still wearing the grubby black suit in which I'd driven up from Blenheim. I'd managed to shave, of course, but I hadn't bathed since Preston. The inn at Arden didn't have running water and I rather got the impression that the Scots don't wash much. Kennedy, perhaps spotting the underling's expression, said, 'The General's working with us, Sergeant.'

This elicited another salute. 'None, sir.'

This seemed surprising. 'None?' I said.

Kennedy interposed. 'I guess they're dockyard workers, not soldiers.'

'Perhaps so,' I responded. I looked over at the patrol boats and submarines secured against the mole. Kennedy and his NCO followed my gaze. 'Where are the crews?'

The answer was prompt enough. 'Guards on each one, sir. Came quietly. No sign of the crews.'

'What about the big one?' I indicated *U-511*, now in the shadow of the *Boston*. Close to she was really quite sizeable. I'm not much of a hand at tonnages, but I'd guess a couple of thousand, perhaps more.[i] Ocean-going. Her deck was just on the level with the dock, and the top of the conning tower might have been twelve or fifteen feet higher, topped with what I took to be a periscope standard. A steel jumping wire ran from the tower to the bows and stern. 'Just a guard, sir.'

Kennedy obviously followed my line of thinking. 'Searched, Sergeant?'

'Top to bottom, sir.'

'Anything of interest?' asked Kennedy.

The sergeant seemed nonplussed. 'Mebbe to submariners.'

For a few moments, Kennedy and I continued to scrutinise

i The mainstay of the British submarine flotilla in the years up to the war were much smaller craft, typically between 500 and 1000 tons.

178

U-511. At length, Kennedy asked, 'What's the thing astern?'

'Search me, Commander,' said the sergeant. 'Subs ain't my line.'

'Did you see what the Jerries were doing to her?' I asked.

The sergeant indicated the railway tracks. 'Storing her, I guess.' By his tone of voice he thought the matter without interest.

Kennedy dismissed him. We walked over to the trucks, standing only feet away from the U-boat. Close up, she seemed even bigger, her grey hull lightly streaked with rust, the paint in places cracked, barnacles just above the water-line. I thought of the havoc that she and her kind had wreaked in the Atlantic in the autumn of 1939 and spring of 1940, and the dozen or so men I knew personally whom they'd sent to their deaths. As though excusing the sergeant's behaviour, Kennedy said: 'The men don't know.'

'Naturally.' I should have been surprised if he'd told them about the bomb.

We stood there looking around for a few moments. I can't say there seemed much to be gleaned. The flat-bed trucks could have carried anything, and the oil wagons presumably carried oil for the U-boat's diesels. Then, remembering the conversation that followed our discovery of the papers in the *Schnellboot* on Thornham beach, an idea crossed my mind.

'You got a Geiger-counter?' I asked.

'Pardon?'

'Geiger-counter.'

'What's that when it's at home?' asked Kennedy.

'Measures radioactivity, they tell me. Might tell us where our bomb is.'

'Never heard of it,' said Kennedy dismissively.

We did no better with the strange vessel that lay immediately astern *U-511*. Close inspection revealed little more than we had seen from the hill. A dirty black tube some sixty or seventy feet long, perhaps fifteen at its widest, tapering towards both ends. One end was rather beamier than the other. With a conning tower it could have been a small submarine, a whale and her calf. Without it, it was just a tube.

As far as we could see there were no hatches or openings. Kennedy said: 'D'you think that's an atom bomb?'

'Too big,' I said, having myself already had and cast away the thought.

'Maybe it's inside?' suggested Kennedy.

It was a reasonable enough idea. 'What good is it in the water?' I asked.

'Can't think.'

'Can you get it on the *Boston*?'

Kennedy gave me a strange look. 'Not much point unless it *is* the bomb. I should look a damn fool if we took it three thousand miles back to Sewells Point[i] to find it packed with cotton wool.'

He had a point. We walked down the quay to the *Boston*, where a couple of ratings were securing the gangway on the shore. Close to, the frigate looked like a stage set from behind the scenes: all props and buttresses holding up the plywood shamming as superstructure and a second stack. The *Boston* only had one funnel. Kennedy had been very ingenious.

It was nothing new, of course. Towards the end of the Great War Q ships had been put into operation. Tramps and trawlers armed to the teeth with guns hidden in fake cabins, odd bits of superstructure and so on. They were live bait. They lured U-boats to the surface for a spot of gunnery action, waited till they were at point blank-range, then collapsed the cabins and opened fire. Accounted for half a dozen Boche submarines until the BdU[ii] got wind of it. Come to think of it Kit had been a midshipman on one right at the end of the war, summer of 1918.

'What next, Commander?' I asked.

The base seemed to be as Kennedy had said. It was in his hands. So were the princesses. So too, perhaps, was the atom bomb. He had done very well. Preferment would follow. It

---

i US Navy base in Norfolk, Virginia.

ii *Befehshaber der Unterseeboote*, U-boat command.

was too bad, I thought. Promoting youngsters beyond their ability always turns out badly in the end.

'Couple of engineers on board who may be able to help us out,' replied Kennedy. 'What did you call it? Geiger-counter?'

With that we made our way over towards the frigate. As we did so, I saw the princesses and Julia coming down the gangway. They were soon spotted by Kennedy's men, who congregated at the bottom of the gangway and gave them a cheer. Strange thing, given their presumably republican sentiments, I thought.

Still, I was quite moved myself to see the girls back on British soil. It took me back to when I'd last seen them on the deck of that wretched *Schnellboot* by the Tower, silhouetted in the moonlight and in the hands of the rascal Skorzeny.

I don't know if that thought put me in mind of the E-boat's mascot, the little liver-coloured dachshund. I thought I heard some barking through the cheering. I dismissed it as a figment of my imagination, focusing on the little pageant unfolding at the bottom of the gangway which offered some hope for the future. There it was again, behind me, a yapping and a yowling. Then, before I had time to turn, the air was rent with a burst of gunfire. I spun on my heel.

When I had last seen her, *U-511* had been lying serenely astern of the *Boston*, barely moving in the sheltered waters behind the harbour mole, not a soul within fifty feet of her. Now, one of the heavy stern hatches on her rusty grey rear casing had been thrown open. Lined up raggedly on the deck abaft the conning tower were a dozen or so men in Kriegsmarine uniform, each armed with a submachine gun directed up at the sky. Atop the conning tower, directing operations, was a man with the build of a tank and a slash of a scar down his face. There was little doubt in my mind who it could be, for in his hands was the liver-coloured dog, barking its head off.

*

I was armed. So were Kennedy's men. But I don't think that a gun was raised against Skorzeny. The princesses were in our midst and the ambush was abrupt. I give it to Skorzeny. It was a clever little operation.

Leaning on his stick, he hailed me from the tower in his all too courteous, just slightly guttural English. There was a smile, a cruel smile in his voice. 'Would you be so kind as to bring the ladies forward, General?' It all had a horrible sense of déjà vu. I suppose he was about thirty feet in front of me; the princesses at the bottom of the gangway forty or so behind. I looked at Kennedy. He seemed utterly crestfallen. He shook his head doubtfully. Yet his men, somehow, knew better. Without any sudden movement or and without drawing attention to themselves, they had edged slowly round the princesses to form a human shield.

This gave me the courage to reply. 'In England the subjects do the monarch's bidding, Colonel,' I shouted. 'Not the other way round.'

At this Skorzeny nodded to the ratings nearest to him on the U-boat's casing. They lowered their guns before firing carefully with a sudden, short burst slightly to one side of the shield of Kennedy's men. The rounds tore into the granite and ricocheted into the *Boston*.

'Get my point, General?'

'Butcher,' I said to Skorzeny.

'I've been called worse things than that,' he smiled. 'You can do better.'

He turned again to the casing, but at this there was another word from the gangway. It was Elizabeth, whose quiet voice rang out clearly enough. 'That's enough, thank you, Colonel.' She had pushed her way to the front of the shield in a gesture of acceptance and defeat.

Skorzeny bowed ironically from his podium. 'Thank you, ma'am.'

Julia and Margaret followed Elizabeth towards Skorzeny and the U-boat. Margaret, I have to say, looked cross. I could think of a number of people worthy of blame for the turn of events, but Margaret turned her fury on Kennedy. 'You bloody fool.' Much else followed. There was a gangplank between the quay and the U-boat's casing. Skorzeny came down and handed the girls on board. They disappeared through a hatch on the side of the conning tower, and Skorzeny's triumph was complete.

We must have stood there in silence for a good quarter of an hour under the eyes of Skorzeny's men. Then I heard the cough of the submarine's diesel engines. A few moments later Skorzeny himself reappeared on the conning tower, still moving with difficulty and aided by his stick. He gave a couple of orders and all but a clutch of the ratings followed the princesses into the bowels of the U-boat. Two had clearly been detailed to cover the men still crowded round the bottom of the *Boston*'s gangway. The other pair set about preparing the U-boat for sea. The remaining fellow dashed down the gangplank and set off towards the port's offices. A few moments later he returned with eight or nine men.

'Your pussycats, Commander,' I allowed myself. Kennedy looked on speechless.

We watched as *U-511* prepared to cast off.

'Obey telegraphs. Let go aft. Let go forward,' ordered Skorzeny. The dockyard wires were lifted off the bollards and fell into the water. The two ratings clumped up the gangplank, withdrew it after them, and stowed it in the casing.

'Slow ahead together.' The U-boat began to slide way from the wall.

'*Auf Wiedersehen,* Colonel,' I shouted as she pulled further away from the quay.

'I think not, General,' retorted Skorzeny. 'This time I feel it is goodbye.'

I have to say I felt much the same as the U-boat manoeuvred out of the harbour. As she did so, it became clear that Skorzeny was paying as much attention to the stern of the U-boat as to the party on the quay. Behind *U-511*, gently at first, then with gathering speed, followed the tow, a wake beginning to curl away from its black prow. In a few moments the whale and its calf had reached the exit of the mole. No sooner had they done so than the bridge party disappeared into the conning tower. I pictured Skorzeny slipping through the hatch into the submarine, and pulling the lid down over his head.

For some moments the U-boat remained on the surface, pulling steadily away from us and turning slowly south towards the mouth of the loch. Then there were some spurts of spray from the casing as the main vents were opened, and the water flooded into the ballast tanks. *U-511* slumped and settled in the water, the bow wave easing as the sea bubbled further up into the casing and forced the air out of the perforations on her deck. Within moments all I could see of her was the tower, the white numerals 511 subsiding gradually under the waves. Then they too were gone.

*

The stewards had cleared the lunch in the *Boston*'s officers' mess, and Kennedy and I were about to settle down to a post-mortem. Suddenly there was a thundering of steel-capped boots on the frigate's decks, and Kit burst into the room with Nancy. His black hair was flying, he hadn't shaved for days, and he was still dressed in his bargeman's dungarees. Nancy looked as though she's been pulled through a hedge backwards, but her face shone.

'Paris has fallen. Most of the Low Countries. London's largely in our hands. Goebbels is dead.'

'Good God,' I cried. 'It's all over.'

'Not quite,' said Kit, grinning under that black thatch of his like a madman, 'but we've got them on the run.'

Kennedy drew on his cigarette, stood and extended his hand. 'Admiral'. If he was pleased to see Kit again he concealed it well.

Kit was like a gushing stream. 'Kitson's got most of the West End, Guderian the East. House-to-house fighting. It's Stalingrad and Moscow all over again. Brunner's dead, too.'

'Wonderful,' I said. Other than the rumours I had picked

up in Preston and Arden, I had heard no news from any reliable source since Blenheim. I had hardly dared to believe that things could have gone so well.

'Antwerp, Bruges and Amsterdam have all gone,'Nancy put in. 'Lyon's in the hands of the *maquis*.[i]The Jerries have fallen back to Geneva.'

'That'll please the Swiss,' I said. 'Sitting on their chocolate bars while the heavens fell around them.'[ii]

'Brought the Geiger-counter, too,' said Kit, as though this was the icing on the cake. 'Where are the girls? Having their afternoon nap?'

I could hardly bear to puncture this balloon of euphoria. Kit, though, was not entirely insensitive to social nuance. He had noticed a lack of enthusiasm in Kennedy's manner. The stream gurgled to a halt with the last interrogative.

'I've blown it,' said Kennedy simply. He described the events of the morning. Kit and Nancy listened with ever-lengthening faces. At the end Kit said charitably, 'I should say you'd been duped.' Kennedy did not seem much consoled. 'Either way,' he said, 'they've gone.'

i A term for the French resistance.

ii An allusion to traditional Swiss neutrality.

V2

There was a long silence as the two parties digested what they'd been told. Eventually, I asked, 'Who's behind this? Skorzeny? Himmler?'

'What does it matter?' said Kennedy listlessly.

Kit asked Kennedy to run over the details of the ambush once again. We went out onto the *Boston*'s flag deck the better to see where it had all happened. The promise of the morning had not been fulfilled. There was a heavy bank of clouds in the west, the waters of the loch were a dull grey, and the air was sharp. Kennedy set the scene.

'Quite an operation,' observed Kit. 'You were lured here by the promise of the bomb, allowed to capture the base and then surprised. Lucky for Skorzeny that the princesses decided to come ashore.'

'Where was Skorzeny hiding?' someone asked.

'Somewhere in the U-boat, I guess,' hazarded Kennedy.

Kit nodded. 'All sorts of odd spaces on a sub. Not one of Skorzeny's little freelance ops, I'd say.'

'Why?' asked Kennedy, with some signs of interest in his voice.

'Too organised. By inclination Skorzeny's a lone wolf. I'm still not convinced that snatching Margaret and Elizabeth at the Tower was more than a bit of opportunism. Perhaps someone tipped him off. Apart from anything else, this one involves the Kriegsmarine. U-Boats are quite difficult to get hold of. I know. I've tried.'

I'd forgotten that Kit had reason to know the Kriegsmarine. It was Admiral Raeder who had had him extricated from the Gestapo.

'So?' I said.

'Major operation requiring official political blessing,' opined Kit. 'I'd lay it at Himmler's door. Perhaps via Brunner.'

'Thought you said Brunner was dead.'

'In his office,' said Kit, smiling. 'Killed while trying to escape. Doesn't mean he didn't do Himmler's bidding.'

We stared out over the grey water. It was difficult to feel that Brunner's death was much of a loss to civilisation. I thought of our last meeting in the War Office, and another thought at once crossed my mind. 'I wonder if there's paper trail.'

Kennedy had been moodily grinding a cigarette butt into the deck. At this he looked up. 'How d'you mean?'

'Oh, I just thought there might be some notes or records in Brunner's office. Jerries are very punctilious about plans. Might suggest where Skorzeny's off to.'

'Worth a shot?' asked Kennedy.

'Worth getting on to Kitson,' I said. 'Got a telex, Commander?'

'Sure,' said Kennedy, with a return to something of his old manner.

'Leave it to me.'

I composed a suitable message for General Kitson, whom I knew of old. We had messed together at Bovington[i] just after the war, and he was a sound cove. A bit gruff, perhaps, man of few words. I think in his twenties he was the youngest MFH in the country. Best judge of horse-flesh I've ever met. Less good with women.

One of Kennedy's ensigns took me down a couple of decks into the radio shack or whatever they called it. I drafted something suitable and got the operator — a lad who looked about 16 — to send it. Back on deck I emerged to see Kennedy and Kit down on the quay. They were fossicking[ii] about with a metal box about the size of a case of wine. It had a pattern of holes on one side, a little like the loudspeaker grille on a radiogram. I clattered down the gangway and joined them.

'This your Geiger-counter?' I asked Kit.

i An army training camp in Dorset, established in 1916.

ii Literally to search for gold, metaphorically anything of value.

'Picked it up in Risley[i] on the way over. Can't get it to work.'

Kennedy seemed equally bemused. Funny, I'd always thought the Americans very technically minded, what with refrigerators and so on. Never saw what was wrong with a pantry myself. Eventually the Commander called down one of the engineers from the *Boston*. As he did so it began to rain. We left him to it and retreated to the bridge, where we could keep an eye on developments. The engineer was a little fellow with glasses, a stoop and one of the most ill-fitting uniforms I'd ever seen. He put the box on a trolley and wheeled it into the lee of the frigate. When he emerged with his prize it was trailing a cable. Someone else was engaged in paying this out. Why it needed two of them I couldn't say. The little chap wheeled the box up and down the quay where *U-511* had been berthed, and examined the dials. He did the same behind the U-boat where the tow had lain; then up and down the railway line. A few minutes later he was up on the bridge with his report: 'Needed plugging in and switching on, sir.'

'Quite,' said Kit.

'Thinking of having kids?' continued the engineer in that strange drawl that infected the *Boston*'s crew.

'Enough already, thanks,' said Kit. He'd had sired a number of children by different mothers.

Nancy scowled.

'Good,' said the little man, not at all over-awed. 'Day down there and you'd be firing blanks.'

'Please explain,' said Kennedy tersely.

'Quay's swimming with radioactivity. Don't know what they've had there. Just keep away from it. Alpha, beta, gamma rays. Horrible.'

'Where precisely?' I asked.

'Not much where the sub was. Loads behind her. Bit less on the flat-bed cars.'

So that was it. We'd found what Kennedy was pleased to call the smoking gun. The bomb — or bombs — had been here

---

i Pioneering centre for nuclear physics on the outskirts of Manchester.

— or if they hadn't, something jolly nasty had been. Within the hour Kennedy had had the *Boston* moved to the far side of the harbour. The quay where *U-511* had been moored was roped off, and the flat-beds were corralled in a siding.

*

I had also heard from General Kitson. He had made an oversight. The men dispatched to search the late Hauptsturmführer Brunner's office could not read German. However, they had found some pictures and diagrams that he felt might be of interest. So intriguing were they, he wired, that they were being flown straight up to Faslane. He thought a plane now had a decent chance of getting though. They would be here by the morning. We seemed to be making some progress after the catastrophe. Kennedy, with an air of someone girding his loins for a decidedly unpleasant undertaking, talked of signalling the President. We would have to do the same with the Prime Minister. The news would have to be broken to them both. One missing atom bomb. Two missing princesses. Stated like that, it sounded bald. It would have to be dressed up a bit, I thought.

*

Kennedy found us some bunks in the *Boston* and the stewards put together a passable meal. I'd forgotten the US Navy was 'dry'.[ii] Kit and Nancy had not. Our 'beefburgers' were washed down with a decent malt — a drink that had the undesirable effect of increasing Kennedy's depression. Kit and I both tried to rouse him, the former with some success. Kit had once stood as Conservative candidate for Devonport, a candidacy fatally flawed by the stories circulating about his private life, not all untrue.

Kennedy's father, the Ambassador Joseph Kennedy, had

ii The consumption of alcohol on board U.S. Navy vessels was prohibited by General Order 99, effective
1 July 1914, issued by Secretary of the Navy Josephus Daniels.

ensured that politics were his children's meat and drink. After the navy, the Commander himself intended to follow suit. As far as tact and loyalty permitted, he was critical of his father's antisemitism and Anglophobia; he talked, as the evening went on and the malt loosened his tongue, of his enthusiasm for the challenges posed by the end of the war. He was no isolationist, and envisaged the United States playing a major part in rebuilding the Old World.

Kit's political ideas were always tinged with fascism, as of course is the whole Navy's. Still, after Kennedy had retired to his bunk, even he conceded that the Commander was a good sort. Nancy was less convinced. He didn't seem very sympathetic to the plight of the princesses, she said. As she pointed out, though the *Boston* wasn't exactly a feather bed, the princesses were likely to be having even less fun on *U-511*.

*

The following morning — according to my diary 9 February — I slept late and woke with the devil of a hangover. I think Kennedy's 'beefburgers' must have disagreed with me. That or the malt. I found Kit in the mess, putting away a disgusting mixture of eggs, tomatoes and something called hash browns. His table manners didn't equate with his rank at all. There was no sign of the courier from General Kitson. For the rest of the morning Kit, Nancy and I kicked our heels. Whatever happened, the *Boston* would be setting sail later that day. Kennedy and her C/O — a shadowy figure who was confined to his quarters with a serious stomach complaint and who we barely saw throughout the voyage — had plenty to busy himself with preparing for her return across the Atlantic, fuelling her, dismantling her trappings and seeing what fresh food could be scavenged from the base. We could do nothing but wait and hope the Jerries didn't turn up. Rumour was that they had their hands full in Glasgow.

It was not long before lunch when the courier finally appeared. Despite the fact that the whole of West London was

190

supposedly in Kitson's hands, the Boche were still holding out in Ealing, Acton and Uxbridge.[i] The courier had eventually reached Hendon at nine, having set off from the War Office at first light. Still he was here, and with him his dispatches. We told him to wait in the ratings' mess lest there was a return message. Then we summoned Kennedy and started sifting the papers.

As befitted the rather scant qualifications of those whom Kitson had selected for the task, they were a pretty mixed bag. Most had clearly attracted attention because they were plans, diagrams or sketches. They were more or less comprehensible whether you understood German or not. From our point of view, the majority of the stuff was dross. Plans of an armaments factory in Solihull, of Dover Castle and the Thames forts, of the airfields defending the Home Counties, and so on. A number were clearly captured British documents. Some, of a later date, seemed to be the product of the Jerries' own efforts. Half a dozen were of greater interest. There was a plan of Horse Guards Parade that detailed arrangements for the ceremony I'd attended on the thirteenth anniversary of Hitler's accession to power and – as it turned out – his assassination. A plan of the Tower seemed to date from the turn of the century, but had been amended by a later hand. Some of the notes were in German, some in English. Perhaps most compelling was a plan of Sandringham. It was of recent date and of sufficiently large scale to include the old stables from which we had made our foray into the house in what seemed another lifetime. Kennedy was fascinated by the Sandringham map. He insisted on showing us in detail how he had disposed his men before seizing the house. I was more interested in why the map was in Brunner's possession, as was Kit. It might argue foreknowledge of Skorzeny's destination after his departure from the Tower in the *Schnellboot*. There again, as Nancy pointed out, it might not. As we understood it, chance alone had taken the *Schnellboot* to Thornham, thence its crew to Sandringham.[ii]

i This is accurate. See Basil Liddell Hart, *The Last Battle* (1952).

ii A point never resolved in the narrative. See Epilogue.

There were two other items. These were the ones to which Kitson had, in an accompanying note, especially directed our attention and which he felt justified the risk of sending a courier. He had added that though one was comprehensible in terms of our observations at Faslane — as he understood them — the other was not. The relationship between the two was not apparent, but they had been found clipped together.

The first sketch was curiously amateurish. It showed in elevation a submarine towing a big capsule or canister, almost a third as long as the submarine itself. It depicted precisely what we had seen with our own eyes the previous day, though it added nothing to our understanding.

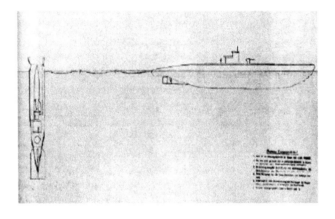

There were two accompanying drawings, clearly part of the same set, which did clarify things. One showed the capsule up-ended, at 90 degrees from its towing position, one end pointing to the sea-bed, the other to the sky. The second was a large-scale cut-away drawing showing the interior of the huge canister. This showed that it was, in fact, something very, very different. It wasn't a submarine at all.

Its shape, though, was instantly familiar from the propaganda films produced by the Boche of Stalingrad and Moscow. It was a thing of elegance and grace, even beauty.

V2

A sharp-pointed nose swelling in two parabolas to the fins forty or fifty feet below. Within the capsule was a V2 rocket, the *Vergeltungswaffe 2* or 'revenge' weapon that had been the scourge of Chuikov in Stalingrad, Paulus's masterstroke in the course of Operation Blau, in Rommel's hands the death-knell of Zhukov in Moscow. The whole caboodle was nothing less than a marine launcher for the V2.

*

For a few moments we sat round that table in silence. To give him his due, Kit was the man who saw in a moment the implications of the whole thing. 'What's the range of a V2?' he asked.

'Not far, I don't think,' said Nancy. 'Couple of hundred miles? Something like that. I took a dekko at some of Brunner's papers once.'

'Couldn't reach Tokyo from Berlin, then?' asked Kennedy, himself displaying a smidgeon of strategy. Perhaps he thought the German-Japanese axis would turn on itself.

'Nothing like,' I said. 'It's thousands of miles. Anyway, Himmler would hardly want to bomb Hirohito, would he?'

'Toyko's on the coast,' said Kit, enunciating each word very slowly and clearly.

It took some moments to register the absolute enormity of what he had said. Kennedy was there before me. 'How many of the world's major cities are within two hundred miles of the sea?'

'Not all,' said Kit.

'No,' I said slowly, thinking things through. 'Most, though.'

'San Francisco, Los Angeles,' suggested Kennedy, 'not Chicago.'

'Washington and New York,' I added. Nancy chipped in with London and Paris.

'Now all within range of V2s,' summarised Kit. 'It means that the Atlantic Ocean no longer exists. It's as if New York was as close to London as Paris or Berlin. Time was Berlin could declare war on the US but it couldn't actually wage war on the States. Take an armada across the Atlantic? No way. Use bombers to bomb New York? No way. It was simple. It was just too far, half a world away. Now that's all changed. It changes the whole face of war. It shrinks the world. It's that big.'[i]

Kennedy pushed his chair back from the table. 'So *that's* what Skorzeny's up to.'

'Presumably with Himmler's blessing,' I added.

'Where?' asked Kennedy. 'London? Where's he going?'

'Any of the world's capital cities,' said Kit. 'London would suit very well, just at present. 'Very *Götterdammerüng*.'[ii]

'No, Kit,' I said. 'Not all the world's cities. It would have to be within range of the U-boat. Which presumably doesn't have limitless fuel.'

'And an enemy one,' added Nancy. 'Has to be an enemy city.'

'Declared or undeclared,' added Kit, I supposed for the benefit of Kennedy. No American would forget Pearl Harbor.

Nancy picked up the plans and re-examined them. As she did so, the final sheet became detached from the clip and fluttered to the ground. It was a small-scale map of a city.

This was the final sheet to which Kitson had drawn my attention. On it had been imposed a series of concentric circles radiating from a central point. I wondered for a moment where I had seen something like this before. It took me back to the trenches. I handed it to Kit.

'Seen one of these?'

---

i Conway was absolutely right. The Nazis were pioneering technology that led to the most important development in strategic weaponry in the 20th century: the submarine-launched ballistic missile.

ii Literally 'the twilight of the gods.' The last opera in Wagner's Ring cycle, used here by Conway in the looser meaning of a disastrous conclusion to events.

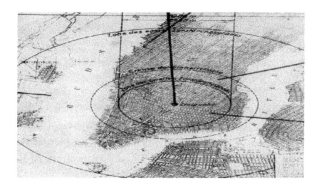

Kit glanced at it. 'Can't say I have.'

'CEP,' I said. 'Circular Error Probable. Shows how likely you are to hit the target when you drop your shell. We used it quite effectively in the Albert Salient in 1917.'

'Big shell,' observed Kit.

I retrieved the map from him. There were half a dozen rings, so I supposed I could see what he meant, more or less. 'Well, it's not scaled. I suppose those things are city blocks.'

He looked out to the grey sea. 'Still looks like about a mile in all directions around the point of contact. Mile radius. Two diameter,' said Kit.

Nancy made the obvious suggestion. 'An atom shell.'

'I think the V2s in Moscow killed everything within a couple of hundred feet of ground zero,' said Kit. A couple of hundred feet in every direction.'

'And how many were killed?' asked Kennedy.

'Hundreds. But it depends entirely on the density of the population. It would kill more in high rises. Places like Chicago. One hit a cinema in Moscow, so the Reds said. Killed five hundred odd.'

'An atom bomb would kill *thousands*, then,' said Nancy, her grey-green eyes wide open.

'I think you've forgotten your maths,' said Kit. He tapped

his finger on the map, 'The area within that circle rises exponentially with the radius. Think that was the phrase. Not thousands. Tens of thousands.'

'*Just with one bomb*?' asked Nancy.

'Think so,' said Kit. 'One bomb.'

There was complete silence in that little cabin. Then someone, I can't remember who, said: 'It'd be like the Somme, over and over and over again.'

'Which city?' asked Kennedy.

Kit scrutinised the map. 'Doesn't say. Perhaps it's just for scaling purposes. Anyway, if it is a particular city, it doesn't mean old Skorzeny's going there. Just at the moment I'd put my money on west London. Do a lot of damage. Providing it doesn't hit Hyde Park.'

'Lemme have a look,' said Kennedy.

Kit handed him the map. As there were no street names on it, it could have been oriented in one of four ways. Kennedy put it on the table and turned it first one way, then another. This way round the city took the form of a wedge. It tapered, I suppose, from north to south and was bounded by the sea — or perhaps a river — on each side. I can't say I've got a photographic memory of the world's cities. It wasn't London, Berlin or Paris, three cities defined by the sinuosity of their rivers. Perhaps it was Hong Kong, an outpost of the empire I've never had the good fortune to visit. I was rather of Kit's party. It was an imaginary city.

'See this,' said Kennedy abruptly. He pointed at one of the narrow lines running up and down the map. 'That's Fifth Avenue.' He moved his finger. 'Central Park. Harlem.' His fingers moved back down. 'The Hudson River … Tribeca, Wall Street.'

He had engaged Kit's attention. The Admiral pointed to the west side of the map. 'Ellis Island, surely?'

'Yes, Admiral,' said Kennedy, with what seemed a tinge of irony in his voice. 'It's New York.'

There was silence again, broken only by the lap of the waves. Then Kit said, 'Oh, I shouldn't think Skorzeny would

196

bomb New York. Even if Himmler does think you stole his princesses. It's a very long way to go and Germany hasn't declared war on the States to my knowledge. Besides, quite often those V2s don't work.'

There may have been a hint of levity in Kit's voice. There was pure anger in Kennedy's response. 'Care to *bet* on it, Admiral?'

The King's Last Word

'We're just about here.' Kennedy indicated a small pencil cross on the chart of the Atlantic. The map was divided into squares on the naval grid square system. The one under his finger was AJ 3996.

It was 20 February. The *Boston* was ten days out of Faslane and had been making slow going against a westerly that had at times blown up to Force seven. The four of us — myself, Nancy, Kit and Kennedy himself — were holed up in the tiny steel grey cabin that the *Boston*'s ailing C/O had designated as our ops room. It was somewhere under the frigate's bridge, too close to the water-line for my liking. President Truman, in his role of C-in-C US Forces, stared down at us from one wall. On the other, a porthole gave one moment on to leaden skies, the next onto the heavy Atlantic swell. I had felt decidedly queasy since we had steamed out of Faslane. Nancy's skin had gone the colour of her uniform almost immediately we cleared Garroch Head in the Firth of Clyde, and she still looked pretty awful. As professional sailors Kit and the Commander feigned immunity to anything less than a gale, but I couldn't see how they stood it — the monotony of the rolling and the shuddering crash with which the *Boston* perpetually buried her bows into the seas, the furniture in the little room continuously creaking and sliding and occasionally breaking right away. You couldn't drink or eat anything without it slopping over your clothes, and you couldn't sleep without being thrown from one side of the bunk to the other.

'Where's Skorzeny got to, then?' asked Nancy, for what seemed the umpteenth time.

On the assumption that *U-511* was indeed making for

New York, Kennedy had been liaising with the Pentagon — that strange new building in Virginia housing the Defense Department — on projecting the course and passage time of the U-boat. They put us onto F-21, the US Navy Atlantic Section Intelligence Center based, I believe, on the old submarine Tracking Room of the British Admiralty. We knew the hour of the Colonel's departure from Faslane to the minute. Everything thenceforward was hedged with uncertainty. Her speed on the surface and underwater; the relative times she would spend snorkelling[i] beneath the waves and forging ahead on the surface in the brutal Atlantic swell; the extent to which she would be slowed by the drag of the V2 capsule; how much the westerly would hold her back. Oddly enough, it was the Americans who had managed to find themselves someone who recalled the voyage of the *Deutschland* in 1916. There hadn't been much talk of this at the time, but Kit professed to know all about her. A blockade-breaking German cargo submarine that had made a couple of voyages between Bremen and Connecticut the year before the US joined the war. The record they found was the first of these. She had left Bremerhaven on 23 June and had arrived in Baltimore on 8 July. A couple of weeks. What sort of a benchmark it was no one could say, but it was a start.

'Can't be closer than here.' Kennedy — glancing up at Nancy - indicated a point on our own track to New York a couple of hundred miles to the east in square AK4599. 'Or further than here.' This was a cross another hundred and fifty miles on.

'If he's not off Start Point,' said Kit. He remained to be convinced of Skorzeny's destination, professing to believe that *U-511* was heading for London up the Channel, past

---

i The snorkel is the tube that allows a submarine to draw air from the surface for the use of its diesel engines while under the water.

the Devon headland. He had failed to persuade Churchill of this argument. Churchill and the President had convinced themselves that Skorzeny was on Himmler's mission to annihilate New York as one last throw against the insurrection.[i] Only in some respects could I hope they were right.

'When do we reckon to overhaul her?' I asked.

'If she's making good time, it's still looking like barely before she's in hailing distance of the Statue of Liberty.'

'And the range?'

'They're still saying 200 miles,' said Kit.

The Pentagon and F-21 had conceded that its intelligence from the Russians on the V2 was patchy to say the least, its various sources inconsistent, and the figures manipulated for political purposes. According to Kennedy, there were those who supposed it would reflect poorly on the great socialist republic if the Jerries' rockets were much in advance of their own. 'Two hundred miles,' confirmed Kennedy. 'If I were him I wouldn't come closer in if I could avoid it.'

Kit pursed his lips. I was more concerned with practicalities. 'How's the reception committee?' I asked.

Kennedy raised his eyebrows and had the decency to look embarrassed, as well he might. 'All over the place.'

*

The *Boston* was a long shot. The prospects of our overtaking and actually finding the U-boat in the wastes of the Atlantic were remote. According to my friend Allen Dulles, when the President, acting on the counsel of both Secretary of State Byrnes and the Prime Minister, had accepted that the threat to the Eastern seaboard was genuine, the Pentagon had

---

i Himmler and Skorzeny are dead and the German archives entirely silent on this matter. However, Albert Speer entirely supports the contention in his memoir *Inside the Third Reich*. The domestic figures surrounding Himmler in his last days also support the contention, as does the historian Hugh Trevor-Roper in *The Last Days of Heinrich Himmler* (1947).

mobilised everything in sight. This order was promulgated on 12 February. In the week that had since passed, that had proved to be remarkably little. Those Pacific Fleet units that had survived Tokyo Bay had returned whence they came, to Pearl Harbor and San Diego. The Atlantic Fleet east coast ports, principally Norfolk and Charlestown, had volunteered half a dozen frigates and a clutch of minesweepers. Inconceivably, none had yet left port. The naval air stations at Newport and Groton had dispatched half a dozen fruitless patrols. The VLRAs,[ii] equipped with submarine detecting equipment flown in from the west coast, were right at the limit of their range at the edge of the Air Gap[iii]. I felt that Skorzeny had a very strong hand and said so.

Kit had begged to differ. 'He's got to do four things. Get within range of his target undetected. Successfully launch his missile. Ensure the thing finds Manhattan. Get it to go off. Hundred to one against. D'you know that thirty per cent of their torpedoes were duds?[iv] I'd be surprised if the V2s did any better. Bit more complicated as technology goes. '

'Bullshit,' said Kennedy. I had some sympathy with his point of view. It was, after all, his country. 'What happened in Stalingrad and Moscow?'[v]

In the absence of Navy Cut, Kit had obtained a supply of Lucky Strikes from the *Boston*'s stores. He lit up before replying. 'I agreed with you some time ago that we should plan for other eventualities.'

ii Very Long Range Aircraft. These were developed in the course of the Pacific War by the US Navy for reconnaissance and submarine detection duties.

iii The area in mid-Atlantic that could be patrolled from neither side of the Ocean because of the limited range of the aircraft. The VLRAs were designed to close the gap.

iv According to Kriegsmarine records recently discovered by the naval historian Richard Woodman, this is — if anything — an underestimate.

v See page 193. The collapse of Stalingrad and Moscow following the deployment of the V2s.

It was time to change the subject. 'Any word on the Rules of Engagement?'

In some respects these were the nub of our problem, or at least the chief among our many problems. Himmler — it will be remembered — had not declared war on the US, nor had President Truman on the Reich. Technically, a state of friendly relations still existed between the two great Powers. Ambassador von Ribbentrop was still in Washington, his counterpart Arthur Bliss Lane in Berlin.[i] We had profound suspicions about Skorzeny and his mission, but Himmler had not actually shown his hand. He had quite a lot to do anyway with the insurrection in Europe and the murmurs of revolt at home. Rumour had it that Rommel[ii] was mounting a coup. For all we really knew, Skorzeny's voyage might be a sea-trial or a voyage into exile.

For these reasons the circumstances in which a unit of the US Navy might open fire upon a unit of the Kriegsmarine were tightly circumscribed. For the *Boston* to do so would be an act of war which would have momentous political consequences. There were, as we now know, a host of advisers counselling Truman in the Oval Office. After Tokyo Bay the United States was a bruised and emotionally defeated nation. At least among the populace, there was little appetite to re-open the war on an eastern front. It is fair to say to say that in the ten days since our intelligence had reached Washington, those sentiments and the advisers who articulated them had stayed the President's hand. So said Mr Dulles. On the other hand, there were those who appreciated the gravity of the threat to New York and who counselled decisive action. Among those to whom the President listened with the greatest attention was Prime Minister Churchill himself. On the morning of which I am now writing, 20 February, he had flown from the bedside of the King in Ottawa to speak in person with the President.

i Respectively the German and American ambassadors.

ii The Potsdam coup of 23 February.

202

The King's Last Word

And therein, like a doll within a doll, lay the kernel of the question. In the remote possibility that the *Boston* actually located *U-511,* the Rules of Engagement as they stood would prevent us giving battle. We could not, as the US Navy standing orders were drafted, stop her unleashing her missile on New York — if indeed it was there that she was heading.

It had been Nancy, four or five days into our voyage, as the full implications of our pursuit dawned on us, who pointed to our conundrum. 'What if we catch her?'

'What do you think?' Kennedy had responded testily. He didn't like women on a ship, I sometimes thought. 'Wait till she fires?'

Kit had been looking out of the port-hole. Without turning round he said, 'What price the princesses then, Commander?'

He turned and faced the three of us, sitting at that little table in the *Boston*'s grey cell on the wintry Atlantic, still a week or so steaming from New York. No one said a thing.

Then Kit answered his own question. Like a poker player laying down a royal flush, Kit said simply, 'New York.'

*

There were, of course, greater minds than ours pondering this question. The technical bods[iii] in the Pentagon were speculating on the degrees of separation between the U-boat and the V2 capsule, and whether it would be possible to knock out one without damaging the other. The problem lay in our virtually complete ignorance of the submarine launching or fire control system. The Soviets had been reasonably helpful on the intelligence they had garnered on land-based V2 rocket launchers around Moscow and Stalingrad, some of which seemed applicable to launching at sea. In many respects you had to take your hat off to the Boche in getting so far. Launching a V2 on land seemed quite complicated enough, what with fuelling it up with stuff like

iii Bodies and by transference people. Contemporary slang.

alcohol and liquid oxygen, getting it pointed in the right direction and firing it.

It seemed that the *Feuerleitpanzer* or fire control vehicle was generally placed within 250 yards of the rocket, but the Department of Defense had also hastily assembled a team of their own rocket engineers and asked them how they would engineer such a system. There was no guarantee that they would reach the same conclusions as their counterparts in Peenemünde.[i] They just might, though, and in the circumstances the faintest of chances was a hope.

On the morning of which I am writing, the conclusions reached were tentative and about as discouraging as possible. Obviously enough, everyone thought that the U-boat would remove itself from the immediate vicinity of the capsule before the launch. Likewise they all assumed that to initiate the launch she would have to be within a quarter of a mile or so of the capsule, and even that was assuming quite a degree of sophistication of the fire control system. And then, as one of those men in white coats in the Pentagon pointed out, if the *Boston* opened up on the capsule with her 10-pounder, would the capsule sink, explode or cause an atomic explosion to be unleashed? As he pointed out, if it was the latter, it didn't really matter if the U-boat was 250 yards away or two and a half miles. The princesses would still be dead.

It all depended on the firing mechanism of the bomb, he said.

'Very helpful,' Kit had commented ironically.

'Yes, Admiral,' Kennedy had said testily, for the two professional seamen were now almost constantly at loggerheads. 'And what are the lives of the U-boat crew and your two damned princesses against the lives of the two million people who live in Manhattan?'

*

i The Army Research Center Peenemünde (Heeresversuchsstelle Peenemünde) in the village of that name on the Baltic island of Usedom.Here the development work on the V2 rocket was undertaken.

The King's Last Word

It was this question that the Prime Minister had been obliged to put to the King.

As Churchill later told me, it was both a constitutional question for the King in his role as monarch and a personal one for him in his role as father. Simple, really. Should the *Boston* locate the *U-511*, on his decision would hinge the future of the free world … It was a nice question.

Having been given the King's response, the Prime Minister was at once flown by the USAAF to Washington for his summit with President Truman. On this meeting hinged the Rules of Engagement.

'What'll Truman do?' asked Nancy.

'God knows,' I said.

'He can't lift the Rules of Engagement,' said Nancy, sweeping the hair out of her eyes. It had grown rather long since I had first seen her out of uniform, on the beach at Foulness a fortnight previously.

'The US is an independent sovereign power,' said Kennedy. 'The President is answerable to no one but the American people. He can do what he likes.'

'Nice point, Commander,' said Kit, drawing on his cigarette. 'Don't you think the President would find himself in breach of international law — among other things — if he knowingly ordered the death of the heirs to our throne? I've known countries go to war over less, haven't you?'

I shrugged my shoulders. I could see absolutely no way out of it. Conversation lapsed. Kennedy had wandered off towards the steps that led to the bridge.

Kit and I had another look at the chart. One of the watch keepers had drawn a semi-circle centred on New York and extending east out into the seaboard. Outside that line we assumed was beyond the range of the V2. Far within it, and Skorzeny's chances of being detected escalated. The intention of the putative 'reception committee' was to patrol just inside the line.

'Pi R squared,' said Kit.

'Beg your pardon,' I said. By this stage, having endured

his company virtually without relief for just nearly three weeks, I was inured to Kit talking nonsense.

'Relationship between the radius of the circle and its circumference. Remember your maths?'

'Vaguely,' I said. I had not enjoyed the subject at school.

'If the radius is 200 miles, the circumference of the circle is 3.142 x the diameter — twice the radius'

'Yes?' Kit at some stage in his career had been a gunnery officer on some wreck or other, so I suppose he knew what he was talking about. Most naval officers can neither count nor write.

Kit found a bit of paper. After a few moments he said: 'I make that 1257 miles. Though of course half of that's on land.'

'Quite a figure,' I said.

'Chances of picking him up in or around it are pretty small, I'd say,' agreed Kit. 'And I doubt whether the Yanks have been able to find an east coast unit that's had any experience of Anti-Submarine Warfare patrols.'

'Ah yes,' I said.

'Best chance is for the airborne patrols to pick him up using those fancy devices for spotting snorkelling subs. HF/DF[i] or something. I think the Yanks did quite well against the Japs in the Coral Sea in the end.'

'How d'you rate the chances?'

No one could have called Kit a thoughtful man, but this did seem to make him pause. It was few moments before he came back with, 'Twenty-five to one.'

Nancy had remained broodingly silent as we mulled over the position, curled up in the corner of our cell as the *Boston* rolled her way towards the oblivion that awaits us all. She said: 'Twenty-five to one against.'

Kit didn't seem to like the drift of this. 'I don't see how you can choose between Margaret and Elizabeth and Julia and half the population of New York.'

Before Nancy had time to reply, Kennedy strode into the room. His thin, ascetic face was like thunder. He bore in his

i High frequency direction finder: an early version of radar.

hands a slip of paper. This he handed to us without a word, and then he stalked out of the cabin.

Kit picked it up and read it to us. It was short and to some ears sweet. The Prime Minister and the President had met.

RULES OF ENGAGEMENT UNCHANGED. DO NOT ENGAGE *U-511*. REPEAT. RULES OF ENGAGEMENT UNCHANGED.

I began to wonder even then about the machinations behind this simple statement, and where the initiative lay between Washington and Ottawa, and between the various parties jockeying for position in the Oval Office.[ii]

Nancy looked up: 'Good.'

'Well old girl,' said Kit, with what seemed a not altogether consoling or helpful remark, 'let's hope push doesn't come to shove.'

---

ii As well the General might.

The Third Letter

I have to say that I don't believe I ever got to the bottom of the decision about the Rules of Engagement. At the risk of interrupting the narrative of the last days of our mission, here is such evidence as I have on the matter. This, Mr Dulles's final letter, is the best fix I believe we are going to get on it, at least until the 'official documents' are disclosed in thirty, seventy or a hundred years' time.[i] As with Mr Dulles's last letter, read into it what you will:

Allen Dulles
Director
Central Intelligence Agency
Room 3663
Rockefeller Centre
New York, New York

General Sir Max Quick
Chief of Imperial General Staff
The War Office
Whitehall
London West

27 March 1946

Dear Max
I'm using one of these fancy new dictaphones.[ii] Excuse the verbatims. I'll take your letter line by line.

i The Freedom of Information legislation does not apply to these papers.

ii The device for voice recording was trademarked as early as 1907. Not until 1946 was a wax cylinder on which the voice recorded replaced by a plastic belt. Hence Dulles description of the device as 'new.'

The Third Letter

First, I take your point. Given where we are now and what the Administration has already divulged. Given, too, it was a conversation between the President and the Prime Minister. Yes, I was there. Byrnes, too. Yes, of course, we thought it was the crux of the whole affair. Strange how things turn out, isn't it?

The President? I guess you see people's mettle in a crisis. Truman was, what, eleven months into the job? Barely got his feet under Roosevelt's desk. To have that thrown at you.

Jesus. An atomic attack on New York.

Just days to prepare for it. Jesus Christ. For a farm boy from Kansas. Maybe that was it. Didn't really get what it all meant. Maybe it was like Stalin. One death's a tragedy. A million a statistic.

Maybe he saw it that way. You couldn't tell. I couldn't.

The afternoon? Yes, the 14th. We'd got Kennedy's signal, what, three days before. Been through every gamut of emotion: Byrnes, myself, Truman and a host of hangers-on. Denial, fury, scepticism, acceptance, practicality.

Give Byrnes his due. It was James who pointed out some of the diplomatic complexities of where we were. President was all for blowing the U-boat straight out of the water. If we could find her, that is. Byrnes painted that picture of Europe on the cusp between the continuation of the dark ages and the enlightenment. Likes history, James. England the linch-pin. The King dying in the next few days. Says James: 'How would it look if the US murdered the heirs to the throne?'

'How would it look if Manhattan was toast?' the President replied tartly.

Still, he got the point. Said he didn't know what conundrum meant. He did, though.

Churchill? Couldn't get away from him. Mother was American, wasn't she? Knew what conundrum meant, the Prime Minister. Don't know how well he knew New York. Had nearly been killed by an auto there. Crossing Fifth Avenue in '31.

Couldn't teach him much about the Rules of Engagement,

either. Said he'd written the Royal Navy's himself in September 1913. Presume he had.[i]

Who suggested approaching the King? Could have been either. Came out of a conversation on the 15th. No minutes of the call. Minutes of the subsequent conversation. Just with Byrnes, I think. Who'd know the King's mind? Churchill, I guess. Who was the most manipulative? Interesting question. Hard call. If anything, I'd say the President. Churchill certainly agreed to approach the King.

No, I doubt whether it was a task he relished, Max. Ask a man permission to kill his two daughters? Ask a king permission to kill his heirs?

I ask you. Ask a dying man the same question. King didn't like the States. Perhaps he was like Stalin, too. Thought a couple of million New Yorkers a statistic. Could I blame him for saying 'no'? Did I blame him for saying 'no'?

As an American I couldn't forgive him. As a man, who could blame him? Seen lung cancer, Max? A horrible disease and a horrible death. Eats a man away. Gnaws at him.

'"Kill my daughters? *Kill my daughters?*"' Who could blame him?

Of course, Truman did for one. Who could blame *him*? Churchill flew down to tell him, himself. Halifax was left with the King.

First time President and Prime Minister had met. Not much in common you'd say. Farm boy from Kansas and Lord Randolph Churchill's eldest son. FDR and Churchill were thick as thieves. Perhaps they were both thieves, eh Max? Didn't make it easy for Truman.

Yes, blood on both their hands. Upwards of a hundred thousand New Yorkers or a couple of princesses.

A hundred thousand New Yorkers against a free Europe. That was Churchill's line.

Worth trying. Didn't wash. Churchill knew New York in a way Truman simply didn't know Europe. Sure, he was

i Entirely correct. See Martin Gilbert, *Churchill: A Life*.

in France at the end of the first war. 129th Field Artillery, I think. The Vosges and Verdun. Nothing more. London, Paris, Amsterdam, Berne, Berlin, Rome, Vienna. Heard of them, maybe. Places on a map. Nothing more.

What other cards could Churchill play?

Not much of a hand, really. The *Boston* was American. Kennedy was American. The picket boats were American. The Rules of Engagement were American. It was Truman's call.

Churchill's ace? Not that I know of, Max. I was there. Discount the rumours.[ii]

I was there. Byrnes was there. Believe me, Max, I was there.

Halifax? Yes. Called from the Oval Office. Yes, after the *Custer* was sunk. Halifax was told to tell the King about the *Custer* and ask again.

Why? Why did he change his mind?

Who knows? Who knows what goes through the mind of a dying man? Who knows what goes through the mind of a dying king?

ii See epilogue.

The Custer

Over the course of the next six days[i] we ploughed east towards New York, following the 45th parallel. The westerly moderated slightly to Force 5 and the *Boston* punched less uncomfortably through the waters. Aboard, the mood was tense and sour. The crew — pre-war servicemen larded with 'hostilities only' east coast fishermen — was supposedly in complete ignorance of our mission but clearly smelt intrigue. They had now been bucketing around the Atlantic for a month, had entertained the heirs to the throne, had lost their C/O to illness, and had now gained a couple of British brass hats and a girl. It had been impossible to conceal my own identity or Kit's, and there was vulgar speculation about Nancy's role in the affair, personal and professional. My attempts to conceal this from Nancy were fruitless. Kennedy, meanwhile, devoted his time to intriguing on the Rules of Engagement, mainly — I believe — through the offices of his father. I found it simultaneously impossible to blame and impossible not to blame him.

I'd never seen Nancy so in the dumps. She couldn't get the princesses in that horrible tin fish out of her head: sealed in a metal container under the Atlantic with a bunch of Jerries on a voyage to annihilate New York, your ultimate fate unknown. Rape or murder perfectly plausible outcomes. They knew what had happened to the Romanovs. Why should the Nazis turn out any better than the Bolsheviks? Look at their record. For all Elizabeth and Margaret knew, they were on the way to their own Ekaterinburg.[ii] What would Skorzeny have done to them? If you are prepared to sacrifice your own life, a submarine's a very easy thing to sink. Kept them under guard

i Apparently February 20-26.

ii The city in central Russia where the Bolsheviks assassinated the Russian Royal family in 1918.

day and night? Drugged them? As a last resort would he kill them?

Even Kit turned snappy. He seemed unconsoled by the continuing absence of any atomic attack on London, or indeed the fairly encouraging news that filtered through to us from time to time about the progress of the rising in England. These were the days when the Boche still held the City and the East End and such cities as there are in the eastern counties: Peterborough, Norwich and Lincoln. Yet Herbert Morrison[iii] and his crew had set themselves up as a 'provisional government' and there was plenty of evidence that the tide really seemed to be turning our way. There was a fair amount of traffic in the wireless office, and it was Kennedy's practice to put up a resumé of the day's events at four bells when the watches changed. This kept the men chattering in the messes in that strange drawl of theirs.

As to Skorzeny, we were restricted to hints. As we closed the eastern seaboard and the Air Gap narrowed, the patrolling Anti Submarine Warfare aircraft of the US Coastguard were able to spend more and more time over what we assumed to be his track. He was never spotted, but there were a sufficient number of questionable HF/DF fixes to convince some that *U-511* really was on her way to New York. Our own radar seemed perpetually on the blink. Knowing Skorzeny and having witnessed the U-boat's departure from Faslane, I have to say I was of that party. Nemesis was fast approaching, and I saw absolutely no way out of our conundrum. In so far as I had a hope it was the rather cowardly one that the US seaborne reception committee, by 26th February mustered into a rather more respectable force of a couple of squadrons of destroyers and frigates led by the cruiser *Quincy*,[iv] would be faced with the unthinkable dilemma. As it was, our own position on Kennedy's chart and the putative position of *U-511* drew ever

---

iii Herbert Stanley Morrison, 1888-1965, Labour politician.

iv A 14,500 ton Baltimore class heavy cruiser.

closer as we neared the US coast. If the Pentagon's calculations on Skorzeny's speed and course had been correct, we would overhaul him at 11.30 GMT on the 27th.

*

An hour before the time, the four of us gathered on the bridge. After the ops room it seemed quite a spacious affair, a steel box perhaps twenty feet square with a low ceiling and a good deal of armoured glass. It was lined with rows of telephones, voice-pipes, radar-repeaters and gunnery-control instruments, with a big chartroom at the back. Normally there were just a couple of lookouts, one on each wing of the bridge. As well as a pair of signalmen, two officers-of-the-watch, two ASDIC/ hydrophone[i] operators and a bridge messenger, Kennedy had drafted two extra lookouts.[ii] The whole bridge party had been told merely that we were looking for a U-boat. Nothing more.

I glanced at the ship's chronometer, a big brass affair on a grey bulkhead. It was just after 10.45. That was clear. Where we were was less obvious. As far as I was concerned we might just as well have been thirty miles west of Faslane as 300 miles from the eastern seaboard of the US. The reception committee picket boats were below the horizon to the north-west and south-west. Absolutely nothing was in sight. The day was overcast, with the cloud down to 1,000 feet. The ASW aircraft patrols were grounded. It was still blowing Force 4 or 5, and the *Boston,* moving at slow ahead, wallowed horribly in the long grey greasy Atlantic swell. I don't suppose anyone on the bridge actually expected to see the U-boat's snorkel on the horizon, but everyone was certainly looking. Personally I'd call the Americans' attitude to discipline rather casual. It was certainly less formal than our own, and there was generally

i Devices that use sound to detect submarines.

ii This is confusing. With the *Boston*'s C/O confined to the sick-bay, Kennedy appears to have assumed command of the frigate.

a fair amount of chatter unrelated to the job in hand. That morning, however, there was absolutely none. The whole bridge party stood in total silence, scanning the grey wastes that streamed slowly past the warship.

The chronometer crept slowly past the hour, then towards the half. There was still nothing. Nothing on the hydrophones, nothing on ASDIC, nothing on the radar, nothing visible to the naked eye. I looked up at the chronometer. It was 11.26. My eyes met Nancy's. I shrugged. The delicate second hand, a black needle, dragged its weary course round the dial. Once, twice, thrice. Then a fourth time. It was 11.30. Seven bells struck. Kennedy consulted his own wrist-watch, then the chronometer. Then he put his glasses back to his eyes. The minutes ticked by. 11.45 came and went. Then noon. It was eight bells.[iii] Scarcely a word was passed. Kennedy left it till 2.30 before he ordered the extra lookouts to stand down. He turned to us with that open face of his and grimaced slightly. 'Dammit.'

Kit was lounging in that irritating, rather negligent manner of his on a console at the front of the bridge, pulling a cigarette out of a packet. 'What did you expect?' he said. 'Surface and surrender?'

Kennedy was too much of a disciplinarian to rise to this in front of the men. He barked down the voice-pipe to the wheelhouse, 'Half-speed ahead.'

'Half speed ahead,' came the echo from the quartermaster.

Kennedy glanced south, up to the skies. 'Maybe it's clearing.'

The Commander may have been a better meteorologist than I, but this seemed like whistling in the wind. It was a desultory afternoon and evening. All sense of purpose seemed to have flown the *Boston*. Her home port was Norfolk, and the crew were clearly hankering to go home. Our orders from the White House were to press on to New York, but their logic seemed to be falling away, certainly as far as the crew went.

---

iii Bells are the strokes on the ship's bell that mark the passage of time.

Towards dusk, Kennedy told us an ASW airborne patrol had managed to get out of Newark. Other than that there was no news. I, for one, turned in early, leaving Nancy and Kit in the little ops room chewing over the chart. Kennedy was nowhere to be seen.

*

I was plucked out of oblivion by a rough shake on the shoulder. Kennedy, fully dressed, was bending over my bunk. 'We gotta fix.'

I was up like a flash, threw on my clothes and stumbled up to the bridge. By night, it had an eerie air. To avoid compromising the night vision of the lookouts and the officer-of-the-watch, the bridge was barely lit. Only the feeble glow of light from some of the instruments gave you enough to see and move. There was Nancy, slumped in a corner, fast asleep. Kit, looking more bedraggled than usual, joined us after a few moments. He had managed to put his blue service sweater on inside out. I glanced at the chronometer. It was 0434.[i]

'We're here,' said Kennedy, pointing on the chart.

I was surprised. We were in square AX 4386, not much more than 150 miles from New York. 'Here's the picket line we crossed yesterday. Here's the *Custer*.' He indicated one of the ships on the southern quadrant of the line. '*Custer's* got an early HF/DF set. Useless beyond 30 miles. The C/O had been briefed to look out for unusual contacts. At about 0200 he picked up one well outside the normal shipping lanes. Just about here.' He indicated a spot some twenty or so miles south-east of the *Custer*.

'Might be anything,' said Kit.

'Check,' agreed Kennedy. 'I know the C/O of *Custer*. Kennan. Good man. He talks to Norfolk. He asks what exactly he's supposed to be looking for. Hadn't been told till then. Big sub and a small sub, they say. Well, Kennan had been

216

in the ops room when the radar fix came up. Funny thing, interpreting radar. Can't do it myself any more than can Kennan. But Kennan *did* ask the radar rating if there was anything distinctive about the fix.'

'Yes?' said Nancy, suddenly alert. I hadn't even noticed she'd woken up.

'"No sir", was what he said. Then, after a couple of moments, he thought again. "Mebbe two objects very close, not one."'

'The whale and her calf,' breathed Nancy.

'Outside chance,' said Kit.

Nancy flared up, her face suddenly animated in the gloom. 'It's all the chance we've got.'

Quietly I asked, 'Where are we heading, Commander?'

'*Custer*'s much the closest. She'll be there within the hour, just about dawn. We're a good ninety minutes away, back-tracking.' I now recognised the throb of the *Boston*'s engines trying to burst their own boilers.

'If she's there and it's here,' said Kit. 'Ships move, you know.'

I'd had enough of Kit by this time. 'So does the infantry.'

It was Nancy who brought us up short. 'What about the Rules of Engagement?'

Kennedy was leaning with his elbows on the chart. He looked up and snapped: 'President's in session now.'

'Oh God,' said Nancy.

'What about Churchill and the King?' I asked.

'Apparently,' said Kennedy, as though he found this difficult to believe, 'the Prime Minister's with the President. Who's the Ambassador?'

'Halifax,' I said, thinking how strange it was that the former Viceroy of India and Foreign Secretary should called after some dreary Yorkshire town. I remembered he'd made himself unpopular in Washington because he knew more about fox-hunting than baseball.

'That's the name,' continued Kennedy. 'Halifax flew up yesterday to be with the King. He's only got a few hours left.'

'Oh God,' said Nancy again.

'What *exactly* is the position on the Rules?' asked Kit.

Kennedy got up from the table. 'Position's unchanged,' he said briefly.

'Just to be clear,' I said. 'That means that even if we locate *U-511*, we can't fire on her?'

'Correct, General,' responded Kennedy.

'Nevertheless,' observed Kit curtly, 'I notice you are making every preparation to engage him.' He nodded at the quarterdeck behind us. In the murky light emanating from the bridge, I could just make out the crew moving around the secondary armament, the depth-charge throwers and the torpedo tubes. Ash cans they called those depth charges. Like dustbins I suppose.

'Rules may change,' said Kennedy shortly.

'And if they don't?' asked Nancy.

It was at this point that Kennedy turned his back on us and strode off the bridge, leaving the officer-of-the-watch in charge. I glanced at my watch. It was now 5.24. Outside, there was the very slightest glimmering of light on the waves.

Kit allowed himself a wry smile.

'What'll he do?' asked Nancy.

Kit glanced carefully round at the rest of the bridge party, as though to remind us that we were not alone. He said, 'His ship.'

'President's decision,' I countered.

'Signals are very confusing,' said Kit, putting his hand to his eye in comic-opera mode. 'I've known them to be misread.'

'Oh God,' said Nancy again.

*

The next hour was utterly unbearable. We followed the *Custer*'s progress on the plot as she approached the last known position of the target. We knew that, at least at first, she would be steaming in at full speed. More than that we couldn't know because she had to maintain radio silence.

If the plot actually was *U-511*, it was obviously critical that Skorzeny remained ignorant of our presence. Kennan on the *Custer* would have been ordered to break radio silence only in extreme circumstances. Despite the straining of the *Boston*'s engines, we ourselves seemed to inch along the plot. Once — it was 0544 — Kennedy looked in on the bridge.

'Signal,' he said flatly.

'Yes?' We all looked up expectantly.

'President's still in session.'

'Thank you, Commander,' I said.

Just after six, the *Custer* should have reached the plot point. Kit glanced out at the waves. It was getting light. 'Visibility's not bad. Maybe six miles. Kennan would be in visual contact any time now.' The *Boston* was at General Quarters as they called it — Action Stations. Looking forward, I saw her bows plunging and rearing out of the seas; to the stern there were half a dozen men round her three-inch guns. Through the haze I thought I saw a glimpse of the first rays of the sun. Maybe Kennedy had been right. It was clearing. Kit nudged me. Again I looked astern. The covers had now been cleared from the two torpedo tubes, the Bofors and the Oerlikons, the depth charges had been swung astern, and the launch unlashed from its davits, ready to be lowered.

'Anything on the radar? asked Kit of Kennedy.

The Commander shook his head. 'Nothing,' he said, spitting out the words. *Boston*'s was not very reliable.

I had read of C/Os going into battle who had had to hold their own legs to stop them from shaking. I had rather come to admire Kennedy. What with one thing and another, his position was utterly impossible. He had developed a nervous tic on his mouth. It was the sort of thing I'd seen often enough in the trenches, often from very brave men.

For precisely nineteen minutes we ploughed on in the ever lighter day towards our destination, the sun almost directly in front of us, a deep orange ball low in the sky. At 0618 an ensign burst on to the bridge with a slip of paper in his hands. This he thrust into Kennedy's hands. Nancy, who had been watching the broad white wake of the *Boston* as it streamed ever smaller into the distance, looked round sharply.

Kennedy took the sheet, read it and read it again.

Without a word, he seized the arm of the officer-of-the-watch and rushed him into the chart-room at the back of the bridge. In passing, he thrust the slip into Kit's hands. Kit read it at a glance, and passed it on to Nancy and me. Before we could read it, Kennedy was back at the voice-pipes.

'Port ten.'

The quartermaster's drawl answered him. 'Ten of port on the wheel, sir.'

The *Boston* veered slightly to the south, so that we were now heading almost straight into the rising sun.

'Midships,' voiced Kennedy.

'Midships — wheel's amidships sir,' came the drawl.

'Steady.'

'Steady.' Again the echo.

Nancy had snatched the message slip. She handed it to me wordlessly.

U-511 LOCATED. 65/31 NORTH, 03/19 WEST. *CUSTER* DIRECT HIT. ABANDONING SHIP.

Kennedy called the ensign over before dismissing him. He stalked over to where we stood.

'I've signalled the Oval Office on the loss of the *Custer*. And I've also requested permission to engage *U-511*.'

'Think they'll get it?' asked Kit.

'If they don't respond, Admiral,' explained Kennedy evenly, 'the fact that a unit of the Kriegsmarine has destroyed a ship of the US Navy places the relationship between the two countries on a new footing. That's an act of war — as well you know.'

There was a moment's silence on the bridge as we digested this statement.

'Not everyone might see it that way,' I said.

'That a threat, General?' asked Kennedy, looking me full in the face. The tic on his mouth twitched.

'An observation,' I replied. 'You're not a free agent. None

of us ever is. '[i]

Before Kennedy could reply, the navigator — who had studiously avoided this exchange —called out, 'ETA[ii] at the datum[iii] thirteen minutes, sir.'

Kennedy pulled up the gun crew voice-pipe on the console in front of him. 'Now hear this. Now hear this. We are closing on a unit of the German Kriegsmarine. Target is U-boat, *U-511*. You have *no permission* to fire on this vessel unless returning fire. No first strike. Repeat, no first strike. ETA on datum twelve minutes. Repeat, twelve minutes.'

Kennedy stepped to the left, to another voice-pipe. To the quartermaster he said, 'Commence zigzags. Mean course as you are.'

'Zigzag. Mean course as you are,' was the echo as the helmsman swung the wheel to confuse Skorzeny on our line of approach.

The manoeuvre improved our position in the sense that at least we weren't staring all time into the sun. Yet we could still see virtually nothing in the waters ahead of us, neither the *Custer* nor *U-511*.

'Sir!' There was a shout from the starboard watchkeeper on the bridge. As one we wheeled towards him, following the line of his pointing arm.

'Keep your quarters,' steadied Kennedy, ensuring the rest of the watch focused on its allotted sectors.

Out of the sun's glare, the object was clear enough. A ship in her death throes. She was an ugly sight. Already down by the head, screws out of the water, the small grey sloop was ablaze from stem to stern. She was billowing so much oily smoke that I couldn't think why we hadn't seen her before. The sun, I guess. It could be nothing other than the *Custer*.

i The General in a surprisingly philosophical mood.

ii Estimated Time of Arrival.

iii Reference point on the earth's surface.

For a minute or so we headed straight towards her before swinging away on the next leg of the zigzag.

'Where the hell is he?' Kennedy muttered. Then, more loudly, 'Slow ahead all. Switch on the hydrophones.'[i]

Kit, too, was muttering, as though to himself. 'If Skorzeny's moving quickly we might pick him up. If he's moving slowly, maybe lining us up a torpedo, we won't.'

We were now about a mile away from the wreck of the *Custer*. The oil from her fuel tanks filled the sky, drifting up lazily in what was now a fairly light wind, no more than a Force 3, though the swell remained. I could see a couple of upturned Carley life-rafts dotting the water, three or four more the right way up that might carry survivors. At this distance it was difficult to tell.

'Hydrophone report,' barked Kennedy.

'Nothing, sir. Just the *Custer* breaking up,' came a drawl.

Then I suppose the wind must have shifted slightly, and with it a black pall of oily smoke.

'Object at Red 80, sir.' It was the port lookout.

This was almost behind the burning *Custer*, and at first I could see absolutely nothing. There were half a dozen pairs of glasses on that bridge, all trained on a single point.

'What d'you make of it, lookout?' This was Kennedy, who had his own glasses.

'Can't make it out at all, sir,' came the quiet drawl.

Kennedy seemed to be doing no better. He turned to Kit, and handed him the glasses. 'Admiral.'

Kit scoured the spot in absolute silence for more than a minute, shifted his focus slightly to the east, then returned the glasses to Kennedy. Making out objects at sea is as much a question of experience as eyesight — or so I had often heard Kit say. 'Submarine trimmed right down. Decks awash. Conning tower and gun platform only above the water. There's another object about thirty yards away. Much smaller. Making a lot of

i At the speed at which the *Boston* had been closing the *Custer* and U-511, the frigate's hydrophones would have picked up nothing but her own propeller noise.

what looks like steam. Seems to be a man on it.'

'Hard a port,' ordered Kennedy. 'All ahead slow.' He was taking us back into the oily smoke-screen. 'Anyone else?'

The port watchkeeper piped up. 'Can't see a U-boat, sir. But there's a sort of block that could be a conning tower. There's a figure on some sort of platform.'

'The capsule,' I said. Nobody said anything at all to that.

'Ensign,' ordered Kennedy after a few moments, 'make a signal to the Oval Office. HAVE LOCATED *U-511*. 65/31 NORTH; 03/19 WEST. COURSE 335. AM PREPARING TO ENGAGE. Got it? Now run.'

There was a voice from somewhere else on the bridge. 'Hydrophone fix bearing Green 70. She's on the move.'

Kit, his own voice rising slightly, said, 'She's seen us.'

Nemesis

Kennedy snatched the voice-pipe. 'Gun crew. Target is a canister behind the U-boat. Bearing Green 40. Range 800 yards. Looks like a fog buoy.[i]Track and hold your fire. Repeat, track and hold your fire.'

'Check, skipper,' came the response.

I heard the grind of heavy machinery and saw the barrel of the 10-pounder gun swing round till it reached the appointed bearing, pointing straight at the capsule.

'Prepare stern torpedo tubes,' Kennedy continued.

'Check.'

'You can't fire,' shouted Nancy. Kennedy, leaning on the console at the front of the bridge, was staring through his glasses at the two targets, watching the U-boat closing on the capsule. He didn't even turn round as he spoke. 'Watch me.'

It wasn't Kennedy who opened the engagement. I saw a flash of flame from the gun on the U-boat's deck. A millisecond later came a roar, and a good hundred yards away from our starboard bow a splash which sent a plume of water forty or fifty feet high above our masts.

Kennedy wasn't going to take this lying down. He pulled up the voice-pipe. 'Give him a warning shot.'

The *Boston*'s ten-pounder roared, and the shell splashed into the water a couple of hundred feet from the capsule.

Just as it did so there was a shout from the hydrophone operator. 'Torpedo in the water! Two!'

Kennedy was commendably calm. Without any great signs of haste he just pulled up the helmsman's voice-pipe. 'Turn her end on.' I felt the *Boston* heel sharply under my feet as the rudder came on. I looked towards the U-boat. Kit still had his glasses on her. He, too, seemed unshaken:

'Tracks in the water. Coming our way.'

I could see nothing. I could only hear the rumble of the

i A large buoy streamed from the aft of a ship to help with convoy station keeping in bad weather.

Boston's turbines as she turned to expose the smallest possible area to the incoming torpedoes. I thought of the tin fish tearing towards us at thirty knots, and the havoc they had wreaked on the *Custer*. Not for long. There was a dull thud from the *Boston*'s stern, and the whole bridge party seemed to turn on its heels towards the sound, to hold its breath and to brace itself for the explosion.

It never came.

'God's own luck,' breathed Kit. 'A dud.'[ii]

'Wheel-house — bridge.'

Kennedy lent over the voice-pipe. 'Bridge.'

'She's not answering to the helm, sir.'

'Switch to manual steering.' Again, quite calmly.

'Manual steering, sir.'

There was a pause and then the same voice came again. 'Wheel-house — bridge.'

'Bridge,' came Kennedy

'Not responding, sir. Guess the rudder's jammed.'

'Very well.'

There was a crack and a roar as *U-511* opened fire again. This shell fell much closer, maybe 75 feet away, in a huge spout of spray, again off the *Boston*'s starboard bows.

Kit was watching the U-boat manoeuvring close to the capsule. 'They've got the man off, Commander.'

'What d'you make of it?' snapped Kennedy.

Another roar. This time the shell fell close enough to splash the *Boston*'s bridge.

'Initiating the firing sequence, I'd say,' said Kit.

'Check,' said Kennedy.

There was another crack of Skorzeny's deck gun, and another huge plume of water splashed over the bridge. The shells were getting closer. An ensign burst onto the bridge. 'Signal, sir.'

Another roar. This one straddled the *Boston*, throwing a huge fountain of water over the depth-charge thrower and

ii An overstatement given the notorious unreliability of the U-boat torpedoes.

drenching the men closed up round her. Kennedy seized the slip, glanced at it and roared into the voice-pipe. 'Free to fire on the capsule. Bearing now Green thirty-five, range 500 yards. Open fire!'

There was an agonising pause as we waited for the frigate's own armaments to respond.

Then from the voice-pipe, 'Can't bring her to bear, sir.'

With her rudder jammed, the *Boston* was barely manoeuvrable. Her main armament, the ten-pounder in the bows, had an arc of fire of about forty degrees either side of the vessel. [i]

Kennedy handed the slip to me. PERMISSION TO ENGAGE *U-511* GRANTED, REPEAT, GRANTED. I passed it to Nancy.

Above the din of another shell coming in, Kit pointed. 'She's withdrawing.' *U-511*, now less than half a mile away, was steaming slowly away from the capsule, her deck gun still bearing on us but for the moment no longer firing. Kennedy turned to Kit and briefly conferred. I couldn't hear what they were saying. For once, they seemed in agreement. Kennedy leaned over the voice-pipe. 'Coxswain, half ahead port engine, slow astern starboard.'

'Half ahead port engine, slow astern starboard.'

The *Boston* slewed slowly round. Her stern had been pointing roughly south-south-east. Now she swung anti-clockwise so that her quarterdeck and its torpedo tubes pointed closer and closer to the capsule. From this I could now see drifting wisps of steam or smoke.

'Ready both torpedo tubes,' ordered Kennedy as the frigate swung closer and closer to the capsule. A few degrees beyond her lay *U-511*, still steaming slowly astern to the north-east. Kennedy was back at the voice-pipes. 'Starboard engine stop.'

'Starboard stop.'

The *Boston* veered slightly to the south, so that we were

i The point being that her armament could not fire at the target.

now heading almost straight into the rising sun.

'Steady,' said Kennedy.

'Steady.'

'Prepare to fire torpedoes.'

The *Boston* was still swinging inexorably round, too fast it seemed to me.

Kennedy seemed to think so too, for he suddenly snapped into the voice tube. 'Fire both torpedoes. Now. Quick.'

But he was too late.

I glanced astern and saw the torpedoes streaking away, leaving a trail of bubbles in their wake. Already the *Boston* had swung past the capsule and was almost bearing on the U-boat. There was a shout from Kit that was at once drowned as the capsule belched fire. For a second I thought we'd hit the V2. As the plume of fire rose from the sea and gathered pace I saw we had not. The charcoal black rocket, miraculously balanced above an orange jet as big as the machine itself rose, at first slowly, incrementally, inch by inch, foot by foot, yard by yard, above the sea, then with ever-gathering pace it soared upwards, piercing the sky until it was just fire in the firmament high above us. The noise was stupendous, a deep-throated roar that seemed to envelop the ship and the surrounding seas to the very horizon. It hit you not so much in the ears but in the chest and your very bones, a gigantic detonation that took me back to Picardy and the Western Front. The V2 was on its way. Surely it couldn't be anywhere other than New York.

I saw the track of the first of the *Boston*'s torpedoes passing a dozen yards in front of the U-boat's retreating hull. The second I thought might do the same. As it was, there was flash of fire and smoke right on the U-boat's bows.

*

I have to give it to Kennedy. He was steadiness itself in the crisis. The roar of the V2 was still echoing in our ears and the U-boat ahead was already down by the head as he gave his orders. Again he was at the voice-pipe, again to the engine-room. 'Half ahead starboard, slow ahead port.[i] Bring her round on the U-boat.'

'Half ahead starboard, slow ahead port.'

Crippled though she was by her jammed rudder, the *Boston* began slowly to turn her stern away from Skorzeny's doomed U-boat. 'Prepare to lower the launch.'

There was a sudden bustle on deck as half a dozen men crowded round the davits of the launch just abaft the main stack. Kennedy's prescience had meant that these preparations had been put in hand before the engagement. The launch had been lashed down for the Atlantic crossing. Before the *Boston*'s turn was complete, she was ready to be lowered from the frigate.

U-511 now swung into view directly in front of us and no more than 200 yards away. She was bow down at an angle of maybe 5 degrees. Kennedy turned to Kit. 'Five minutes?'

Kit had seen ships sink before. 'If that,' he said.

'Coming?' asked Kennedy of me.

The launch was already in the water when the four of us bundled out of the bridge. There was a small hatch close to the *Boston*'s waterline which at sea was normally secured. We thundered down the iron steps and into the bowels of the frigate. At the hatch a rating was struggling with the clamps that held it fast. He swung it open onto the launch. It was manned by a dozen bullet-headed ratings. Down we piled. We were scarcely aboard when the coxswain at the wheel gunned the throttle and left the *Boston* behind us.

The crew of *U-511* had clearly left the rescue of the hostages to their assailants, for there were at least a dozen them already on the stern casing, making ready to abandon ship. I couldn't make out the bridge party, but whoever it was had extracted some sort of rubber boat from a hatch behind the conning tower. As we closed the U-boat it looked as though a couple of ratings were trying to launch this onto a swell that must still have been six or seven feet.

---

i The *Boston* was now being manoeuvred only with her engines.

Kennedy was looked speculatively at the grey mass of the U-boat. 'She'll go with a rush when she does.'

We were now no further than fifteen feet away and the coxswain throttled back and prepared to lie us alongside the submarine. He was taking her in just forward of the bridge party, as close as he could to the conning tower.

'Arm yourselves,' shouted Kennedy.

Kit and I drew our revolvers, and a couple of ratings cocked their machine-guns. As we did so two figures scuttled out of the conning tower to join the ratings on the U-boat's casing. One had the unmistakable profile of Skorzeny, standing out head and shoulders above his companion. The other I had to look at twice to identify, a diminutive figure in a dirty-grey boiler-suit. It was Julia.

'Yours, I believe, Admiral,' remarked Kennedy as we drew alongside the U-boat.

'Very well,' replied Kit.

We couldn't get within six or seven feet of the U-boat without the launch striking the ballast tank that bellied out from the craft's water-tight pressure hull. Dead in the water, she rolled ten degrees this way, ten degrees that, her casing never in the same place at once in relation to the pitching launch. We threw out a gang-plank. It swayed, very uneasily and unsteadily, between the two boats, looking about as safe as a high-wire over Niagara. There was no time for niceties. The coxswain threw himself across the lifeline. Kit, Nancy and I followed suit. I lost my footing and almost my leg in the suddenly closing gap between the launch and the U-boat's casing, over which some of the bigger waves were now breaking. As I did so, the submarine lurched and its bows settled appreciably.

Kit shouted, 'She's going.' He hared round the conning tower with Nancy in pursuit to the stern casing, where Skorzeny and Julia were standing.

As he did so, Kennedy shouted, 'Let's chance it.'

There was a ladder of half a dozen or so steel staples let into the side of the conning tower. He was up these and through the conning tower hatch before I could reply. I followed, tumbling down eight feet of ladder into what must have been the U-boat's control room. It was a compartment about the breadth of a tube train, fifteen or twenty feet long, and fitted out with everything that made it the infernal machine it was: a riot of pipes, valves, electric wiring, switches and junction boxes, dominated by the bronze column of the periscope. Barely lit by emergency lamps, it was deserted. Already the floor was sloshing with filthy brown water reeking of sewage. At each end of the compartment was a watertight door, secured with a couple of clips and a control wheel.

'Any idea?' I said to Kennedy.

He indicated the door heading towards the bows of the boat. 'If they're forward of this door, and it's flooded, they're dead. If we open it and it's flooded, we're dead.'

'What about the stern?'

'Can't be flooded,' he said. 'They'll have closed all watertight doors when she was hit. Should have, anyway.'

I seized the clamps on the door and tried to shift them. Kennedy lent his own weight. They wouldn't move an inch.

I stepped back. 'Suppose they're alive behind the forward door?'

With a courage for which I will always admire Kennedy, he just swung round and seized the two levers on the forward door and pulled them down and open.

All hell broke loose. There must have been thousands of gallons of water behind that door, half way up the forward compartment. Opening the door was like unleashing a river. One moment we were on our feet in the control room. The next we were swilling around on the floor in two feet of freezing Atlantic brine.

Kennedy was quicker than me. Against the onrush of water he was on his feet, forcing his way forward, pulling himself through the door with his hands as the first of the flood abated. I was at his heels. The compartment into which we had forced ourselves was far smaller than the control room. It comprised a corridor through to the next water-tight door and

230

— I'd guess — the boat's wardroom.[i] There were half a dozen bunks grouped round a table. Curtains screened the bunks, and the lower set was under water on which floated a flotsam of socks, underclothes, photographs and bits of filthy paper. By what instinct God knows, Kennedy tore open the curtains. There lay Elizabeth and Margaret, asleep, drugged or dead.

We seized them as though they'd been bags of coal, threw them over our shoulders and struggled back to the control room, then to the bottom of the ladder. There was now a good three feet of water in the control room, well up to our waists. Live electrical contacts were spitting venomously as the level crept up the control panels. We looked up the ladder to the little circle of grey sky at the top of the hatch. As we did so, *U-511* seemed to settle deeper into the water. I looked at the girls. They were dead to the world. Alone, Kennedy and I could make it. With those two on our backs it was another matter.

'Up you go,' cried Kennedy. 'I'll push 'em up.'

How he did it I'll never know. I got myself to the top of the conning tower ladder and reached down. He stood on the bottom and walked the bodies first of Margaret, then Elizabeth up towards me as the waters rose around him. At last I had them both beside me on the U-boat's steel casing. There at my side was Kit. 'Get up, man!' I shouted down to Kennedy. The launch, engines running, seemed feet away, and the casing was now awash.

Kit manhandled Elizabeth over the casing and across the heaving gangplank to the safety of the launch.

I threw Margaret across my shoulders and staggered across.

I turned, and as I did so I saw Kennedy's head emerge from the hatch. Then the U-boat lurched again and the great grey mass slid easily and smoothly beneath the Atlantic waves. I turned as I heard the slashing of an axe against the

---

i Officers' dining room and lounge, usually doubling as a dormitory. A generous description of the hutches on submarines typical during WW2.

line that secured the gangplank to the launch. When I turned back, Kennedy had gone.

It was then that I saw, east from where we lay, a sight the like of which I had never seen and never wish to see again. There was a sudden flash of light so searing that I clapped my hands to my eyes, yet the light was so bright that I could clearly see the bones through my closed eyelids. Along with the light came a sudden flash of heat so intense it felt like it would burn right through me. After several seconds the light slowly began to fade, and I opened my eyes. Before me, rising majestically into the air, was a roiling, boiling mushroom cloud. The column from the ground was glowing orange like a billowing fire, rising and disappearing into the rolling mushroom head. The head was glowing a hideous purple colour. After about 30 seconds the blast hit me. It wasn't like a strong wind, more like someone trying to throw me off my feet. A thunder-like roar arrived with the blast wave, continuing for nearly a minute. The mushroom cloud still hung above, but it had stopped growing and the upper parts were starting to drift to one side with the wind. I thought it was the end of the world.

The Four of Hearts

So I come to the events of Victory Day.[i]

What happened in the days immediately following the sinking of *U-511* on 28 February is too well known for me to recount other than with the utmost brevity. The US Department of Defense provisionally concluded that the V2 had exploded some seventy-five or eighty miles east of Manhattan at an altitude of between 10,000 and 8,000 feet. The population of New York was of course spellbound by the monstrous spectacle that unfolded before their eyes. Physically, though, they were unhurt.

Dozens of theories were formulated to explain the failure of the rocket to reach its target. Some in the Pentagon took the view that it was an extraordinary achievement for the Nazis to have come so close to achieving their objective of destroying New York. Certainly the more you pondered the problem the more difficult it seemed.[ii] Of course, as a simple soldier I was prepared to take what the technical bods said at face value. Still, I could never understand how the Jerries could hope to orientate the rocket with any accuracy in an Atlantic swell. One moment it was heading for New York, the next Philadelphia, the next Boston. Why did it explode thousands of feet above its target? God knows.

The huge mushroom cloud of radioactive fallout that we had witnessed from the launch of *U-511* was swept principally to the east by the weather system prevailing on the day. Radioactive particles were detected just outside Reykjavik in Iceland, in County Waterford on the west coast of Ireland, on the hill farms in Wales, and in the southern fjords of Norway.

i 9 March 1946.

ii See epilogue.

The relief of the free world at New York's reprieve was tempered by the realisation that an awful power had been unleashed on the world and by Stalin's announcement that the Soviet Union had itself perfected an atom bomb.

This was in fact communicated by Ambassador Gromyko[i] to President Truman within hours of the loss of *U-511*. According to Mr Dulles, this development had long been anticipated. The propagandists in the Truman Administration withheld the facts from the public at large until the ultimate fate of the Reich became apparent in the aftermath of the Potsdam coup of 23 February. The extraordinary dispatch with which Field Marshal Rommel, Count Von Staufenberg[ii] and Admiral Canaris disposed of Himmler and the remaining Nazi leaders convinced both President Truman and the Prime Minister that the Thousand Year Reich had utterly foundered. I believe this event also persuaded Truman and Churchill that the free world was ready for the announcement of the Soviets' possession of the bomb — intelligence that in any case could not be concealed for much longer.

As it was, Churchill and the President of course discovered that this barely dampened the spirits of the peoples of Western Europe, now freed — or who had freed themselves — from the grotesque and unspeakable evils of Hitler's regime. Whether they were right in regarding the threat of communism as remote and abstract remains to be seen. In the meantime, they were more than content to be rid of their immediate oppressors and the hideous machinery of a police state: the Gestapo, the Abwehr, the SS, Vine Street and Prinz Albrechtstrasse, and concentration camps from Malvern in the west to Sobibor in the east.

It is perhaps best to draw a veil over the subsequent treatment by the indigenous inhabitants of their former

i Andrei Gromyko, 1909-1989, Soviet diplomat and politician.

ii Claus Schenk Graf von Stauffenberg, 1903-1972, German aristocrat, soldier and patriot.

oppressors. The French called it *L'épuration*, and its methods ranged from the lynch mob to the gallows. Women guilty of fraternisation with the enemy were tarred and feathered — or worse. Much the same treatment was meted out to collaborators — or supposed collaborators — all over England and continental Europe. There was a particularly ugly case in the Yorkshire Dales involving the gang rape and murder of a young woman who had supposedly been the mistress of the Gauleiter of Newcastle, Sir Edward Monkton.[iii] She turned out to be entirely innocent, and his niece. Displaying the naked bodies of Mussolini, Daladier and Quisling in public seemed a descent into just that same barbarism that I had supposed we were fighting against. It was this sort of episode that gave the public holiday declared by Churchill in Ottawa and echoed throughout the Continent a hollow ring.

The return of the Cabinet from exile on 5 March lent urgency to the preparations in London, though I have to say I'd have thought they would have had more important matters on their hands. Not least the restoration of democratic government to a country that had laboured under the yoke of Heydrich and Mosely for five years. Still, something had to be put on, I suppose.

I was loath to play a public part in the celebrations, but the Prime Minister and — I have to say — Nancy persuaded me otherwise. By this time a good deal of rumour and gossip had accumulated about what was beginning to be called the February Rising, the odd grains of truth hidden in a morass of misapprehension and misunderstanding. They used to say that truth is the first casualty of war, and they were right. Some strange stories had been brought to my ears about what I was supposed to have been doing over the past two months. Kit and I were both persuaded — I against my better judgement — that our appearance on a public platform with the Cabinet and members of the Royal Family might be of value. It would dispel speculation, rumour and indeed the fabrication of

iii Edward Piers Monkton, 1883-1946.

235

which the BBC in the days after Goebbels's execution was patently guilty. The original plan was that we should join the main party on the balcony of Buckingham Palace, but I demurred. Even Kit thought this inappropriate. Instead it was agreed we would be on hand in the drawing-room from which the balcony opened. Depending on the mood of the crowd, we might be asked to join the party on the balcony very briefly. I reluctantly accepted this as a contingency.

When we discussed these matters at the Metropole[i] in Northumberland Avenue a couple of days before V-Day, I rather thought Kit had the fever of limelight upon him. As I left him that day on the steps of the hotel, we agreed to meet for a sharpener at the Rag[ii] just before noon on the day itself. From then, on, he said, we would let events take their own course. Very philosophical, I thought.

*

I woke up that day in a happier frame of mind than I'd done for five years. I dare say I shared that mood with the rest of the nation.

Hitler was dead. Himmler was dead. Order, in the form of a military government, had been restored to Germany. Those who had perpetrated the occupation in England were dead or behind bars. Winston was back. I had myself played a small part in the return of the rightful order. I had done my duty, it seemed. As I shaved in the shabby old bathroom at Cambridge Gardens, with Nancy still fast asleep, it occurred that God was in his heaven and all was right with the world. As it so turned out, this was not quite so.

*

i Once fashionable hotel, close to Trafalgar Square.

ii Nickname of the Army & Navy Club in St James's Square.

The Four of Hearts

Nancy's mother was in town for the celebrations. At least in some senses this was too good an opportunity to miss. I had not seen Lady Bibury since Nancy and I had run up to Harrogate and announced our intentions immediately after our return from New York. We had arrangements to discuss. I was also interested to see if Honoria had reconciled herself to the marriage. George, the late Lord Bibury,[iii] had always spoken ill of me to his wife. So Nancy said. This seemed harsh recompense for the efforts that I had made at the beginning of rearmament in 1936 and 1937 to advance his career. He should have blamed his own incompetence.

In what seemed to me a craven effort to pander to Lady Bibury's prejudices, Nancy and I arrived separately at Fortnum's.[iv] There, amidst the gathering crowds, we aired our plans for the wedding. It was a relief to see the tea-rooms empty of Wehrmacht field-grey, but Erwin Rommel himself would have been more civil than Lady Bibury. She had written that the liaison between myself and her daughter caused her 'quite inexpressible pain' By half-past eleven the gloss of the morning had worn decidedly thin. I made my excuses and left them to settle the bill. I had made arrangements for Nancy to meet her at the Palace. Her mother had the gall to hint that she might accompany us there.

I was going to use the Piccadilly exit from Fortnum's but when I saw the crowds I thought better of it. They must have been ten deep right along both sides of the street from Green Park up to Piccadilly Circus. An absolutely extraordinary gathering of what Marx called the *Lumpenproletariat*. Duke Street was hardly better. A street vendor was doing a roaring trade selling Union Jacks, and elsewhere I heard snatches of song. I'm not musical myself, but the atmosphere was infectious. They sang, I believe, *The White Cliffs of Dover* and *Rule Britannia* and *When the Lights Go on Again* and anything

iii Lady Honoria Bibury, 1899-1952, in her day a leading member of the Quorn Hunt.

iv Fortnum & Masons, the famous store on Piccadilly.

else that came into their empty heads. As I threaded my way down to St James's I thought of another such walk I had made, one evening in the snow, half a mile away across St James's Park.

I reached the Rag. For five years it had been infested with the Wehrmacht. Now it was back to its old self. Macintosh was on the door, Parsons was doling out the poison, and sundry familiar figures were propping up the bar as though not a thing had changed since 1940. Yet there were ghosts there too, the ghosts of Alec and Wingate, Stewart-Richardson and Hore-Belisha and dozens of others, all of whom were now dead.

I glanced at my watch. It had just gone noon when Kit eventually turned up. Already rather the worse for wear, I thought, and of course as scruffy as they come. Doesn't brush up very well, Kit.

I was going to say something about the scenes at Buckingham Palace for those who weren't there. Then I realised there's no point. That day, it seemed that the whole country was there, a sea of humanity that was a battered yet somehow heroic expression of our nationhood. As to the Palace itself, it had become the stage on which the players in the February Rising would have their entrances and exits.*

We met Nancy at the garden gate in Buckingham Palace Road, about the only approach possible given the extraordinary crowds massing everywhere — from St James's, Buckingham Gate, Constitution Hill and the Mall. We were admitted by a guardsman and made our way over to the main building. The household had begun the work of expunging all signs of the Nazi occupancy from Nash[i] and Blore's creation, but their work was far from complete. The great corridors through which we were led were still hung with swastikas, portraits of the Royal Family had yet to replace those of early Nazi Party members on the brocaded walls of the State apartments, and much of the period furniture in which our late King took

i Edward Blore (1787-1875) completed the designs for the Palace originated by John Nash (1752-1875)

such delight apparently remained in Goering's country place, Karinhall.

At the double doors that led into the drawing-room on the first floor my hand instinctively moved to straighten my tie. I have to say my creases weren't as sharp as I'd have liked and I could have done with a haircut. Still, there we were. The doors were thrown open and we were ushered into a room empty of people but filled with sound. The whole party was on the balcony, beyond the billowing curtains of the drawing-room, outside with the tumultuous crowd. I smiled at Nancy and at that moment a shadow fell on the curtain, a hand drew it aside, and we found ourselves in the presence of the Queen. She was in her old ATS[ii] uniform, her mourning signified by a black arm-band. Nancy curtsied, Kit and I bowed. I began to mumble something about her father, and then she just embraced me. I've never been so surprised in my life. Before I had time to say anything, Margaret was at her side. She greeted us with a graciousness that was new, and I have to say that neither looked much the worst for their experiences over the previous month. Margaret couldn't keep the smile off her face. Perhaps cheating death gives you a better sense of being alive.

The curtain twitched again and a cigar led the Prime Minister into the room. The build was heavier, the face more jowled than when I'd seen him last, but the eye was as bright as ever. 'General,' he said, 'we have come through.'

*

It was evening, the early spring sun was setting over the Palace Gardens, and the crowd was beginning to disperse, when the Prime Minister led me aside. 'Let's have a drink, shall we, General.'

We settled ourselves in the corner of the drawing-room.

---

ii The Queen joined the Auxiliary Territorial Service — which acted in support of the Army - at the beginning of the war. She was a driver.

Nancy, Kit, Elizabeth, Margaret and the Queen Mother were nowhere to be seen. Off to powder their noses, I supposed, Kit excepted. The Prime Minister poured himself a couple of fingers of Scotch and splashed in some soda. Then he put his hand inside his jacket pocket and drew out what I thought at first was a slip of paper. Then I saw it was a playing card. He laid it down on a small table by his seat. It was the very same card that had been planted on me in Horse Guards in what seemed another lifetime, the card that had sent me on my way to shoot Hitler. It was the four of hearts.

'Interesting man, Conway,' said the Prime Minister in his rather ponderous way.

So confused was I by all that was implied by Churchill's possession of the card that I was struck dumb. If this showed on my face, the PM chose to ignore it. With difficulty, I pulled myself together. 'Remarkable,' I said. 'For all his faults.'

The Prime Minister peered into his drink. Then he sighed and looked up at me. 'I must tell you, General, that the Opposition are making mischief about you and Conway.'

For a moment, I couldn't think what he meant. 'Opposition?'

'Morrison and his awful crowd. Bevan,[i] Attlee.[ii] Communists. Provisional government or whatever they called themselves until our return.'

I tried to focus my mind. 'What mischief?'

'They have got hold of a very garbled version of the events of the Rising, General. It traduces the true facts of the story. The story of Colonel Skorzeny and our friend the late Commander Kennedy. They have allowed themselves, I greatly fear, to be misled by the Colonel. We should have had him shot, you know. You may regret not having done it yourself.'

I could barely keep my voice steady. I thought of Skorzeny as I had last seen him in New York, diminished but not

i Aneurin Bevan, 1897-1960, Welsh labour politician.

ii Clement Attlee, 1883-1967, labour politician.

defeated, being escorted down the *Boston*'s gang-plank.

'They are politicians,' agreed the Prime Minister. 'Able politicians in their own way. They have their own morality. Their ends justify their means.'

'What are they saying?'I asked.

Churchill paused and helped himself to another couple of fingers of Scotch. 'That you two are traitors who betrayed the princesses to Skorzeny and the Americans.'

'We betrayed the princesses? *We betrayed the princesses?*'

'I won't bore you with the detail of their fabrications, General. They argue that Skorzeny's appearance at the Tower early in your adventure was less than fortuitous, the disclosure of their location in Sandringham to the Americans less than coincidental, the trap laid for Commander Kennedy at Faslane the product of inside knowledge. They say you and the First Sea Lord are double agents.'

'This is utter nonsense. I don't believe a word of it. Not a damn word!'

While I was beside myself, the PM was calm itself. 'I don't myself, but it was necessary that you should be made aware of this mischief. Nothing will come of it, of course. I doubt whether even Morrison believes it. Still, I fear we have not heard the end of it yet.'

'What else?' I asked. I couldn't conceive now where this would all end. Today of all days.

Churchill picked up the playing-card and began to finger it. 'Betraying nuclear secrets to the CIA.'

'Who in their right minds would believe such a story?' I cried.

The PM shrugged. 'Well, the Americans also now have the secrets of the bomb.'

'Good Lord!

'You will hear the story on the BBC tomorrow,' added the PM.[iii]

I was so flabbergasted by this cascade of accusations and revelations that I found myself barely able to speak. My mind was a whirl of contradictions and outlandish thoughts. All

iii The announcement was indeed made on 10 March 1946..

the events of the past month rose up in my mind, the order and sense that I had made of them utterly at odds with what I had just heard. What the Prime Minister had said was literally incomprehensible.

We sat there, the two of us, in complete silence as the room darkened around us. Churchill, lost in his own thoughts, took occasional tugs at his cigar.

I suppose it must have been a little before six o'clock when one of the footmen came in with the wireless. For the announcement, he said: the BBC relay of President Truman's broadcast. These words brought us both out of our reverie. I got up and stretched my legs. The PM stayed seated while the footman fiddled with the wireless. He had some difficulty tuning in — rather to the PM's annoyance — and when he finally succeeded we just caught a few of Truman's phrases in that homespun voice of his. 'This is a solemn but glorious hour. My only wish is that Franklin D. Roosevelt had lived to witness this day... our rejoicing is sober and subdued by the supreme consciousness of the terrible price we have paid to rid the world of Hitler and his band. Let us not forget, my fellow Americans, the sorrow and heartbreak in the homes of so many of our neighbours — neighbours whose most priceless possession has been rendered a sacrifice to redeem our liberty.'

At the end of the broadcast I switched the thing off. The words had made me think of poor Kennedy, and his own sacrifice to save the princesses. And it was in a strange, jumbled way that this thought prompted another that came quite unsought into my mind. 'Prime Minister, can I ask you why the President changed the Rules of Engagement on that last day?'

The great man looked sharply at me, and his expression broadened into a smile that played across his lips for a second. 'You have seen the reports in the Press. In accordance with the final wishes of the late King.'

For the very first time that afternoon I began to doubt the truth of what I was being told. Perhaps I should have begun to doubt it sooner. Quite a lot sooner. 'That was it, was it?'

The Four of Hearts

Churchill's mind already seemed to be drifting elsewhere. 'I have already given you my answer,' he replied.

I pressed home. 'It wasn't for another reason?'

Now I had caught his attention. He turned to face me. Bluntly he replied, 'What else could possibly have caused the President to have changed his mind?'

Before I could answer, the door to the drawing-room burst open and the princesses tumbled in, followed by Kit and — to my pleasure and but not altogether surprise - Lady Julia. I had not seen her since New York.

The Prime Minister had glanced indulgently towards the source of the disturbance. Now he looked back at me with a smile. 'What does that old play say, General? "What you know, you know"? Yes, I think that was it. What you know you know.'

Then, in the wake of the others I noticed another entrant to that wonderful room on that day on which we witnessed and gave thanks for the victory of the forces of good over evil. A dog. Just a small dog. A small, liver-coloured dachshund. When it saw Kit it gave a sharp yap, rushed over and jumped into his arms.

Epilogue

At which point the General's narrative closes — leaving the reader in difficulties.

If the story has reached a natural conclusion, the memoir leaves unresolved all sorts of questions major or minor that demand an answer. Intrigued as I was by the account when it was first given to me in 1999 by N------, the General's great-nephew, it became apparent fairly quickly that without unravelling at least the principal points that the narrator leaves open I would not be discharging my duty as Editor. The difficulties in so doing gradually became equally clear.

If the problem of discovering the actual course of events was sufficient in itself, once I had done so the implications of these facts for the reputations of nationally and globally respected figures made the matter doubly or triply so. I had to discover what actually happened and I had to persuade any publisher — ever mindful of the law of libel — of the veracity of my understanding. It is for both these reasons that publication of a manuscript discovered in 1999 has been delayed for more than two decades, and the coffers of Learned Counsel duly enriched. My God!! The time I have spent in Chambers with … But no, I will draw a veil over the iniquities of the legal profession that are too well-known to merit repetition. Rather, I must turn to that palimpsest of the truth that the exigencies of the lawyers allows us.

Simply discovering the facts indeed posed plenty of problems. With the exception of Her Majesty the Queen, none of the principal figures in the account remained alive to answer my enquiries. The General himself died — appropriately enough — on Armistice Day in 1984; Churchill of course predeceased him by twenty years. Admiral Conway was killed in 1953 in one of those crashes that beset the early days of the pioneering Comet jet airliner. The Duke and Duchess of

Epilogue

Windsor were dead, Colonel Skorzeny had been killed water-skiing in Argentina in 1979. The American Allen Dulles died of cancer in 1969. Such was the necrology.

Before her death, poor Lady Quick was this side of the grave but the far side of human consciousness. Her Majesty could — or would — only refer me to her official biographer Philip Ziegler. Sir Philip in turn was able to inform me that the earliest date at which the Monarch's official papers on the Rising would open for public scrutiny would be 2046 — a year neither I nor I suspect my publishers expect to see. Churchill's official biographer Sir Martin Gilbert provided me with a similarly dusty answer and refused to respond to questions concerning his long-awaited work. The CIA took the line that Dulles's papers were embargoed until 2026.

If at one level this was all profoundly discouraging, on another it made me believe that there was much to conceal.

As indeed there was. If the obvious and official lines of enquiry were of little use, the byways and footpaths of scholarship were productive. I discovered a plethora of widows and widowers, sons and lovers, colleagues and employees for whom discretion was no longer a virtue. Once they understood that the General's remarkable narrative was being readied for publication, they became reconciled — and in some cases anxious — to gloss the account with their own facts, ideas, understandings, points of view and — often enough — contradictions. Names, dates and places cannot be disclosed, but I can say that from their insights a coherent understanding of the story behind the story began to emerge.

It was buttressed by the archives of the world. If there remains — in a nation increasingly careless and ignorant of its own or any other past — little official enthusiasm for accounts of the Occupation and the Rising, it was gratifying to discover so much tangential material that threw light on the General's escapade. From the Bodleian, the Naval Historical Institute, the archives of King's College, London, the papers of the physicist Sir John Cockcroft, other records lodged at Yale University in New Haven, the military archives in São Paulo and the Bundestag and the Kremlin, a thousand apparently unrelated sources crystallised my understanding of the General's partial and near-sighted account.

*

The villain of the piece was of course Churchill. Or is villain the word? What of the cards he was given and the cards he played? When the General saw him on V-Day in Buckingham Palace fingering the four of hearts that supposedly sent Air Marshal Sir Alexander Howe to his death and the General himself to his appointment with destiny, our good narrator seems to have assumed the Prime Minister's guilt. The record demands qualification. The General assumed that Churchill had masterminded Operation Scylla to kill Hitler and left the Air Marshal, Admiral Conway and the General himself the task of executing the plan.

Not so.

The General notes that he and the Admiral assumed that the Air Marshal had emerged unscathed from the Gestapo. The Prime Minister knew better. He knew that Sir Alec had been turned by the Germans and had betrayed his colleagues. Churchill's plan was to place the Air Marshal in a position in which he was obliged to execute a plan to assassinate his new master – supposing it would lead to his removal or death. Just so. The Air Marshal wasn't seized by the Gestapo; he simply crossed the Rubicon. Neither did he die at the Germans' hands. For all I know or have been able to discover, the Air Marshal is still alive. Churchill's agent in this was of course Admiral Conway, a card player of great accomplishment who could – and did - give his former colleague every card he chose. Conway's own men then planted the card on the General, so providing Churchill with what he believed to be one loyal team of good marksmen with the courage and conviction to assassinate Hitler - should the Sappers who had mined the Victorian memorial where Hitler would address the troops fail in their task.

Epilogue

It was the Prime Minister's misfortune that the Admiral had also been turned. Conway was not what he seemed, – least of all to General Quick.

For all the Admiral's insouciance, effortless superiority, love of women and the bottle, Conway was a man of very considerable courage and personal loyalties. Despite the latitudes of his personal behaviour, he was a devoted husband and father. It was this that Admiral Raeder was clever enough to discover when he held Conway in custody in Portishead at the beginning of the Occupation in the early autumn of 1940. Conway was given the simplest of choices. To work for the Reich or to see his wife and children – two sons and one daughter – gassed. I believe that one of the reasons he acceded was because he had observed all too closely what the death of Quick's own family had done to the composure of the General. Yet of course Conway – unlike Howe - did not precisely accede. A man of that nature would scarcely betray his country without a struggle. And struggle he did throughout the Occupation and most particularly the Rising. Indeed, it was on Conway's deeply divided loyalties that – utterly unbeknownst to Quick — most of the rest of his own narrative hinges.

For it was of course Conway who told Skorzeny of the attempt that was to be made to free the two princesses. But Conway also ensured that Skorzeny's E-boat was intercepted six miles off Great Yarmouth just as it was heading east to the Elbe. He was not of course to know that Skorzeny on his incapacitated Schnellboot would seek shelter in the Wash and that he might end up in Sandringham, but he must have had a shrewd guess. To the east lay the only shelter and King's Lynn was the only obvious port. So his conscience was squared.

The fog of war. As far as I have been able to discover, it was then a simple mischance that the Americans discovered the location of the princesses by breaking the SOE radio codes. It had long been their habit to listen in on the transmission of friend and foe alike, an arrangement that – I believe – still continues.

Both Churchill and Conway must then have felt that events were taking their own course. There seemed to them little to choose between the heirs to the throne being in the hands of the Reich itself or in the hands of a United States intent on supporting the Reich. I have in front of me an SOE situation report entitled – without great originality – 'The Devil and the Deep Blue Sea'. Yet the stakes could scarcely have been higher. I have every reason to believe that Churchill meant every word he said in the w/t conversation attributed by Quick to the morning after the seizure by the Americans of the princesses. Churchill believed that the future of the free world was hanging in the balance, a balance to be torpedoed one way or the other by the two fragile lives of the sisters. Of course he may have been quite wrong. But I do believe that that was what he believed. It was time for desperate measures. Those were of course the secrets of the atomic bomb. For Churchill, they were the last resort, the last throw of the dice.

Churchill's man was of course Cockcroft. Sir John had managed to keep the Prime Minister very largely apprised of developments while he collaborated with the Nazis in his own Cambridge Laboratories. Churchill was entirely ignorant of the existence of the papers on Skorzeny's E-boat, but he knew the papers existed and he knew that Cockcroft and his German colleagues had manufactured two atomic bombs. He also knew where they were. And it was of course Churchill who alerted the White House to the presence of the bombs in Faslane. They were the bait and he thought there was a good chance that the Americans would deploy Kennedy and the *Boston* to fetch them.

Of course he was quite right. Churchill could see and he could judge but he was not omniscient. He wasn't to know what Conway would make of the plans, or that Skorzeny might decide to add to his aura in Germany when he returned with both plans and princesses. Neither was the PM to know that Skorzeny suspected Conway of being behind the interception of the Schnellboot. On the morning after the Americans' raid on Sandringham, Conway thought it judicious to rescue Skorzeny and his men from the Sandringham cellar. It wasn't. In the next few days Conway got wind of the Americans' plan for Faslane and collaborated with Skorzeny on his ambush.

248

Epilogue

What Skorzeny hadn't bothered to tell Conway was the little matter of the V2. The Admiral had been told that the princesses were being taken to safety in the United States. He may or may not have believed this story but he certainly didn't suppose he was sending them to their deaths. When he realised that the Free World was being given the choice between the princesses and half the population of New York, he knew that the time had come to sacrifice his own family. It was of course Conway who was the most vehement in urging Churchill to give the Americans the secrets of the bomb in exchange for the lives of the princesses. It was this decision that saved him from the gallows and indeed public disgrace. Churchill knew perfectly well that the publicity of a court martial would be to no one's advantage, least of all his own.

Oh and the dog, Skorzeny's dog that leaped into Conway's lap on V-Day in Buckingham Palace. Lady Conway's hobby was breeding dachshunds. The Admiral had presented Skorzeny with the dog at an Anglo-German military conference in 1938 at Wilhelmshaven. Conway and the dachshund were – as the saying goes – just old friends.

Jim Ring, Burnham Overy Staithe, June 2020

WriteSideLeft

2020

https://www.writesideleft.com

Lightning Source UK Ltd.
Milton Keynes UK
UKHW011825190820
368504UK00001B/49

9 781916 261037